DEAD RAT

A PULSATING THRILLER SET IN THE MURDER
CAPITAL OF THE UNITED KINGDOM

DEREK FEE

❀ Created with Vellum

For Aine, Bobbie and Sean

PROLOGUE

B elfast is an unforgiving city in winter. Atlantic storms enter via Donegal Bay and head across country until they hit the Black Mountain and disgorge their cargo of rain upon the citizenry. But the Irish are inured to rain, even when it's ice-cold rain. More pervasive is the wind from the Arctic, which howls down Belfast Lough and brings biting cold, hail and occasionally snow to the city before continuing on its way south. The residents of the city had already suffered three of what the television weather presenters termed 'cold spells' this winter. The fourth arrived that afternoon when the mercury began its fall to the bottom of the thermometers. A light dusting of snow followed, with a more appreciable fall on the top of the Black Mountain. By evening, the peaks wore their white caps like a group of old men huddled around a turf fire. The temperature had passed through zero at midnight on its way to minus five degrees, accompanied by a wind-chill factor of minus ten.

Hugh Royce bundled his padded jacket around him. He didn't do cold. He pushed himself further into the recess at the rear of O'Reilly's pub in North Belfast. He was only five minutes out of his car and already his feet felt like two blocks of ice, but at least he was sheltered from the wind. He looked across the empty parking lot and coughed. He had just recovered from a bout of the Australian flu and standing in the open during one of the severest cold spells to hit the city was not what he needed. He removed his hands from his pockets and blew into them. 'Should have invested in a pair of gloves,' he murmured to himself.

The building behind him was closed and lightless. The area in front of him had a soft covering of snow, and the footprints from his car to the point where he now stood were clearly visible. He looked at his watch, four minutes past twelve. He would give it a quarter of an hour. The trip back was going to be a bitch if there was ice on the road. His hands shook as he removed a cigarette packet from his pocket and eased a cigarette out. The first match he struck was extinguished immediately by a gust of cold wind. He bent his head to bring the tip of the cigarette closer and cupped the match in his hands. The cigarette caught. As he raised his head, a shadow flitted across the parking lot, but no one came forward. Must be seeing things, he thought, or maybe I'm going crazy. What sort of idiot agrees to a meeting outside a dark pub at midnight on the coldest night of the year? But he had come to Belfast to sort things out and if that meant freezing his balls off in the process, then so be it. He pulled on the cigarette, filling his lung with the sweet smoke. As he exhaled, he peered into the darkness. Nothing. Where the fuck are you, man? It's not the night to be late. He looked at his watch again. The minute hand had hardly moved and the cold was creeping up from his feet, spreading the sharp pain all the way to the crown of his head. What if the bastard doesn't show? As far as the others were concerned he was a flea on the arsehole of the world, a meaningless blast from the past. He thought about the shit decisions that had led him to be standing in an empty parking lot in the middle of a cold dark night in an effort to atone for his sins.

He turned his head quickly at a sound, but there was nothing there. Was he just imagining these fleeting shadows and scratching noises? Fear crept up his spine. His inner voice told him it was time to leave. Now all his attention was on his ears. There was definitely something out there in the darkness. He pulled on the cigarette. Fuck it, he thought. I'm out of here in two minutes and they can live with the consequences. He started counting off the one hundred and twenty seconds in his head.

As he reached one hundred he heard a definite noise from the other side of the pub. He turned his head and saw a black figure rounding the corner and heading in his direction. He smiled. Maybe everything was going to turn out and soon he'd be heading for the warmth of his billet. He peered through the darkness. The man who turned the corner had his face covered by a scarf and wore a beanie on his head. Royce's smile faded when he saw the man remove a gun from his pocket. 'In the name of God, man, don't. You don't have to.' The shots came before he could get his hands up in a vain effort to defend himself. He felt the bullets slam into his chest and his legs were no longer capable of supporting the rest of his relatively light body. His last thought was that it was a hell of a night to die. He fell forward, then nothing.

The man who had shot Royce drew level with the body, pointed the gun at the dead man's head and fired.

CHAPTER ONE

Detective Superintendent Ian Wilson stood at the window of his apartment and surveyed the city of Belfast. It was seven o'clock and the city was just waking up. The snowy scene was straight out of a Christmas card. Snow temporarily covers the dirt and grime before it adds to the mess by becoming slush, he thought. He and his partner, Stephanie Reid, had returned to Belfast two months previously, having laid Stephanie's mother to rest in California. The last few weeks in Venice Beach had been a whirlwind of funeral arrangements and the filing of legal papers. The upshot was that Stephanie was now a very wealthy lady having been left the bulk of her mother's estate. It was a chalice that she didn't really want. They could have stayed on, but Reid had felt she needed to get back to the routine of cutting up dead bodies for a living.

Wilson had been a little more reticent about his return to Belfast to resume leadership of the PSNI Murder Squad. The day he'd left Belfast for California he'd learned of the death of Noel Armstrong, a government minister whom he suspected of murdering two prostitutes and whom he had established was being protected by the security services. Armstrong's death had left him dissatisfied. There was a certain rough justice in his demise, but he would have preferred to see Armstrong stand in the dock and be judged for his crimes. But that was never going to happen. Wilson had long ago given up the naïve idea that justice always prevailed. In his experience, it was generally perverted by one of the participants in the game. That was his main worry since he returned. Armstrong had been in the service of the British security service for more than fifteen years. Throughout that time, he had also managed to convince his colleagues in the Republican movement of his commitment to them. Until a few months ago. Somehow, they had learned of his treachery and they had executed him for it. How exactly had they discovered his duplicity? It was a question that had dominated Wilson's thinking since he'd watched Armstrong's funeral on television. It wasn't the usual send-off afforded to a stalwart of the struggle to free Ireland. Where was the tricolour-draped coffin carried by the luminaries of the party Armstrong had served? Where was the volley of shots as the coffin was lowered? It all pointed to the fact that somehow his speculation about Armstrong's double life had been passed on to the man's comrades. Yet Wilson had told no one outside the investigation of his suspicions. The fact that he might have been the source of the leak nagged at him. He didn't like to think a member of his squad was unreliable. He had turned those thoughts over in his mind a thousand times without coming to a conclusion. A secret in Belfast was something that only one person knew. Despite the so-called return to normality, the security services still kept a close eye on happenings in the province. It was also possible that Armstrong's friends in the security services may have put the finger on him. Maybe they'd grown weary of cleaning up his mess. But the timing was ominous. Or coincidental, except that Wilson didn't believe in coincidence.

Since his return Wilson had been watching the members of the squad to see who might have passed on the information.

The obvious candidate was Siobhan O'Neill, a young Catholic detective constable who had recently joined the squad. Everything about her behaviour since his return ran against that supposition, and coming to that deduction required a level of religious profiling that was anathema to him. She was one of the most conscientious members of the squad. He'd run a check on her to see whether she had any Republican contacts and it had come up negative. He'd also been watching the reaction of the three men on the squad and again had registered nothing. Perhaps he had called it wrong. He certainly hoped so.

'Breakfast?'

Wilson turned and saw that Reid was already standing in the small galley kitchen. She looked radiant. He sometimes wondered what she saw in him. 'Why not.' Reid stayed over most nights although so far there had been no indication that she wanted to make the arrangement permanent. Bar her demand for wardrobe space. She had kept her apartment close to the Royal Victoria Hospital and stayed there when she wanted what she called 'me time'. Wilson was not going to push the issue. He was happy with the current arrangement and if it was going to change, he wanted it to be a natural progression, not something that was forced by either party.

Reid popped four pieces of bread into the toaster. 'Avocado toast and poached eggs,' she announced.

'How very Californian.'

'You obviously haven't looked outside.'

Wilson realised that he had been miles away. Armstrong was no longer any of his business. The body had been dumped a couple of hundred yards inside the Irish Republic, which meant that the murder investigation was in the hands of the Garda Síochána. More particularly in the hands of DCI Jack Duane of the Irish Special Branch, or whatever they called the group he worked for. He thanked God for small mercies, walked into the kitchen and kissed Reid. 'I'll make the coffee and set the table.'

'I've got to hurry,' Reid said, cracking an egg into the simmering water. 'It's a busy day and I hope the gritters have been out.'

Wilson slid his hand round her waist. 'Maybe we should have stayed in California, you weren't so rushed there.'

'Maybe we should have.'

'You really mean that?'

'Sometimes, especially when I think that we could be having our breakfast sitting outside in the garden and looking forward to a day of sunshine.'

'And now we're back in grey cold Belfast.'

'It doesn't have to be like that.'

'What do you mean?'

'Don't tell me you're completely happy here.'

He was shocked. Was he completely happy in Belfast? He hadn't really thought about it. 'I thought you loved it here?'

'You mean the part where we wake up in the morning in the dark, go to work in the dark and come home in the evening in the dark. Is that the part you think I love?' She put the plates containing their breakfast on the table and started to eat.

'There is an upside.' He started on his meal.

'Really? I'll give you an hour or so to think about that.'

He could feel one of those uncomfortable moments hanging in the air. Where were they going? They would never be the couple next door, going to work in the morning and raising their children before the final act of drawing their pension. Reid had already led an exciting life. She'd travelled, experienced civil war. And her work at the Royal mattered. 'It's where we're from. We're at home here.' He didn't even sound convincing to himself.

'I would probably have agreed with you this time last year, but now I'm not so sure.' She finished eating and drained her coffee, then leaned forward and kissed him. 'I'm late, you clean up.'

He watched her as she put on her coat, wrapped a scarf round her neck and covered her short blonde hair with a woollen bonnet. She waved from the door and was gone.

He finished his coffee and collected up the dirty dishes before stacking them in the dishwasher. There was no doubt in his mind that Reid had been distracted by her time in Los Angeles. He was a little out of sorts himself and he hadn't lost his mother. But there was something she wasn't telling him, and he was wondering what it was and why she was so reluctant to discuss it.

CHAPTER TWO

The temperature was hovering around minus one when Wilson left for the station. The snow was sticking but the gritters had been out and the early morning traffic had helped clear the roads. The residents of northern Europe would laugh at the level of panic a couple of inches of snow can cause in Belfast. The schools had been closed and consequently the traffic was lighter than usual. It was a good day for the locals to take a 'sickie'. He was crossing the Lagan when his mobile phone rang. He recognised Detective Sergeant Rory Browne's number and pressed the green phone icon.

'Where are you, Boss?' Browne was breathless.

'Crossing the river on my way in.'

'We've got a dead body. Cleaner opening O'Reilly's pub on the Antrim Road found a guy in the car park. He thought it was a tramp until he saw the blood, and the bullet-hole in the head. The uniforms who responded called it in to us.'

'I'll head there straight away. You pick up a car and collect Harry. I'll meet both of you there. And make sure the uniforms seal off the area and don't screw up the crime scene.'

'Already done and we're on the way.'

Wilson glanced at the clock in the car. It was approaching

nine o'clock. That meant there was no way he was going to make the senior staff meeting. He sighed with relief. There was nothing in his life worse than listening to some inspector trying to climb up the arse of the chief super. He knew where O'Reilly's pub was so he took the M2 and fifteen minutes later he pulled in behind two police cars stationed across the entry to the pub and its car park. He got out of his car with some reluctance and walked to the boot, crunching the frozen snow underfoot. He took out a pair of blue plastic overshoes and slipped them on.

As he approached the strand of crime scene tape, a uniform lifted it to permit him to enter. He signed his clipboard and handed it back. 'Where is he?' Wilson asked.

'Around the side, on the edge of the car park,' the officer replied. 'There's an old Volkswagen Polo parked fifty yards away. Looks like he might have arrived in it.'

'Where's the cleaner?'

The officer winked. 'In the pub, he insisted he was shocked and needed a drink.'

Wilson looked over at the two police cars.

'They're inside,' the officer said. 'It's Baltic out here, sir. We're taking it in turns to man the tape.'

Wilson nodded and started to walk around the edge of the pub. The snow had been disturbed – so much for preserving the crime scene. He'd just turned the corner when he saw the body. There was no snow on it. The snowfall the previous day had abated about ten o'clock in the evening, which meant that the man had been killed after ten. Wilson stood over the body, which was frozen solid by a combination of the low temperature and rigor mortis. Reid might have some difficulty in estimating the exact time of death. He looked towards where the car was parked and saw the line of footprints. Only one set, which meant they probably belonged to the victim. He heard another car screech to a halt and turned back to the front of the pub in time to see Browne and Graham exiting the vehicle.

His feet were already beginning to sting from the cold and he sympathised with the uniform at the tape.

'Get yourself inside and tell one of those other slackers to get out here,' Wilson said as he passed.

'Thank you, sir,' the uniform said before walking briskly into the pub.

'Mornin' Boss,' Graham said. 'Bit of a cold one.'

'You could say that. There's a Volkswagen Polo in the car park. Skirt around the edge and take a look. Call in the registration to Plate Recognition and find out the name on the book. Don't go near it until Forensics have had a look. Rory, you and me inside. We need to have a word with the guy who found the body.'

Wilson felt instant relief in both his feet and his hands as he entered the pub. The heating wasn't exactly blasting, but the temperature was a good ten degrees higher than outside. Four men were gathered at the bar. Three uniforms were cradling what looked like coffees, and a civilian had helped himself to a large brandy.

Browne took out his warrant card and showed it to the civilian. 'I'm Detective Sergeant Browne, this is Detective Superintendent Ian Wilson, and you are?'

The man finished his brandy and poured himself a refill. He pointed at Wilson. 'Aye, I've seen him on television. I'm Joe Hanley, I'm the dogsbody in this pub.'

Wilson estimated Hanley to be somewhere between fifty and sixty years old. He was slight with a pinched face, protruding eyes and a head of fuzzy grey hair. 'You found the body?' he asked.

'Aye.' Hanley sipped his drink. 'And I'm not the better of it yet. I saw him as soon as I turned the corner of the pub.'

'You didn't panic though. You've probably seen dead bodies before?'

'Aye, I worked in a funeral parlour in Glengormley,' Hanley said. 'But it's the first one I saw shot through the head.'

'You examined the body?' Wilson asked.

'Not a bit of it. I took a wee look at him and that was all.'

'Did you recognise him?' Wilson asked. 'Was he one of the regulars?'

Hanley took a drink and then shook his head. 'Never saw the bloke before.'

A radio crackled and one of the uniforms pushed the button and listened. He turned to Wilson. 'Bit of a commotion at the tape, sir, they want you outside.'

Wilson nodded at Browne, who slipped quietly away.

'So, you have no idea who he is?'

Hanley shook his head.

'Give your address and phone number to my sergeant before you go anywhere.'

Hanley nodded and finished his drink. He was about to pour himself another when there was a shout from the door. 'Put that bottle away or I'll break your fuckin' arm.'

Hanley immediately replaced the bottle and put his glass on the bar. 'It was the shock, Mr O'Reilly,' Hanley said. 'It was purely medicinal.'

Wilson turned to look at the new arrival, who was dressed in a warm jacket and jeans and wore a Russian-style fur hat. His most prominent facial feature was his nose, which was purple-red either from the cold or a fondness for whiskey.

'This is the owner of the establishment, Owen O'Reilly,' Browne said.

O'Reilly marched over to the bar. 'I heard that there was a situation at the pub, police cars and the like, and I came right over.'

'Everything is under control,' Wilson said. 'We have a dead body in the car park and the pub will be closed until our forensic people have completed their examination of the crime scene.'

'Fuckin' hell,' O'Reilly said. 'A dead body! Are you sure he didn't die of hypothermia? It was bloody cold last night and we often have vagrants sleeping out around the place.'

'Certain,' Wilson said deadpan. 'There's a bullet-hole in his head.'

'Holy God. How long do you think we'll be closed?'

'When we're done, you'll be the first to know. In the meantime, how about a cup of coffee for me and my sergeant?'

O'Reilly moved behind the bar, lifted up the bottle of brandy and examined the level. He stared at Hanley. 'Purely medicinal was it? No one needs that amount of medicine. It'll be comin' out of your pay at the end of the week.' He moved to the coffee machine.

Harry Graham entered the pub blowing on his cupped hands. 'Checked the registration with the station. Last registered to a guy named Adam Donaldson with an address in Argyle Street.'

'Get a phone number for him,' Wilson said, taking a cup of coffee offered by O'Reilly.

Graham continued blowing on his hands. 'Any chance of a coffee for me?' he asked O'Reilly.

O'Reilly nodded and went back to the machine. 'I assume no one is paying.'

Wilson took a ten-pound note from his pocket and put it on the bar. 'Never let it be said.'

O'Reilly pushed the note back. 'On the house.'

Graham took out his phone and sat at one of the tables across from the bar.

Wilson and Browne moved away from the uniforms. 'Any news on Forensics and the pathologist?' Wilson asked.

Browne sipped his coffee. 'Forensics are on the way. The pathologist is doing an autopsy and will be along as soon as she's free. What are we looking at here, Boss?'

'Somebody wanted this guy dead. The head shot was the clincher. There are two exit wounds on his back, so it was two to the body and one to the head.'

'A professional?'

'Someone who knew what they were doing.'

'Poor sod, what did he do to deserve being murdered?'

'That's something we're going to have to find out. There's a CCTV camera outside covering the car park. Before you leave, make sure that you take the disk with you.'

Browne made a note in his day book.

Graham joined his colleagues. 'I got a number for Donaldson, but nobody is answering. Could be our boy outside.'

A uniform came through the door and one of the three others at the bar reluctantly left the warmth to take his place. The new arrival came over to Wilson. 'Forensic van just rolled up.'

Wilson turned to Graham. 'Harry, get on to the station and organise for uniforms to do a house-to-house.'

Graham nodded. 'There weren't many folk about last night. It was a perfect night to kill someone.'

'You never know,' Wilson said. 'Some old guy out walking his dog might have seen something. I'd best brave the cold and have a word with the new arrivals.'

CHAPTER THREE

The forensic team were already suited up and unpacking their gear when Wilson joined them at their van. He knew most of the FSNI personnel, but the man in charge was new to him. He turned as soon as Wilson approached. 'Detective Superintendent Wilson I assume,' he said.

'You have me at a disadvantage.'

'Michael Finlay, most people call me Mick. It's frigging Baltic out here. What have we got?'

Finlay's accent wasn't from the north of Ireland. It was somewhere south of the border, but Wilson was unsure of exactly where. Finlay was just under six feet tall with a neatly cut goatee beard. It was difficult to get a fix on his body size as he had so much padding under his suit.

Wilson explained the situation. 'The body hasn't been moved. There's a blue Volkswagen Polo in the car park that we assume belonged to the deceased. We've traced the owner listed with the DVLA and tried to call him, but there's no answer. If there's any identification on the body, I need it post-haste. There's a coffee machine in the pub if you want to take a break from the cold.'

Finlay turned to the two members of his team. 'Let's get

the scene of crime photos done straight away.' He turned to Wilson. 'Pathologist?'

'Busy with an autopsy. She'll be here as soon as she can.'

The three forensic officers picked up their gear and Wilson led them around the corner to the site of the body. Finlay looked at the Polo sitting alone in the car park. 'I'll organise transport for the car. No doubt you'll want it thoroughly examined and it's best to do that back at our facility.'

Wilson nodded. He was glad the new guy was on top of things. The team were already putting down yellow numbered markers and taking photos. As another cold blast of wind hit him, he didn't envy them their task. His phone rang and he saw it was his boss on the line. He pressed the green call button and started walking back towards the pub. 'Ma'am,' he said. 'I'm outside, let me get in out of this bloody wind.' He moved to a quiet corner of the pub and spent the next five minutes briefing the station commander, Chief Superintendent Yvonne Davis, on what they had found.

'No political overtones?' Davis said. She had almost taken up religion when the body of Noel Armstrong had been located on the southern side of the border. The Armstrong affair, as she now referred to the case, had looked for a long time like it would end her career in the PSNI.

'Not on the face of it, but it's early days and this is, after all, Northern Ireland. It looks like the killer knew what he was about. Harry's put in a request for uniforms to help carry out the house-to-house, so I'd be grateful if you'd expedite that. The uniforms chosen won't thank us because it's freezing outside, but we have to get on with the investigation.'

'I'll have a word with Castlereagh. We missed you at the senior officers' meeting this morning.'

'I was looking forward to it myself. Pity this poor man's murder got in the way.'

Davis laughed. 'You're an absolute devil, Ian. Keep me informed.'

'Yes, ma'am.'

Wilson walked across to Graham, who was just finishing his coffee, and told him that Davis would be expediting the uniforms for the house-to-house. 'Sorry, Harry, normally I wouldn't put a dog out in weather like this, but we need to canvas the area before people forget what they might have seen or heard. I want a report on the house-to-house by this evening. What about this Donaldson fellow?'

'I've given that phone number a few more tries, but there's still no answer and there's no answer machine. This is a strange one, Boss. Out on a night like last night – must have been important.'

Wilson didn't like the word 'important', but Graham was right. There had to be a very good reason for someone to be out and about on the coldest night of the year. 'Maybe Forensics will come up with something.' He turned to Browne. 'In the meantime, Donaldson is your baby. Go to his address and see why he isn't answering the phone.' Browne didn't look pleased. 'And while you're at it, think about poor Harry and the uniforms freezing their balls off knocking on doors.'

CHAPTER FOUR

Professor Stephanie Reid arrived at O'Reilly's pub just before midday. She had already carried out an autopsy on an apparently healthy athletics coach who had dropped dead. The cause of death turned out to be a minor heart malfunction that would have been easy to repair had it been detected. It just proved the old adage: when you time is up, your time is up.

Wilson came up behind her as she was putting on her white plastic suit. 'About bloody time,' he said, helping her pull the suit up.

'Some of us have real jobs.' She picked up her bag. 'Lead on, Macduff.'

They walked around the pub. 'Cause of death is pretty easy,' Wilson said, 'half his head is blown off. My guess is that he might have been already dead from the shots to his chest, and I certainly hope so. Time of death might be a little harder to determine because of the freeze.'

The forensic team had turned the body over. Wilson stared at the face of the man. He looked familiar. He envied those people with a photographic memory for faces or names. He was in a people job and their faces and names registered only during the time he dealt with them before being consigned to some psychological dump. Despite this failing, he was sure that he had met this man before, and in his mind there was no association with the name Donaldson.

Finlay joined them and introduced himself to Reid. 'Nothing in the pockets other than these.' He held up five small plastic bags and handed them to Wilson.

Wilson checked the contents of the plastic bags: a packet of cigarettes, a box of matches, a ten-pound note and some loose change, a car key on a Volkswagen fob and another small key. 'That's it? No driver's licence, credit card, bank card or letter from Social Services?'

'No identification whatsoever,' Finlay said.

'Strange in this day and age,' Wilson said, thinking about the different kinds of identification that could generally be found on the average person. 'He wasn't robbed, but perhaps the murderer searched him and removed his identification.'

'It's a possibility,' Finlay said. 'But it doesn't look like the body was moved after he was shot. We've processed the area around the corpse, so as soon as the professor has finished, he can be removed.'

'No shell casings?' Wilson asked.

Finlay shook his head. 'Looks like he took his brass with him.'

It was another indication that the killer knew what he was doing.

Finlay continued. 'It looks like the victim was smoking when he was shot. We found the cigarette butt under the body. I can't say for certain whether someone emptied his pockets. His clothes look undisturbed.'

'What about the rounds he took in the chest?' Wilson asked.

Finlay shook his head. 'They passed through so they're out there somewhere. When we're through here we'll carry out a detailed search. We did recover this.' He held up a plastic bag containing a mashed slug.

Wilson took the bag and looked at the piece of deformed metal. 'Looks like it could be a nine millimetre.' He handed back the bag.

Finlay dropped it into his satchel. 'I agree.'

Reid stood up. 'I'll arrange transport for the corpse. Time of death is going to be problematic. Right now, I would say anywhere between ten o'clock yesterday evening and two o'clock this morning.' She saw the disappointment on Wilson's face. It was a pretty wide window.

Wilson looked across the car park where the Polo was being winched onto a low-loader. 'When will you be through?' he asked Finlay.

'We're breaking for lunch. We'll process the rest of the site this afternoon and hopefully we'll turn up the slugs from the chest shots.'

'Can you get the scene of crime photos to me by this afternoon?'

'We'll send them to your computer over lunch.'

Wilson slapped Finlay on the back. 'Good man.'

Reid packed her bag and started to walk away. Wilson joined her.

'That Finlay is an impressive young guy,' Wilson said.

'He seems nice,' Reid said.

'You have anything planned for lunch?' Wilson asked.

There was no point in going back to the Royal so close to lunchtime. She looked at a sign on the corner of O'Reilly's advertising all-day lunch specials. 'I suppose a pub lunch is out of the question.'

'It is at this pub, but I know another good bar on the way back into town, and I hope to God they've lit their turf fire at this time of the year. If we hurry, we might just be able to get a table close enough to thaw us out.'

CHAPTER FIVE

Detective Constable Peter Davidson dropped by the station early in the morning and found the squad room deserted except for Siobhan O'Neill, whom he was beginning to suspect was permanently attached to her chair. She was the squad 'brains', dipping in and out of her computer to supply the 'real' detectives with information. At least that's what he assumed she did since he had had only limited contact with her. On the few occasions that he had availed of her skills, he had been impressed. Davidson was crawling towards retirement and was being treated by Wilson as a kind of free electron, running a small side investigation into the supposed suicide of politician Jackie Carlisle. The investigation had led him to form a liaison with Carlisle's wife, the comely Irene. The investigation had also reminded him that Wilson's intuition was still operational because it was becoming clear that Jackie Carlisle had been murdered. Davidson had also been feeling that his own powers were in serious decline, but the investigation had convinced him that there was life in the old dog yet, both in terms of his job and his ability to please a lady. The Carlisle investigation was off the books because it was delicate. So bloody delicate that it was dangerous to the health of whoever was working on it. And that was Peter Davidson. While Wilson had been sunning himself in California, Davidson had been treading water. Wilson was the only one who knew what he was up to, and he wasn't going to put himself at risk without some kind of safety net. In the meantime, the widow Carlisle was getting restive. She had a lot of insurance money riding on the investigation proving that her husband was murdered. Wilson and Davidson were weaving a fragile web that could break and dump them both on their arses at any moment. 'Nobody about?' he asked as he passed O'Neill's chair.

'Body found outside a pub on the Antrim Road.' O'Neill thought Davidson was a funny old bloke, but he'd more than thirty years' experience on the job and had forgotten more than she would ever learn. Lately, he had been sprucing himself up. It was obvious to her that there was a lady involved. Everyone in the PSNI knew of Davidson's chequered past, but O'Neill was in her twenties and she found the image of people as old as Davidson going at it repugnant.

'Death never sleeps.' Davidson was feeling profound. 'Is it possible to pull up information on one of our colleagues in the Special Branch?'

O'Neill looked up from her computer. 'I have no idea.'

'Would you like to try?'

She thought about it for a moment. 'What's this in aid of?'

'The investigation whose name is so sensitive that we may not speak it.'

'The Carlisle investigation?'

'That's the one.'

'Give me the name.'

'Sergeant Simon Jackson. Remember, absolute discretion is necessary. If there's any chance at all that he can discover what we're up to, stop immediately.'

'Okay.' She watched Davidson go to his desk and sit down. She'd been studying her colleagues attentively since Wilson had returned from his break. She was aware that her boss was observing her more closely than before. She wasn't naïve and knew he must be considering whether one of his team had leaked the information about Noel Armstrong to the IRA. She was the obvious candidate. She had emphasised the matter of her security to Ronan Muldoon, but he had the brains of a gnat, and the IRA leaked like a colander. In retrospect, she should have thought of a more subtle way to make Armstrong pay for his crimes. If Wilson did manage to connect the dots, she might get away with perverting the course of justice, but it was more likely that she would be an accessory to murder. And that would mean a great deal of jail time. So, it was important that the dots not be joined up. Her mother had recently entered a care home and she had made sure that the monthly fee would be paid irrespective of what might happen to her. She didn't like the fact that she had, in a certain manner, betrayed her boss and her colleagues. It left a nasty taste in her mouth. But she wasn't sorry that she had ensured that Armstrong wasn't going to get away with murder. She wasn't the first police officer in Northern Ireland to leak information and she certainly wouldn't be the last. She was remaining as calm as she could. The Armstrong business would fade away eventually, but in the meantime she was going to keep her guard up.

CHAPTER SIX

O'Neill and Davidson were the only two members of the squad in the station when Wilson returned from lunch. Graham was probably freezing his arse off rapping on doors on the Antrim Road, while Browne was following up on the ownership of the Polo. Wilson wasn't one for taking vacations. He often thought of the number of days he might be owed if he were to count up his overtime. He didn't feel comfortable away from the office. While he'd been in the States, Davis had put one of her CIs in charge of the squad. The man she chose had no investigative experience and, in Wilson's opinion, zero leadership ability. The upshot was that the squad had been just about keeping its head above water for the three weeks he'd been away. He looked through the glass surround of his office. A good example of what he meant was Peter Davidson. Nothing appeared to have happened on the Carlisle investigation since he'd left. He caught Davidson's eye and motioned him to the office.

'Boss,' Davidson slipped easily into the visitor's chair in front of Wilson's desk.

'Why is nothing happening on the Carlisle investigation?' Wilson asked.

'I've asked Siobhan to get me whatever she can on Jackson. You told me he was dangerous, so I've been waiting for your return to proceed. It's not like the investigation has been approved, and I've been feeling the cold wind of exposure blowing up my arse.'

Davidson was right. Wilson had started out intending to light a fire under him, but he had placed Peter in a difficult position. They had identified Sergeant Simon Jackson, a Special Branch officer, as a prime suspect in the murder of Jackie Carlisle. Wilson had experience with Jackson and was sure that he wouldn't have acted without orders from someone higher up. Jackson was an operator not a director. There was a danger in investigating Jackson, but there would be extreme danger if the plot to kill Carlisle was orchestrated by someone further up the food chain. 'Understood, but we have to push the investigation along. You've probably got the best contacts in the PSNI of any of us. Isn't there someone you can tap?'

'Not that I can think of offhand, but I'll set my mind to it. It'll be a difficult trick to zone in on Jackson without setting off an alarm somewhere. In this city the walls really do have ears. And if our boy catches on that we're looking at him, I'm a bit too old for the rough and tumble.'

'You don't look it.' A couple of months ago Davidson had seemed down in the dumps and retirement was looming, but carrying out an investigation on his own seemed to have given him a new lease on life. But Wilson was forced to agree. Davidson was exposed, and maybe it was time to replace him with a younger officer. But Wilson was going to need both Graham and Browne on the Antrim Road investigation. And possibly Davidson too. 'Okay, let's proceed quietly. Get what you can on Jackson. Was the neighbour who saw the car with the two men able to identify him?'

'He's been away since. He's a vet working on some kind of aid project in Uganda. He's back next week.'

'Show him the photo and get a statement. The more paper we have the better if we're going to drag Jackson in.'

Davidson nodded. 'Next week, Boss, for sure.'

'Also, get on to the tech guys. That phone made only two calls before going dead, one to the hospice to cancel the appointment and then one when the job was done. Get them to pinpoint the location of both the sending and the receiving phones for the second call.'

'I'm on it. What's with the business on the Antrim Road?'

Wilson filled him in on the body at O'Reilly's pub. 'Harry's in charge of the house-to-house and Rory is trying to lay hands on the registered owner of the car.'

'If it was a professional hit, the guy must have some connection to organised crime, and in this city that means Davie Best.'

That thought had already occurred to Wilson. 'That's a distinct possibility. But first we have to identify the victim. Then we might be able to find some connection to Best's operations. I might need you at some point on this investigation.'

'You know where I am.'

Wilson smiled. 'I never know where you are these days. Just push the Carlisle investigation forward, but carefully.'

Davidson stood up. 'I'm on it.'

FINLAY WAS as good as his word. The photos were on Wilson's computer by early afternoon. He brought them up one after another and examined them in detail. He couldn't shake the feeling that he had met the victim, but he had no idea where or when or, indeed, in what context. He sent the file on to O'Neill with a request to start a whiteboard on the crime.

CHAPTER SEVEN

The squad stood around the whiteboard for the evening briefing. Four crime scene photos shot from various angles were attached to the board. Wilson turned to Browne. 'Any news on Donaldson?'

'There's no one at the house,' Browne said. 'The neighbour says that he's away a lot and the physical description doesn't tally with our victim. They haven't seen the Polo for at least a couple of days.'

'Donaldson could have sold his car on to either the victim or a third party,' Graham said, 'and they haven't bothered to re-register the car with the DVLA.'

'Our victim isn't Donaldson,' Wilson said. 'It's our primary task to find out who he is. If we had a name, it might give us some idea as to why someone wanted him dead.'

'This is the clearest picture we have of his face,' O'Neill attached a photo on the board. 'It's not one that the public would like to see, but giving it to the media might be the fastest way to find out who he is.'

Wilson looked at the photo of a face with the rictus of death clearly on it. The media would love it, but he doubted that PSNI media affairs would agree to the release.

Davidson was standing at the rear of the group. 'I've seen the guy somewhere before. I think he might have been a copper.'

'I've had that feeling since I saw the corpse this morning,' Wilson said. 'But if he's a copper, surely someone would have come forward and said that he was missing.'

'Maybe he's no longer a copper,' Davidson said. 'I'm trying to dredge him up from somewhere deep in my memory. Name is something like Harry or Hubert. My memory is gone to pot.'

'We're nine hours into this investigation and we haven't managed to identify the victim,' Wilson said. 'Not exactly a stunning performance.' He knew what the hierarchy in Castlereagh would make of it. Deputy Chief Constable Jennings would use it as a stick to beat both him and his chief super.

'Not our fault, Boss,' Graham said. 'No identification on the body, and the car's registered to a guy who's missing and obviously isn't the victim. The stations won't take a missing persons' report for someone who hasn't been missing for more than twenty-four hours. What are we supposed to do?'

'The people upstairs won't be interested in our excuses,' Wilson said. 'We need to get our thumbs out of our arses on this one. Someone will be going on TV tomorrow and we better have a name by then.'

Browne took a disk from his pocket. 'This is the CCTV from the pub.'

'Give it to Siobhan,' Wilson said. He turned to Graham. 'Anything from the house-to-house?'

'Nothing, except five very disgruntled uniforms. It wasn't the day for knocking on doors.'

'Maybe we should get a leaflet out,' O'Neill said.

'I think the media is a much better bet,' Wilson said.

O'Neill was working on her tablet. 'Look at this, Boss.' She held the tablet up for Wilson. It was mobile phone footage of the scene outside O'Reilly's pub. It showed clearly the body lying face down in the snow. 'It was uploaded this afternoon on the *Chronicle* website.'

'The cleaner,' Wilson said. 'That Hanley character, we should have known better.'

'Nothing we can do about it now,' O'Neill said. 'The TV stations will pick it up for the news this evening.'

Wilson tried to hide his annoyance. The ubiquitous mobile phone was everywhere these days. That wouldn't stop him giving Hanley a rocket the next time they met. 'So much for having a bit of time to get the investigation on the road. Hanley would be smart to keep away from me for the duration.'

'Just someone looking for the main chance,' O'Neill said. 'These days there's always someone around with a mobile phone with a camera. He probably made a few hundred quid from that bit of footage.'

'Not Harry or Hubert,' Davidson said, more to himself than the group. 'The guy's name was Hugh something or other. I think he used to work drugs when I was in Vice.'

'Are you sure?' Wilson said.

'It was a while ago, but I'm pretty certain. The surname will come to me eventually.'

'Siobhan,' Wilson said. 'Get me someone in the Drugs Squad on the line.'

O'Neill went to her desk and picked up the phone. Wilson watched her speaking and working on her computer at the same time.

'I sent the photo over by email for confirmation. The victim was a former detective constable named Hugh Royce. He left the PSNI four years ago.' O'Neill said when she re-joined the group.

'Okay,' Wilson said. 'Everyone has overtime. I'll square it with the chief super. Before we leave here tonight I want everything we have on former Detective Constable Hugh Royce.'

. . .

YVONNE DAVIS WAS GENERALLY in the station way beyond closing time. Either that, or she was in some meeting in Castlereagh that lasted well into the evening. There was no such thing as overtime for senior staff, high levels of dedication were expected.

Davis didn't mind staying late at the office, or sitting listening to colleagues spouting rubbish at a meeting. It was better than the alternative, which was sitting in front of the television with a microwaved meal on her lap. Somewhere along the way the life that she had foreseen for herself hadn't quite panned out. She had kicked her husband to the kerb because of his marital transgressions. It was one of the great ironies of life that the breakup had led to an improvement in his situation while her life had crashed. To her children, she was the mother who was never at home. Because of her absences on PSNI business there was the inevitable drift of the children towards their father. When he left, they hung on for a while before moving to live with him. The lesson she learned was that it pays to be the bastard in the relationship. She was thinking about how twisted life could be when she heard a knock on the door. 'Come in.'

Wilson entered and sat on the chair in front of her desk. 'We've identified the victim. He's a former PSNI detective named Hugh Royce. He used to work in the Drugs Squad.'

She ran the name through her mental Rolodex. 'Never heard of him.'

'I thought I recognised the corpse this morning, but it was Peter Davidson who identified him during the evening briefing. We're looking into his life now.'

'His connection with the PSNI makes things awkward. I'll have to pass this information upstairs. How long ago did he leave?'

'We're checking that now. Siobhan O'Neill said four years. Hopefully it wasn't last week.'

'We're going to be dragged into it?'

'Possibly, it depends where the investigation goes.'

'You and I are hanging on here by a thread. The Armstrong affair was the last straw for some people.'

'Meaning DCC Jennings.'

'While you were sunning yourself on a beach in California, I was faffing around here trying to come up with a reasonable answer for what happened. For God's sake, a government minister you were investigating for murder was abducted and executed. I found myself in the middle of a shit storm.'

'It looks like you coped well, and it was probably character building.'

'With more than a little help from the chief constable.'

'You make a lovely couple. And just for the record, I wasn't sunning myself, I was watching my partner's mother die, and then I helped bury her.'

Davis moved a stray hair away from her face. It was her nervous tell. 'I know and I apologise for the remark. We do, however, seem to be staggering from one crisis to another.'

'Noel Armstrong murdered two young women. He was also responsible for the deaths of people in his own organisation, and he was protected, possibly by someone in our organisation. They should be asking questions of the people who covered up his crimes not the ones who were trying to put him away. But I suppose that would be too much to hope for.'

She stared at him. 'In the meantime, Jennings has the whip hand on us. I hope to God the Royce killing has no political overtones.'

'On the surface it doesn't look like it.'

She opened her top drawer and took out a bottle of whiskey. 'Can I tempt you?'

Wilson shook his head. 'As they say in the States, I'll have to take a rain check. The rest of the team are still working and I should be there with them.'

She poured herself a shot of whiskey but didn't drink. 'We're not out of the woods on the Armstrong affair.'

'Do you think someone might have leaked my theory about Armstrong?'

'I've been thinking about it. I don't suppose you have anyone in mind?'

He didn't answer immediately. 'I'm keeping an eye out, but so far I don't think anyone on the team was responsible.'

She picked up the glass and drank it in one swallow. 'We've survived the initial storm. Don't create another one. Armstrong is in the ground and a couple of cases have been closed. His colleagues are not making any noise for obvious reasons. I hope the people upstairs are ready to let sleeping dogs lie.'

Chance would be a fine thing. Wilson stood and nodded. 'Have a nice evening, ma'am.'

She put the glass into the bottom drawer of her desk. 'You too, Ian, thanks for keeping me informed.

CHAPTER EIGHT

Two men sat in the empty car park of Cliftonville Golf Club. The course was closed due to the inclement weather, and the clubhouse was deserted, which suited the occupants of the car perfectly. Eddie Hills sat behind the wheel of the 750 Mercedes while his boss, Davie Best, sat in the passenger seat. Best was the chief of the mob that controlled much of the crime in Belfast. He glanced to his side as a silver BMW 325 pulled up alongside. He watched as a man got out of the BMW, opened the back door of the Mercedes and settled into the back seat.

'About time,' Best said.

'I was held up at the station.' DCI George Pratley sat back and rubbed his hands together. He was glad the engine was running and the heat was turned up. It was brass-monkey weather outside.

'George, I'm afraid you might have fucked up,' Best said.

'That's your opinion. I did what had to be done.'

'That's the problem. It didn't have to be done. And if it did, it wasn't your place to make the decision to do it.'

'I suppose it would have been handled better by your pet Doberman,' Pratley said.

Hills took his hands off the steering wheel and turned to look at Pratley. It was a look that would send a shiver through the strongest of men. Best put a hand on Hills' shoulder. 'Did anyone ever tell you not to poke a bear?'

'Royce was about to rat us out,' Pratley said. 'I took an executive decision to eliminate him.'

'Who told you that you were a fucking executive?' Best said. 'You're so far down the chain of command that there isn't even a name for the position you occupy. We understood that Royce had the potential to become a risk to the organisation and we would have taken care of that risk when it became overt. If he was going to be eliminated, I should have been consulted.'

'Nobody knew Royce better than me,' Pratley said. 'I worked with that man for three years. Hell, I was the one who recruited him. He was a junkie, and junkies can't be trusted. Royce knew things that could get us all put away.'

'Royce knew things about *you* that could get *you* put away.' Best turned to stare at Pratley. 'You're the only one who knows the next step on the ladder.'

Pratley felt a tingle run up his spine. The inference in Best's words was clear enough. 'I was protecting our arrangements. Royce was hell-bent on going to the authorities and spilling his guts. That would put the focus on the drug business and my squad. Right now, you're raking in the money because of my cooperation. What happens if I go down?'

'We'll deal with that problem when it arises,' Best said. 'Stick to your own business and don't even think of taking another executive decision. We're way beyond the days when you used to sell Rice and McGreary their own gear back. You're a partner in the firm now, a very junior partner.'

'Don't worry,' Pratley said. 'The hit was clean. It will be another unsolved murder to add to the list. What's done is done. A possible rat has been eliminated. It should encourage a spurt of loyalty in the rest of your employees if nothing else.'

'You go back to your cosy little house,' Best said. 'And keep doing what you've been doing. We'll let you intercept a shipment soon so that everyone will think what a great job you're doing. But we'll want the gear back, mind.' Best put his hand out and felt the material of Pratley's coat. 'Nice coat, cashmere if I'm not mistaken.'

Pratley nodded.

'We're done here,' Best said. 'Get the fuck out.'

Pratley opened the door and slid out into the cold night. He shivered as the cold hit him. McGreary and Rice were schoolboys in comparison with Best and that crazy fucker Hills. He climbed back into his car and turned on the engine. He needed a drink. No, he needed a lot of drinks.

'I don't like it,' Hills said as soon as the back door closed. 'Mad Mickey was one thing. Royce is another. Peelers tend to stick together and although Royce was a wrong one, they're not going to let it go easily. Wilson is no dummy. He'll soon start to add two and two together and he might end up with five.' Hills moved the Mercedes away from the edge of the car park. He made a point of shining his headlights on the man in the BMW. 'I think the wrong man might have been killed.' His voice was soft but full of menace.

'You might be right there,' Best said.

CHAPTER NINE

The team, minus Peter Davidson who apparently had a meeting that couldn't be cancelled, had been at their computers and on their phones for almost two hours when Wilson called a halt. Davis would be screaming at him for approving overtime without consulting her first. He had phoned Reid to explain the late night only to find that she was happy to remain at the Royal. He wasn't the only one with a backlog and hers was considerably larger. They'd agreed to meet later for a drink at the Crown.

The whiteboard was gradually filling up. The victim was already named at the top and beneath was a photograph that had been emailed over from HR at Castlereagh. It showed a very different Hugh Royce from the one Wilson had seen at the crime scene. The photo had been taken seven years earlier for Royce's warrant card, when he was a clean-shaven man with carefully coiffed fair hair above his clear blue eyes, straight nose and dimpled chin. A lot of water had flowed under the bridge since, and its effect on Royce hadn't been positive. O'Neill had managed to pull Royce's service record from the main computer. PSNI officers' personnel files are confidential under the Data Protection Act. They contain annual appraisals and hierarchical notes and memos, and because of the legislation can be viewed only by the individual officer and approved personnel. There was a rumour in the force that another more secret personnel file existed, but that was only a rumour, or was it? So what O'Neill had was a resumé of Royce's career in the PSNI. She had already transferred the information to the whiteboard. Harry Graham had busied himself called up contacts to see if they had any anecdotes to offer on Royce, or his working environment.

Wilson reconvened the team in front of the whiteboard. He tapped the HR photograph. 'Hugh Royce was born in 1978 in Strabane and joined the PSNI in 2008. He spent the first three years as a uniformed officer in Derry. In 2011 he became a detective constable and was posted to the Drugs Squad here in Belfast. That's when this photo was taken. In 2014 his career came to a dramatic halt when he was accused of corruption. He quit the force rather than face conviction and jail.'

'He wasn't the only one, Boss,' Graham said. 'There was a major anti-corruption push at the time, especially in the Drugs and Vice Squads. A couple of guys were arrested and tried, but the cost was astronomic. Someone across the water hit on the ploy of getting anyone accused of corruption to just resign. It was called the '23 pence solution' because at the time that was the cost of a stamp.' Graham didn't bother to add that, Peter Davidson was one of those who had been presented with the resignation letter but he had refused to sign. It turned out to be the best strategy.

'We need to find out how Royce went from this,' Wilson pointed to the HR photo, 'to this.' He moved his finger to the crime scene photo. 'Starting tomorrow we are going to comb through the life of Hugh Royce. He was married but divorced late in 2014. There were no children. We need to find his wife. We need to find out how he came by the car. So we still need to interview Donaldson. We need to find out where he was living and see what we can find there. Did he have friends in the Drugs Squad? Was he still in touch with them? Where did he work? Somebody killed him for a reason and we need to find that reason.'

'Siobhan and myself have been through the CCTV from the pub,' Browne said. 'We have the patrons leaving early at eleven o'clock. Then the Polo rolls up at eleven fifty and parks where the camera can see it. A man gets out, probably Royce, and walks into the lee of the pub where he disappears, and that's it. No sign of the killer, or Royce, after that because the camera is fixed and didn't catch the action.'

'We have to check for CCTV along the Antrim Road,' Wilson said. He turned to Browne. 'Harry got the shit end of the stick today, so it's your turn tomorrow. If there's any CCTV out there, I want to see it.' He looked around at the faces of the team. Had one of them leaked the information on Armstrong? He might have done so himself if he'd had the opportunity – the idea had certainly occurred to him, so maybe he was as guilty as the real culprit. 'Away home with the lot of you, we have a lot of work ahead.'

CHAPTER TEN

The barman nodded at Wilson as soon as he entered the Crown, a signal usually indicating that his snug was occupied but available. Wilson pushed open the door expecting to see Reid's beautiful face and was instead confronted by journalist Jock McDevitt's not exactly ugly, but certainly not beautiful, mug. The ruddy colour on McDevitt's face indicated that he hadn't just arrived.

'Thanks be to God,' McDevitt said as soon as Wilson was seated. 'I thought my lonely vigil was going to last the whole night. Don't you ever look at the messages on your phone?'

'I was busy.' Wilson had received eight messages from McDevitt in the course of the afternoon and evening. 'I thought I might have met you at the Antrim Road crime scene this morning.'

McDevitt pushed the bell and ordered two pints of Guinness. 'Too bloody cold. I sent along an intern. My body is still in California in terms of heat. But I don't need to stand in the cold when my very best friend is the SIO.' McDevitt had been in Los Angeles at the same time as Wilson trying to sell his book on the Maggie Cummerford case to a movie company. 'Wasn't that a wonderful meal we had in the Ocean Club in

Malibu? They're talking about Colin Farrell playing you in the movie.'

'If that's your attempt at indicating that I owe you, you're knocking on the wrong door.'

The barman arrived and distributed the drinks. McDevitt handed over the money. 'Poor bastard, shot on the coldest night of the year. The coldest night ever, for all I know.' McDevitt was looking sideways at Wilson, who was sipping his drink. 'You know who he is, don't you?'

Wilson toasted McDevitt. 'Cheers.'

McDevitt raised his glass and smiled. 'The people who say the Chinese are inscrutable haven't met Lisburn man. You know I'll find out.'

'Aye, you will, when the press release is issued by the media service.'

'So, my very best friend is not going to help me.' McDevitt put on his sad clown look.

'Not this time, Jock, it wouldn't look good if you were way ahead of the posse.'

'Yes it would because I'm always ahead of the posse.'

Wilson realised that he had finished his drink. He was about to ring for another round when he thought that McDevitt probably had enough.

McDevitt suddenly sobered up. 'Get the next round in. I was on water until you arrived. I've had a lousy cold since I returned from LA, so make mine a hot whiskey.'

The door of the snug was ajar and Reid pushed in on the two men. 'Did someone just mention hot whiskey? I'd love one thanks.' She bent and kissed Wilson before sitting beside him.

Wilson pushed the bell and ordered the drinks.

McDevitt looked at Reid. 'Did you ever hear that when the American Indians saved the life of one of their tribe they were responsible for that person?'

Reid shook her head. 'Apropos of what?'

'Your partner saved my life, and now he won't help me.'

The drinks arrived and Wilson paid. He distributed the glasses. 'Forget it, I'm not giving you the name of the victim. You'll have it tomorrow along with the other media outlets. The subject is now closed.'

'How did it go in LA?' Reid asked.

'We pitched the studios,' said McDevitt. 'There's a lot of interest, but we'll just have to wait and see. It's a shot in the dark, so I'm still buying lottery tickets.'

Wilson's stomach rumbled. 'Let's drink up and get something to eat. Tomorrow is going to be a busy day.'

CHAPTER ELEVEN

When Wilson arrived the next morning, the only person missing from the squad room was Browne. The cold spell was continuing and Browne would not thank his boss for giving him the job of searching for possibly non-existent CCTV footage. The other three members of the team were working at their desks. Wilson went into his office and fired up his computer. He checked his emails and saw that Finlay had already compiled a draft forensic report. The conclusion was that the killer had left no evidence except a badly deformed slug that had passed through Royce's head and hit the concrete path outside the pub. The other two rounds had not yet been located. The slug was a nine millimetre and the markings indicated that it was fired from a Browning Hi-Power. That would be confirmed when Finlay found the other two slugs. The autopsy was scheduled for midday and Wilson decided to send Graham to attend. In the meantime, it was full steam ahead on finding out everything there was to know about Royce.

Wilson was just finishing the forensic report when O'Neill knocked on his door. He motioned her to enter.

She stood with a sheaf of papers in her hand. 'I've been

tracing Royce. I've checked the usual government channels, the Department of Social Welfare and Her Majesty's Revenue Commissioners. Luckily there was only one Hugh Royce listed for the province. The problem is that there's nothing recent. He's not drawing the dole and he's a bit behind with his tax declarations. I'm sure HMRC have been anxious to speak with him. I tried the housing register for his address while in the PSNI, but he no longer lives there. I have his birth certificate, his marriage certificate, his decree nisi and even his A level results.' She put the relevant documents on the desk in front of Wilson. 'There were three different addresses associated with his annual declaration for tax purposes. I did a search on them and they're rental properties where he no longer resides. Next, I looked at his ex-wife. Her maiden name was Sharon Feeney and there's no one of that name in Belfast, neither is there a Sharon Royce. I looked for marriages over the past five years for her married and maiden names. There were seven in total but only two in Belfast. The husbands' names are Roger Appleton and Bruce Parnell. I called the phone numbers associated with both. Sharon Feeney is now Sharon Parnell and she hasn't spoken to or seen her husband since the day he signed the divorce papers. I told her that he was deceased and her only comment was "good riddance". She doesn't want to talk about her ex.'

'That's not her choice, we'll talk to her whether she wants to or not. Give Harry the address and the phone number.'

'It's already in the murder book.'

'Good job. We have no idea of his current address?'

'He doesn't own a property so I'm assuming he rents. If that's the case, his residence could be anywhere.'

'Any sign of him on social media?'

'Nothing, he has no social media footprint, no Facebook, Twitter, nothing.'

'Does he own a mobile phone?'

'I've checked with the networks and he doesn't have a contract. Might have a pay-as-you-go though.'

'Looks like you've covered all the bases so far.'

'There's one more piece of information I unearthed. Royce was an orphan since the age of eighteen. The Royces were in their forties when they married. John Royce died from prostate cancer when his son was twelve. His wife, Diana, had early dementia and died six years later at the age of sixty-three.'

'Fatherless at an impressionable age, motherless before he reached full manhood – not the ideal start to adulthood,' Wilson thought of his own situation. He had lost his father and was estranged from his mother when he was scarcely eighteen. Maybe he and Royce had more in common than he would like to think. He was lost in thought when O'Neill spoke again.

'Anything else?' she asked.

'No, not right now, but I'm sure you'll find something useful to do.'

'I suppose you're going to make a request for information from the public.'

Wilson turned to his emails and opened a message from Public Affairs. 'There's going to be a press conference downstairs at high noon, just the chief super and me. The hierarchy are treating us like pariahs since the Armstrong affair.' He looked up to see her reaction. There was none. 'Print me up a batch of copies of that HR photo, on proper glossy paper. The request for information from the public will go out on the evening news channels. We'll have to downplay the fact that he was a PSNI officer who left in disgrace.'

Graham came to the door as O'Neill exited. 'I've been ringing around trying to find out what Royce did to get himself fired. Nobody seems to know, or at least that's what they're saying. I know this is going to hurt, but you're going to have to contact someone in Professional Services to access the file.'

Wilson frowned. 'There's no way that PS will respond to

me, given our chequered past. I'll have to ask the chief super to approach them.'

Wilson was frustrated with the rate of progress. They knew who their victim was, but nothing about him, especially not where he lived. There was little or no forensic evidence at the scene, and there had been no word yet from Browne concerning additional CCTV. The house-to-house had come up empty and they were going to look like a crowd of clowns on TV begging for the public's help. But it was what it was. His watch showed it was fifteen minutes to eleven. Maybe something would break in the next hour.

He phoned Davis and brought her up to date, then he asked her to use her influence to have the PS file released to him. They needed to know why Royce had signed his career away. He forwarded the forensic report to the members of the team and asked O'Neill to include it in the murder book. He sat back and prayed for a miracle.

The phone rang half an hour later. It was Finlay and the content of the call wasn't the miracle he'd been praying for. The initial search of the car had come up empty. They had found eight separate sets of fingerprints and they would eliminate Royce before checking the rest with the database. Wilson typed up the content of the call and forwarded it to O'Neill and Graham. He went into the washroom and splashed water on his face. Two weeks back in the job and all the benefit of the trip to the States had disappeared. He combed his hair and started down to the cafeteria, which had been commandeered for the press conference. A media person in the form of a young female officer was setting the scene up and ushering a group of journalists into their places. Two television cameras on tripods were facing the table on which a series of micro-phones and miscellaneous recording devices had been set. Heads turned as soon as Wilson made his way forward. Jock McDevitt winked as Wilson passed. Wilson ignored him and sat off-centre at the table.

Next Davis strode into the room in full uniform carrying a file under her arm. Her gait said that she meant business. She sat in the centre facing the cameras and looked at her watch. 'I think that we're ready to go,' she said, nodding at the TV cameramen, who signalled back that they were ready.

She began reading from a note attached to the top of the file. 'Yesterday morning the body of a man, now identified as Hugh Royce, was found outside O'Reilly's pub on the Antrim Road. Mr Royce had been shot three times and was declared dead at the scene. We have established that Mr Royce was murdered at some time between eleven o'clock the previous evening and two o'clock yesterday morning. Detective Superintendent Wilson and his team are investigating the crime. Perhaps you would like to say something, Detective Superintendent.'

'Thank you,' Wilson said. 'We are anxiously seeking anyone who might have been in the area of the Antrim Road when this crime was committed. Because of the foul weather, this normally busy thoroughfare was practically empty. If you saw anything, even if you didn't recognise its importance at the time, please contact us at the number appearing now on your screen. We are also appealing to anyone who has information on Mr Royce, or his movements on the day of his death, to contact us urgently.'

'There will be no questions,' Davis said and stood.

Wilson followed suit. They started to leave the room. Several journalists shouted questions after them. As soon as they were outside Davis turned to him. 'You can't have Royce's file from Professional Services, but someone will be in your office at three this afternoon.'

CHAPTER TWELVE

Peter Davidson has spent what passed for a life as an RUC and PSNI officer. In the late 1980s he had been a uniformed officer policing sectarian violence. He often wondered what effect this seminal experience had on his low opinion of the human race in general. He became a detective constable in the 1990s, working in Vice. He lost his sergeant's grade in the 2000s because of his liking for what the Toms were offering. To a large extent Ian Wilson and the Murder Squad had resurrected him. It didn't quite return him to the naïve young man who had joined the force, but it at least gave him some belief in the decency of human nature. On the way there had been two wives and three children, but Davidson was never cut out to be a family man. He paid the wives off monthly and sent his children a present of money on their birthdays. He was beginning to give up on having a future when he met Irene Carlisle. She had given him a new lease on life, even though he feared it would be only a temporary one. Davidson fancied that he knew women, he'd had enough experience of them to make that assertion, and he feared that Irene's dalliance with him was a passing fancy. As soon as she had the insurance money in her hand, he would be dumped.

He was ruminating on this part of his future as he turned off North Street and headed up Union Street in the direction of his objective, the Sunflower Pub. Irene had bought him an expensive Barbour jacket as a Christmas present and he snuggled deeper into it as he faced into the cold wind that blew in his face as he turned the corner. He pushed in the door of the bar and felt instant relief from the cold. The man he had arranged to meet was sitting in the corner close to a compact stage area that was dominated by the large banner advertising Black Bush. He walked across the room and sat down at the small circular table.

'Peter, you old rogue, I thought you'd be retired by now,' the man said as Davidson took his seat.

'Aye, Jamsie, and I thought you'd be dead by now.' Davidson didn't know what age former Detective Inspector James Gibbons was, but he was certainly more than eighty. Gibbons had a head like a bowling ball and his bald pate was covered with liver spots. He sported two patches of facial hair on either cheek like some character from a Dickens novel.

'I won't last much longer,' Gibbons said. 'I told my children this was probably my last Christmas. That's a fine jacket you have on you there.'

'Christmas present. What can I get you?'

Gibbons glanced at the advertisement on the stage. 'And make it a double.'

Davidson went to the bar and returned with two glasses of Black Bush.

'Your health,' Gibbons toasted and sipped his whiskey. 'What do you want with an old fogey like me, young Peter?'

Davidson sipped his drink. 'You still have contacts in the Branch?'

'A few, but the good ones are dead and gone. What's on your mind?'

'I'm looking for information on one of the current mob.'

Gibbons sipped his drink. 'Bad idea.'

'I'm trying to do it delicately.'

'You couldn't do it delicately enough. Those boys don't like outsiders rooting around in their business. Take my advice and give it a miss.'

'I just need a bit of background information.'

Gibbons emptied his glass and handed it to Davidson, who went to the bar and procured a refill.

Gibbons took the glass. 'I still have a few contacts. What's the guy's name?'

'Simon Jackson.'

Gibbons sipped his drink. 'Simon Jackson.' He rolled the name on his tongue. 'Don't know him. He's after my time. The new ones are a different breed. I'll ask about him very delicately.'

Davidson took a card from his jacket pocket and pushed it across the table.

Gibbons took it and slipped it into his pocket. 'Have you been to Windsor Park lately? Linfield are a disgrace this season.'

CHAPTER THIRTEEN

B rowne came back to the office after lunch complaining about the pain in his feet, which he felt might be the beginnings of frostbite. He also came back empty handed. Many of the residents of the Antrim Road had installed CCTV systems, but in every case the camera was pointed at their gate. Nobody in the vicinity of O'Reilly's pub had installed CCTV. It was a dead end. O'Neill had contacted Traffic and they promised a disk with whatever footage was available for the hours in question. It was going to be an unenviable job to go through the footage. Wilson was finishing his cafeteria lunch of tuna salad on soggy white bread and weak tea when Graham knocked on his door. He dumped the remains of his meal into the wastebasket and decided he was finally finished with cafeteria food. 'You've nearly got your colour back,' he said when Graham entered.

'I hate that place.' Graham didn't bother to sit. 'Dead bodies don't bother me, but when I see the chest opened and all the crap that's inside my stomach does somersaults. Why is it always me that has to attend the autopsies?'

'I thought I did you a favour, keeping you out of the cold.'

'Thanks for nothing.'

'How did it go?'

'The professor did her normal efficient job of slicing and dicing. Royce wasn't exactly the healthiest man alive, but he had a lot of years left in him. The two shots to the chest did for him, the shot to the head was for good measure.'

'Anything else?'

'Royce had been a junkie. His arms are covered with old needle marks. The professor estimated that the track marks could be as old as two years. She wasn't able to narrow the time of death down more than eleven p.m. to two a.m. The full report will be here this evening and Professor Reid said, if you want, you can contact her with any questions. How did the press conference go?'

'We managed to avoid the issue of Royce being a former PSNI officer, for now. The journos will be all over this by the end of the day and I wouldn't be surprised to see that fact highlighted in tomorrow morning's newspapers.'

'The phones will be going crazy. It'll be on the radio by now and TV this evening.'

'That's not your problem but following up on those calls will be.'

'Thanks, Boss, you're really giving me some class jobs. Every crazy in Belfast will be on the line peddling whatever half-assed theory they have concerning the murder. It's the ones who claim to have the alien responsible in a kitchen cupboard that I can't stand. A lot of people out there need professional help.'

'First priority is to discover Royce's address. Any call that gives us a location gets priority. In the meantime, I want you to contact the former Mrs Royce and tell her that, despite her reticence, she's going to be interviewed by us either at her home or at the station; the choice is hers.'

'On it,' Graham nodded and left.

So Royce had been a junkie but was clean for at least two years. Wilson wondered whether that happened before he was drummed out of the force or after. He supposed it was an occupational hazard for members of the Drugs Squad. The job obliges them to be around drugs and pushers who spend money like water. The temptation must be there daily. He knew that Davidson had encountered similar problems when he was in the Vice Squad. The thin line between the police and the criminals goes a long way back, and there is plenty of historical evidence to show that the line has often been crossed. That thought cut deep with him. His own father was committed to justice but managed to betray that commitment. Given that fact, he wasn't going to judge Hugh Royce too harshly.

CHAPTER FOURTEEN

A t exactly three o'clock there was a knock on Wilson's door. He looked up to see an attractive young woman and motioned her in.

'Detective Sergeant Lucy Kane, Professional Services,' she said as she walked forward with her hand outstretched.

Wilson stood and shook. 'Detective Superintendent Ian Wilson, please sit down.' Kane looked to be in her early thirties. She had short dark hair, a pale Irish face that was attractive rather than beautiful and a slim lithe body that was shown off by a blue trouser suit. She was either a regular member of a gym or a dedicated runner.

'Apparently your chief super has been speaking to mine,' Kane said, taking a seat directly facing Wilson.

'That's the way it usually works.'

'Unfortunately, we're not able to release files that we've been working on, but I've examined the Hugh Royce file and I'm permitted to answer your questions up to a limit. The case was before my time, so everything I tell you is what I learned from the file.'

'And the limit is?'

'I can't name any of the witnesses.'

'That's reasonable. Tell me why Royce was asked to leave.'

'There was an allegation from a fellow officer that seized drugs had disappeared from storage and been replaced by sachets of flour. When the allegation was investigated, it was shown to be true. There was evidence that the thefts were systematic. We were about to launch a full-scale investigation of the squad when Royce's name came to the fore.'

'Was there any specific evidence against him?'

'Only the allegation by a fellow officer.'

'So what happened then?'

'Royce was presented with the allegation and what little evidence we had. He was told that Professional Services was about to launch a full investigation and if it was established that he had stolen the drugs, he would be charged with corruption and if found guilty, would receive a long custodial sentence.'

'Were you confident of a successful prosecution?'

'From what I've read, I'd say the investigation would have been costly and might not have been successful.'

'So the option that was put to Royce was to resign or risk jail on a corruption charge?'

'That is my understanding.'

'So presumably he was asked to sign a prepared letter, and he just did?'

'Apparently.'

'Was the signing of that letter not an admission of guilt?'

'Not in law. We had no direct evidence against him. He was simply resigning from the force.'

'Was the full investigation ever completed?'

'No, the fact that Royce accepted retirement was construed at the time as a valid reason to short-circuit the investigation. I got the impression from the file that my colleagues were overjoyed because the budget for the full investigation might not have been approved.'

'Who made the decision to offer Royce retirement?'

'I have no idea.'

'It's not in the file?'

'No.'

'What happened to the officer who made the allegation?'

'I can't answer that.'

'Do you know that Hugh Royce has been murdered?'

'Yes.'

'I'm going to ask you for a favour. You can refuse and I won't be offended. If it compromises you in any way, I'll understand. I don't want the name of the officer who made the allegation, but I would like to know what happened to him. You can look at his record. I'd like to know if he's still in the Drugs Squad, or even still on the force.'

'Why do you want to know?'

'Royce was shot twice in the chest and once in the head, which indicates that someone wanted him very dead. The killer left almost no forensic evidence, down to taking his shell casings with him, which suggests either a professional hitman or possibly a police officer. Royce was a former Drugs Squad officer drummed out for corruption on nothing more than an allegation, and the autopsy shows that he was an addict but has been clean for at least two years. Something is stinking to high heaven here, and it just could lead back to the PSNI. I think that it's in everyone's interest to look into what happened in the past. I don't need the name, only what happened to him.'

'I may have to discuss this with a superior.'

'Be my guest. Don't forget, we're all on the same side.'

She started to rise. 'While I was at it, I took a look at your file. You sail pretty close to the wind.'

'But I'd never sign a retirement letter without substantial evidence against me.'

She smiled. 'You obviously weren't guilty of sexual harassment.'

'That was the conclusion of the investigation.'

'I hope your luck hasn't changed.' She turned towards the door. 'I'll be in touch, maybe.'

'Thanks.' Wilson watched her leave the office. She was a step up from Coyne and Gillespie, the two assholes who tried to railroad him for the screw-up in the Worthington investigation.

He reflected on Royce's retirement. It was a bit too pat. Royce was presented with a series of allegations, and immediately folded. Yet the man had been a detective constable, hardly the type to throw himself under a bus. In Wilson's experience, men who end up under the bus were thrown there by someone else. He was trying to reconcile the man in the HR photo with the dishevelled figure in the snow outside O'Reilly's. Royce looked like he had fallen on hard times. There was clearly a lot more to learn about him and Wilson had a feeling that most of it would not be pleasant.

His computer made a ding indicating the arrival of an email. It was the autopsy report from Reid. He downloaded the file and started reading. Ten minutes later he had finished and forwarded the file to the rest of the team. Royce wasn't about to die naturally anytime soon, and if it wasn't for three nine-millimetre slugs, he would still be in the pink. The contents of his stomach showed that he'd dined royally on fish and chips and a cola. His body was covered with old needle marks. He had serious gum disease and tooth decay. The good news was that he hadn't gone the full distance with the drugs. Something had happened to make him stop. A good man had gone bad and then had somehow restored himself. Wilson needed a drink. He took out his mobile phone and texted Reid: *The Crown six thirty?* He had an immediate positive reply. Maybe the Royce autopsy had depressed her as well. He wondered, and not for the first time, how she could do her job.

CHAPTER FIFTEEN

The evening briefing had taken place in an air of disappointment. They were thirty-six hours into the investigation and they still had no line on Royce's address. The picture of the man was coming together very slowly. The victim was a welter of contradictions, and more worryingly, the years since his departure from the PSNI appeared to be a total mystery. Wilson had relayed the content of his discussion with Kane and it was clear that there had been some corruption in the Drugs Squad that Royce was involved in. Why else would he have rushed to accept the resignation letter? It was becoming increasingly important to learn about Royce and the missing years. None of the information they had amassed so far could be construed as being the basis of a motive for his murder. Wilson had informed Davis of the progress so far and indicated that the response to the appeal would be critical. Graham had stayed on to handle whatever calls had come in and the rest of the team had headed for the exit.

Wilson went straight to the Crown, where he found his snug unoccupied and settled himself to await the arrival of Reid. He had just started on his first pint when the door opened. The smile faded from his face when he recognised the new arrival as DCI George Pratley, the head of the Drugs Squad. They had never worked together but had met on a senior officers' management course a few years previously.

'I heard this was your regular watering hole,' Pratley said as he entered the snug. 'Mind if I join you?'

'I was wondering when I was going to see you,' Wilson said.

Pratley sat down and laid the glass he was holding on the table. 'How so?'

'Hugh Royce was one of your guys.' Pratley had put on some weight since Wilson had seen him last. He took in the cashmere coat, the English leather shoes and the expensive looking watch. They must pay higher salaries in the Drugs Squad, or else Mrs Pratley must be bringing home a lot of bacon.

'Poor Hugh,' Pratley sipped his whiskey. 'He had a hell of a lot of potential. I even thought that someday he might replace me as the head of the squad.'

'They rise high before their wings melt and they fall to ground. How did it happen?'

'No idea. Maybe he needed money at home. Maybe it was because we were after the likes of Gerry McGreary and Sammy Rice and they managed to corrupt him by force. I never found out.' He leaned back for the bell. 'Can I get you a drink?'

'No,' Wilson said. 'I'm okay for the moment.' He watched as Pratley ordered himself a refill.

'I looked at his record,' Wilson said. 'He was a smart boy, too smart to screw up his career for a couple of quid.'

'Word has it he lifted two kilos.'

'That's a lot of weight to move.'

'Not if you sell it back to where it came from.'

Pratley's drink arrived and he paid for it. 'Are you sure you don't want one?' he asked Wilson before he let the barman go.

'Absolutely. Did you stay in contact with him after he retired?'

'For a while,' Pratley drank half his glass. 'Bitch of a wife divorced him a few months after he left. She didn't understand the phrase "for better or worse". You talk to her yet?'

'No.'

'If you do, don't believe a word the bitch says.' He took out his mobile phone and brought up a picture of the dead body that had been circulated on the Internet. He turned the phone to show Wilson. 'I never thought that Hugh Royce would end up like that. What line of enquiry are you following?'

'We're looking at everything right now. The last years are a bit of a mystery, but we're trying to fill in the gaps. Someone wanted your pal Royce dead.'

'He's not my pal.'

'Sorry, I got the impression that you were close. If you were building him up to take over the squad, you must have been mentoring him. What went wrong?'

There was a knock on the door and Reid put her head round the corner. 'If you're busy, I'll wait at the bar.'

Pratley stood. 'No, no, I've got to be away, things to do, places to be.' He finished his glass and manoeuvred himself passed Reid without touching her. At the door he turned back to Wilson. 'If I can help.'

'I'll be in touch,' Wilson replied, making room for Reid.

'Who was that?' she asked as she settled herself and leaned over to kiss Wilson.

'That was DCI George Pratley, the head of the Drugs Squad.' He pushed the bell.

'Double gin and tonic. And what was he doing here with you?'

'That's a very interesting question. Ostensibly he was telling me how much he cared for poor Hugh Royce, but he never once exhorted me to find the bloody murderer. Mind you it's been a few years since they served together.' The barman arrived and he ordered the drinks. 'We're off home after this one. We're both bushed and an early night is on the cards.'

'Is that a threat or a promise?'

'Probably both.'

The drinks arrived and he paid.

'I saw you on the news, very senatorial. Davis looked a little stressed.' She clinked glasses and drank.

Wilson finished his pint and put the glass away. He was still thinking about his conversation with Pratley.

PRATLEY LEFT the Crown and hailed a black taxi. He sat in the back, gave his address and pulled the glass divider across. He took out his mobile phone. 'It's me. I just had a drink with Wilson. He's nowhere on the Royce business.'

'We know, now get off the phone.' Davie Best cut the communication. Fucking mobile phones, there was always someone listening somewhere, worst invention ever. Who was he kidding? In the course of the past year, he had set up an intelligence operation to rival that of the PSNI and the British military. He hated to admit it, but Pratley had been right about Royce. The stupid bugger had gone rogue and was about to spill on their drugs operation. There was no way that could be allowed to happen, and it was probably necessary for Royce to die. There was big money involved and the people further up the line who financed the operation wouldn't hesitate at taking a serving copper out. Mr Wilson had better be wary.

CHAPTER SIXTEEN

Wilson returned from his run to find not only his breakfast on the table but also a copy of the *Chronicle* with a handwritten message on the top: *Compliments of your pal, Jock, call me*. He called out for Reid, but she had already left for the Royal. He wolfed down a bowl of cereal while he read McDevitt's front-page article. The *Chronicle* saw Royce's death as the start of a turf war between different drug gangs. Wilson was sometimes amazed at McDevitt's ability to get at information and then twist it in ways that only a journalist could. The article emphasised Royce's past as a Drugs Squad officer and even had outline details of his fall from grace. Royce's face stared out from the first page under a headline 'The First of Many?'. At least McDevitt had included the PSNI's call for witnesses. Wilson ignored McDevitt's 'call me' request; he didn't need to speak to McDevitt at that moment. It would not be a civil conversation.

THE TEAM ASSEMBLED before the whiteboard at nine o'clock. Some of the details from the forensic report and the autopsy had been added.

'Anything from the phones, Harry?' Wilson asked.

'They're not exactly flooding in, Boss,' Graham said. 'It appears that our friend Royce kept himself to himself.'

'Either that or he mixed in company that doesn't want to communicate with the PSNI,' Wilson said. 'Any anonymous callers?'

'Most are anonymous,' Graham said. 'The only ones who give their names are the flakes. The bottom line is that we haven't had one call that gives us an address.'

'Shit,' Wilson said. 'Royce wasn't sleeping under a bridge. We need to find out where he lived and who his associates were. Has the wife been contacted?'

'Yes, Boss,' Graham said. 'She's expecting us to call to her house this morning.'

'Okay, keep at it. Rory, follow up on the forensic report. The sooner we have news on the gun the better. Siobhan, get me what you can on DCI George Pratley and follow up on the CCTV from Traffic.'

Davidson joined him on his walk back to the office. 'I'm meeting some of the Technical Branch guys today about locating those calls. What if they ask me for paperwork?'

'Tell them it's a murder investigation. We don't need paperwork.'

Wilson sat at his desk. It was forty-eight hours since he had stood over the dead body of Hugh Royce, and they had made only minimal progress. He was about to start on his emails when the phone rang.

'Did you like the article?' There was a trace of mirth in McDevitt's voice.

'Feck off. And thanks for raising the scare level of Joe Citizen. After reading your piece, they'll be expecting a re-run of the St Valentine's Day Massacre.'

'That's what newspapers are for these days. The blokes at the top want the general population to be pissing in their pants. By the way, you didn't bother to call me. That was very remiss of you, because I'm about to pull you out of the quick-sand again.'

'How so?'

'I want you to meet a mate of mine. He's very shy and he won't meet you at the station or anywhere there are a lot of people. But he knows things about your friend Royce.'

'Where and when?'

'You know the car park at the entrance to the Black Mountain?'

'I've been there. When?'

'Eleven, and come alone. My mate is not only shy, he's also very nervous.'

'I'll be there and this had better be good.'

'It will be.' The line went dead.

Wilson tried to concentrate on his administrative tasks but his mind was flying around like a ball on a squash court. Maybe McDevitt was right about a potential turf war and perhaps Royce wasn't the first victim. He was certain that the body found in the burned-out BMW at Helen's Bay was that of Mad Mickey Duff, a known character in the drugs business. Perhaps Mad Mickey was the first victim. Belfast definitely didn't need a turf war between drugs gangs. It would litter the street with bodies. Davie Best had taken over the drugs operation of the Rice and McGreary gangs. But who else was on the scene? And in the background there was the armed vigilante group Republican Action Against Drugs, which had admitted responsibility for killing several drug dealers. The more they progressed on the Royce murder the more muddy the waters became. He gave up on the administration. He'd have just enough time to interview the former Mrs Royce before meeting with McDevitt and his mate.

MRS SHARON PARNELL, lived in a two-storey semi-detached

house on the Shore Road in Greenisland, a small community north of Belfast.

'Come on in.' Parnell opened the door to Wilson and Graham. She was in her late-thirties and casually dressed in loose jeans and a blue cotton top. Her hair was dark with a reddish tinge and she had a pleasant open face.

Graham showed his warrant card as they entered.

'It's okay.' She looked at Wilson. 'I saw you on the telly.'

'Always wise to check,' Wilson said, following her into a small living room to the left of the entrance hall.

'It's still freezing out, so I suppose a cup of tea wouldn't go amiss? The kettle is already on.' Parnell appeared nervous, but then again no one likes a visit from the police no matter how innocent they are. 'Please sit down, I'll be back in a minute.'

Wilson and Graham sat together on a couch and listened to the sounds of a kettle being boiled and crockery being loaded onto a tray. Parnell returned after a few minutes with a laden tray. She played mother then sat when both police officers had cups of tea in their hands. 'I really don't know how I can help. I haven't seen Hugh in years.'

'We're still at the stage of building up a picture of Hugh Royce.' Wilson sipped his tea. 'You were still married when he retired from the force?'

'Yes, we lived in town at the time. I married Hugh when I was twenty-one and he was twenty-six. I was a bit naïve I'm afraid.'

'He liked being a police officer?' Wilson asked.

A wistful look came over her face. 'Loved it, couldn't have been prouder when he was made a detective constable. His heart was nearly bursting out of his chest when he received the letter.'

'You had no family?'

'No, at first we waited and then we tried. Nothing happened. We were talking about IVF, but it isn't cheap. About that time Hugh started to change.'

'In what way?' Wilson asked.

'He became more secretive. There was always something happening in the job that kept him out late and on edge. I had to learn to walk on eggshells around him.'

Wilson had the feeling she wanted to say more. 'This is a murder enquiry. We want desperately to find the person, or persons, who murdered your ex-husband, so if there's anything that you think might help us, I'd like to hear it.'

She didn't reply and sat with her hands resting on her lap.

'Something happened when he was in the Drugs Squad?' Wilson asked to break the silence.

'He wasn't happy there. We had more money coming in because of all the overtime he said he was doing. But I think the overtime was bullshit. I smelled other women on him. He'd changed and it wasn't a change for the better.'

'You know that he was accused of corruption,' Wilson said.

'Yes, but that wasn't the Hugh I knew.'

'He signed the resignation letter.'

'That broke him. He came home the night he resigned and shut himself off in the bedroom. I went to comfort him and I heard him crying.'

Wilson put down his teacup. 'I don't understand how someone who was so positive about the job would have signed the letter so willingly.'

She thought for a moment. 'Have you met George Pratley?'

'Yes,' Wilson said.

'I think that man is in league with the devil,' she said.

'Why?'

'It was Pratley who changed Hugh. I don't know about any corruption, but I know that Hugh wouldn't have done anything without Pratley's say-so. Pratley wasn't just a boss, he was a kind of guru who dominated Hugh.'

Wilson and Graham looked at each other.

'Pratley went up and up, and Hugh was just the fall guy,'

she continued. 'Why Hugh? Why didn't they look at some of the others in the squad? I'm sure that Hugh wasn't the only one involved.'

'What happened after Hugh retired?' Wilson asked.

'Money kept coming in from somewhere, but our relationship floundered. Hugh wasn't the man I married and when he started to use, I decided that I'd reached the end of the road and I got out. It was bad enough to see Hugh heading for the gutter, I wasn't going to follow him there.'

'The autopsy report mentioned that Hugh's body was littered with needle marks. What was he on?'

'I didn't see any needle marks. I thought he might be snorting cocaine or doing pills. I'm not up on drugs so there might have been other stuff. I got out pretty soon after it started.'

'And you haven't seen him since?'

'Once or twice at the court hearings. He didn't fight the divorce. There were no kids and we both went our separate ways.'

'And you never met again?'

'I saw Hugh one time I was in town. He was with a group of men walking along Donegall Square. I ducked into a shop to avoid him.'

'Do you know where he was living?'

'No, sorry.'

Wilson stood up. 'Thanks for your help. I don't think that we'll be bothering you again.' He and Graham started to leave the living room and Parnell followed them.

She put her hand on the door handle. 'Hugh wasn't a bad man. He certainly didn't deserve to die a violent death. I hope you get the man who killed him.'

'So do I,' Wilson said as she opened the door.

THE BLACK MOUNTAIN is probably the most prominent

feature of Belfast's landscape as it towers over the city from the west. Wilson deposited Graham at the station and drove west skirting the Peace Wall before heading through Whiterock Grove and Hannahstown to reach his destination. There was still a covering of snow on the peaks and the clouds were hanging low over the hills, threatening some form of precipitation. Wilson pulled into the car park just off the Divis Road and saw that it was empty. He was ten minutes early. As he waited the first spits of sleet began to fall. Twenty minutes later he was contemplating leaving when McDevitt's car pulled up beside him. Wilson turned and looked into the Mercedes. McDevitt was in the front seat. His passenger was in the rear and was wearing a black balaclava with holes cut for the eyes and the mouth. Wilson got out of his car and slipped into the passenger seat of McDevitt's car.

'No one about?' McDevitt asked.

Wilson wiped the sleet off his jacket. 'You must be kidding. Nobody is stupid enough to be up here in weather like this, present company excepted.'

The man in the back seat of the car laughed.

'This is Mouse,' McDevitt said. 'Mouse and I go way back. He's one of my major sources for information on the drugs trade.'

'Hello, Mr Mouse,' Wilson said.

'Good to meet ye, Mr Wilson.' The accent was West Belfast.

'The floor is yours, Ian,' McDevitt said. 'If Mouse can help, he will. If it's too sensitive a question, he may decline to answer. The main point is that Mouse will not incriminate either himself, or any of his confederates, is that understood?'

'Understood,' Wilson said. 'I'm not interested in drugs except where they intersect with the investigation into the death of Hugh Royce.'

There was no sound from the back seat.

'You were acquainted with Hugh Royce?'

'Aye, I knew him.'

'Do you know where he was living?'

'Aye.'

'Where?'

'Mr McDevitt has the address.'

Wilson looked sideways at McDevitt, who was smirking. How I would like to stick a charge of interfering with a police investigation on that smart bugger Wilson thought. He knew it wasn't going to happen and wondered what quid pro quo the journalist was going to extract from him for Royce's address.

'How do you know where Royce was staying?'

'He hadn't been around for a wee while, more than a year maybe. So when I saw him in town I wondered why he was back on the scene, and so I followed him.'

'Was Royce a member of your firm?'

'No.'

'But he was a member of a rival firm?'

'Aye, he used to be. That's why I followed him.'

'He worked for Davie Best?'

Mouse laughed under his balaclava. 'Nah, he worked for a bigger firm than Bestie.'

Wilson was momentarily nonplussed. As far as he knew, Davie Best ran the biggest firm in Belfast. The combination of the old Rice and McGreary mobs had to be the biggest firm in the city. 'If it's not Davie, who's the biggest firm in the city?'

In the silence of the car, Wilson could hear the steady beat of the sleet hitting the roof and the windshield.

'I'd have thought that someone who's been around as long as you would know who the biggest firm in the city is,' Mouse said when he finally spoke. 'You ought to know because you're a member. The PSNI is the biggest firm in Belfast. That's the firm that Royce belonged to.'

'What do you mean?' Wilson's voice was strained.

'Think about it,' Mouse said. 'You boys can take anyone in competition off the streets. You decide what shipment gets through and what shipment gets stopped, what runners get lifted, who is left alone. You can fabricate evidence against a rival to your firm and put them out of business. You can form alliances with other firms and kill off new firms before they get established. You guys are *the* firm. And Hugh Royce was working for you.'

'He retired from the force,' Wilson said.

'But he didn't retire from the firm.'

'Do you know who is in charge?'

Mouse tapped McDevitt on the shoulder. 'We're done here.'

'No, we're not,' Wilson said sharply.

'No breaking of the rules, Ian,' McDevitt took a slip of paper from his pocket and handed it to Wilson. 'We can talk about what you owe me later. Mouse has done his part and now you have to do yours. Have a safe trip back to Belfast.'

Wilson took the slip of paper and looked at the address. He opened the door and was hit by a blast of ice-cold rain. He turned back and looked at the man in the rear of the car. 'You wouldn't be bullshitting me?'

'No bullshit, Mr Wilson.'

Wilson stood outside the car, letting the rain beat against his bare head. McDevitt reversed past him and drove out of the car park. He looked down over the city with the sleet stinging his eyes and drenching his clothes. He knew of the venality of politicians and of most of the hierarchy of his own organisation, but the thought that the corruption ran so deep shocked him. He ran his fingers through his hair. He had a feeling he had just opened Pandora's box and what he was going to find inside scared the hell out of him.

CHAPTER SEVENTEEN

Wilson drove back to the station. On the way, he had called Graham and told him he had Royce's address. He arranged to pick him up and told him he should bring along the key found in Royce's pocket. The address on the paper turned out to be a large three-storeyed red-brick house in the Malone Road area that had been turned into a homeless shelter. They parked in front and entered the building. There was a young man on the reception desk and Graham produced his warrant card as they approached.

'What can I do for you gentlemen?' the young man had a lanyard around his neck that gave his name as Nick Baily.

'Good afternoon, Nick,' Graham said. He introduced himself and Wilson. 'We're making some enquiries about someone who has been staying here.'

'Most of the residents are out for the day,' Baily said. He pulled a registration book out from under the counter. 'Give me the name and I'll see if he's still with us.'

'Hugh Royce,' Graham said.

'The name seems familiar,' Baily said. He started to scan the pages, then stopped. 'He booked in with us three days ago.'

He looked puzzled. 'But he doesn't appear to have stayed overnight. What's this about?'

'Mr Royce was found murdered on the Antrim Road two days ago.'

'Yeah,' Baily said. 'I remember it now. It was on the news yesterday.'

'And it was in the papers,' Graham said. 'We were asking for information on Mr Royce and his possible whereabouts.'

Baily could see the way the two police officers were looking at him. 'Because of the weather we've been busier than usual. The name didn't register with me until you said it. I don't read the papers and there was nothing on my newsfeed.'

Holy God, it wasn't on his newsfeed, Wilson thought. But he was willing to bet that what the Kardashians had for breakfast was.

'Was he assigned a bed?' Graham asked.

Baily consulted the register. 'Yes, on the second floor.'

'We'll need to take a look,' Wilson said.

'Of course.'

Graham produced a plastic evidence bag containing the key. 'Does this look familiar?'

Baily held out his hand and took the bag. 'It could be one of our locker keys.'

'Can you check in your book if Mr Royce had a locker?' Wilson said.

Baily was getting nervous. 'Yes, he had a bedside locker.'

'Has his bed been reassigned?' Graham asked.

'I'm afraid so.'

'How about his locker?' Wilson asked.

'I don't know.'

'Take us upstairs,' Wilson said.

Baily led them up a flight of stairs. The first floor had been converted into a series of dormitories with beds in rows. At the foot of each bed was a locker. Baily checked the numbers on the side of the metal-framed beds and stopped near the far wall of the room. 'This was Mr Royce's bed.'

'Did Royce stay here regularly?'

'I have no idea,' Baily said. 'I'm a volunteer so I only work here when they need me. There are some regulars, but an effort is made to house them. We mainly deal with people who are happy enough on the street but who want a bed when the weather turns nasty.'

Graham had inserted a key in the locker at the side of the bed and turned the key. He opened the door and put on a pair of latex gloves before reaching inside. He pulled out a small kit bag, laid it on top of the bed and opened the zip. He took out a clean polo shirt, a pair of cheap jeans, three pairs of underwear and three pairs of socks, laying each item on the bed as he withdrew them.

'Is that it?' Wilson asked.

Graham turned towards his boss. 'Royce travels light.'

'Most of the men don't have a great deal of possessions,' Baily said. 'But a small kit bag is a bit extreme.'

Wilson nodded at the locker. 'Anything else in there?'

Graham dipped into the locker and took out three books. One was instantly recognisable as a leather-bound Bible. The other two were paperbacks. He placed the books front cover up on the bed.

Wilson looked at the paperbacks. The author was Richard Pearson and the titles were self-explanatory: *God at My Right Hand* and *The Hard Road to God*. He'd never heard of this Pearson character, but the religious genre wasn't his usual bedside reading. 'See is there anything inside.'

Graham picked up the books and flicked through the pages. 'Nothing, but they've been well-read.'

'Bag them.'

Graham put the books in individual evidence bags before carefully repacking the kit bag.

'We're taking this stuff with us,' Wilson said when Graham was finished.

'Can we have the locker key back?' Baily asked.

'Not for the moment,' Wilson said. 'We'll drop it by when we're finished with it.'

'What do you make of it, Boss?' Graham said as soon as they were in the car and on their way back to the station.

'He didn't look much like a street person,' Wilson said. 'The clothes in the kit bag were washed and ironed, and I've never seen so few possessions. It's the kind of thing you'd bring on a weekend away.'

'My thoughts exactly, but it doesn't solve the problem of finding the place Royce calls home.'

'There are lots of people like Royce out there. Their lives disintegrate on them and they just drop out. The majority of them are gamblers, junkies or alcoholics. Royce could be calling a deserted hay barn outside Strabane home. And if he is, we'll never find it.'

Back at the station, Wilson went directly to his office. He was beginning to get a picture of Hugh Royce. He was the only child to older parents, had no siblings, he was probably searching for a father figure when he encountered Pratley, who proceeded to mentor him. Perhaps he had been groomed in the same way a paedophile grooms a child. Wilson was beginning to believe Mouse's story about the PSNI being a firm. Pratley had a lot to answer for.

The white envelope on Wilson's desk had his name on it. He opened it and took out the single sheet of paper it contained. It was a photocopy of an article from a newspaper dated four years previously. The headline of the article read 'Freak death of PSNI detective'. The article went on to report that Colin Payne, a detective constable working in the Drugs Squad of the PSNI, had died while helping to clean a slurry tank on his aunt's farm. It was the twentieth death related to the cleaning of tanks on farms in the past ten years. An autopsy had shown that Payne was not overcome by fumes, as in other cases, but had been drowned in the slurry.

Wilson motioned to O'Neill and she entered the office. He picked up the envelope. 'Who delivered this?'

'I've no idea. A uniform came up and dropped it on your desk.'

Wilson picked up the phone and called the duty sergeant. 'An envelope with just my name on it was delivered in the past few hours, any idea where it came from?'

'No idea, sir, it's been pretty busy here this morning. Someone must have dropped it in.'

'There was an officer from Professional Services here yesterday, DS Lucy Kane, any sign of her today?'

'Sorry, Boss,' the duty sergeant said.

'Okay, it's not important.' Wilson put the phone down. He saw that O'Neill was still in the office. 'Thanks.'

'No problem.'

Wilson was certain that the envelope had come from Kane and that Colin Payne was the officer who had reported the corruption in the Drugs Squad. He was also sure that Hugh Royce had been thrown under the bus to spike any further investigation of corruption in the Drugs Squad. But where did that leave him with the motive for Royce's death?

CHAPTER EIGHTEEN

Peter Davidson sat across from the two young officers from Technical Branch manning their computers. He was from the generation that had to work hard to use a mobile phone, and he had never gone beyond using his computer as a word processor. What happened inside the machine, and the wonders that it produced, were beyond his comprehension, and of no direct interest. The room was like something out of *Star Wars* with the walls covered in screens on which arrays of numbers were displayed. As far as Davidson was concerned, the age of the nerd had well and truly arrived. He had already outlined his mobile phone problem and the two young men had nodded sagely as he told them what he would like from them.

'No problem,' the serious one with the wire-rimmed glasses said as soon as he was finished.

'Should this request come through official channels?' the equally serious bald man asked.

'It's a murder enquiry.' Davidson didn't consider these technical guys to be proper coppers. They wouldn't know an arrest if it jumped up and bit them on the leg. But obviously they had been tarred with the bureaucratic brush. 'If we make a request through channels, some bloody bureaucrat will leave it on his desk for a week. And we're going to lose precious time. I thought that you guys were outside all that "through channels" bullshit.'

The two young men looked at each other. They were computer geeks first and police officers second. Davidson had hit just the right note with them. 'Okay,' the first serious one said. 'Give us the phone number and the date.' His fingers flashed over the keys.

Davidson put a piece of paper on the desk with the number and date on it. Fingers continued to move faster than he could follow. These guys were cut from the same cloth as O'Neill. This was the new world of policing, and he wasn't a part of it.

'The base number was pinging off a tower in Hillsborough,' glasses serious guy said. 'It was static for quite a while. There was one call made.' He called out a number and Davidson wrote it carefully in his daybook. 'The receiving phone was at Belfast International Airport. The call lasted less than thirty seconds and the receiving phone went dead five minutes later.'

'Has the number been reactivated?'

'No, my guess is that the receiver ditched the SIM card, the battery and possibly the phone.'

If the investigation into Carlisle's death wasn't so bloody dangerous, Davidson thought, it could actually be fun. He now had another phone number that he could investigate. His next stop would be Belfast International to see whether any discarded mobile phones had been found on that date. 'Thanks guys, it's been an education.'

'This one was on the house, ould lad,' the second young officer said. 'The next time, go through the normal channels.'

Davidson bristled at the 'ould lad' remark but realised he

must look like a fossil to the two young men. He smiled benefi-
cently and stood up. 'Fucking arsehole,' he said as he left the
room.

CHAPTER NINETEEN

Deputy Chief Constable Royson Jennings was examining the latest reports on the progress in the Royce murder enquiry submitted by Yvonne Davis. If he'd been given the chance, he would have counselled against taking Royce out, but Pratley had jumped the gun. He was still regrouping after the Armstrong fiasco. He had no idea what had gone wrong, but he had a feeling that whatever it was, Wilson was at the centre of it. If only he could prove that Wilson was involved somehow in Armstrong's death. The bastard had somehow covered his tracks. Dublin had reported that they were certain that the IRA had discovered Armstrong's treachery, and he had been murdered because of it. Luckily Armstrong would soon be ancient history, making it highly unlikely that his role in protecting him from prosecution for killing two prostitutes would ever see the light of day. It had been a close call, but Armstrong's demise would eventually suit all their ends. It was an ill wind that didn't blow someone some good. And now there's this business with Royce. Ever since Wilson had stumbled inadvertently across the Circle, things had been deteriorating. Meanwhile Chief Constable Baird was cementing his power. There was a knock on Jennings' door.

'Enter,' Jennings looked up from the reports to see George Pratley closing the door behind him. 'Sit.'

Pratley took one of the visitor chairs. 'You wanted to see me.'

'You're surprised?'

'Royce was a danger to all of us.'

And you in particular, Jennings thought.

'He couldn't just have stayed lost,' Pratley continued. 'Everything was going ahead smoothly and then he reappears like some long-lost prodigal.'

'And that's why you decided he had to die?'

'He threatened the whole operation.' He was going to use the 'executive decision' explanation but decided against it.

'And who made you God?' Jennings crashed his fist onto his desk. 'You don't make life or death decisions. You follow fucking orders. Didn't you ever get that message into that thick skull of yours? And now we have Wilson and his crew on the trail.'

'Then get him off it.'

'Easier said than done, you numbskull.'

'You're the bloody deputy chief constable.'

'Even with that grandiose title my powers are limited.'

'Then we need to give him something else to worry about.'

'What do you have in mind?'

'Drugs could be found in his apartment, or his car.'

'You'd have to have a valid reason to search.'

'Not having a valid reason never stopped us before. We need to fit Wilson up and we have plenty of guys on the force with experience in doing that. If he's fighting a drugs charge, he won't have any time for investigating Royce's murder.'

Jennings thought for a few minutes. He was aware of Helen McCann's plan to destroy Wilson by making him the one who exposed his father's involvement in murder. It was a subtle plan that depended on attacking Wilson psychologically. There was merit in Pratley's idea but very little subtlety.

If it were managed properly, it might ruin Wilson professionally and even force him out of the PSNI. And that would be a
happy day for all concerned. 'Have you discussed this with
anyone?'

'Nobody other than you.'

'Put a plan together and I'll pass it upstairs.' Jennings knew
that McCann would jump at any plan that involved Wilson's
demise. The woman had developed a pathological obsession
where Wilson was concerned. He smiled when he realised
that so had he. 'I want every possibility covered. Wilson is as
slippery as a snake and I don't want him slithering out of this.
And I want total personal coverage – there can be nothing to
link me with this plan.'

'I'll put something together in a few days.'

'Make it a priority. I want to rubber stamp every iota of the
plan before we pass it up.'

'Understood.'

'You can go.' Jennings watched Pratley leave. He was a
good man to have at the coalface dealing with the likes of
Davie Best and his gang, but he wasn't a strategic thinker. That
was Jennings' area of expertise. Pratley and Best would use a
sledgehammer to crack a walnut. Helen McCann would put
subtle pressure on the nut so that it cracked itself. He lay somewhere between the two. Setting up Wilson wasn't going to be
easy and wasn't without attendant risks, but it was certainly
worth a try.

CHAPTER TWENTY

W ilson cancelled the evening briefing. He needed to reflect on the day's happenings. He knew that he should inform Davis immediately, but that was the last thing he was going to do. The Armstrong affair had freaked her out, and he could just imagine what a murder case possibly involving police corruption would do to her. Since her arrival as Spence's replacement, his squad appeared to be lurching from one crisis to another. Then again why should he believe a single word that came out of Mouse's mouth? The guy was obviously a minor criminal and a snitch. He was trading information for money with McDevitt. The best strategy was to continue investigating Royce's death as a simple drug-related killing. He had already identified several possible scenarios that didn't involve police corruption, but he knew in his bones that Pratley and his crew were up to their necks in it. They may not have been the ones that pulled the trigger on Royce, but he had an inkling that someone from Pratley's squad had done for Payne. He needed to share, but whom was he going to share with. He trusted Donald Spence, but the path they were about to embark on was dangerous and Spence had earned a peaceful retirement. He was going to have to play his cards close to his chest and pray that Republican Action Against Drugs claimed the killing. Unfortunately, he knew that wasn't going to happen.

Browne knocked on the door and pushed it open. 'News from Forensics, Boss, they found the spent slugs and the gun used to kill Royce was definitely a Browning Hi-Power and it was clean. There's no sign of it on the database.'

'There's still no sign of that Donaldson guy?'

'Not a whisper.'

'Okay, Rory, that's enough for today. We'll start again tomorrow.' He looked into the squad room and saw that O'Neill and Graham were still at their desks. 'Tell the others they can go.'

'You off too, Boss?'

Wilson nodded at the pile of paper on his desk. 'This is what's waiting for you at the end of that promotion ladder.'

'I don't like that game, there are too many snakes.'

'Truer words were never spoken.'

DCI JACK DUANE sat in a hired car outside Tennent Street station. He had taken up his position at five o'clock on the dot and watched as the day shift disgorged from the building on their way home. As soon as he saw Siobhan O'Neill exiting the door, he started the car and began to inch forward. He pulled level with her and lowered the passenger side window. 'Looking for a lift?'

O'Neill stared into the car. She'd seen Duane in Wilson's office and was aware that he was a policeman from down south, but she'd never been introduced to him. 'I'm okay, I only live a short distance away.' She continued walking.

'I really think you should take the offer of a lift,' Duane said, keeping pace with her. 'We have something to discuss.'

For the first time in weeks, O'Neill felt a dart of fear. She stopped and the car stopped too. She knew she really didn't have a choice. 'Who the hell are you?'

'A friend. Now open the door and sit in.'

She held the handle for a few moments before pushing the catch and opening the door. She sat in the passenger seat and closed the door behind her.

'Busy day?' Duane asked.

'Yes.'

'I think we should go somewhere we can have a drink and a nice chat.'

They drove in silence until Duane pulled up beside Kelly's Cellars in Bank Street. They got out and entered the pub.

'What can I get you?' Duane asked.

'Bloody Mary, double.' Her confidence was returning. The pang of fear she had felt on the street had been replaced with the resolve to stay cool and not give anything away. Duane was smooth. He dressed well and was handsome in a rugged kind of way. But he was also old enough to be her father. That might appeal to some women but wasn't really her thing. He took their drinks from the barman and moved to the end of the room, away from the crowd gathering at the bar. They sat at one of the round tables.

'Sláinte,' Duane raised his pint glass and O'Neill lifted hers and touched his. They both sipped their drinks. 'For such a nice wee lassie, you caused me an almighty amount of shite,' Duane said.

'I have no idea what you're talking about.' The pang of fear returned.

'You know who I am?'

'You're a peeler down south.' She drank to hide her nervousness. There was something about this man that bothered her. She felt he could be dangerous.

'I am that. But I am also your best friend if you're honest with me, and a fearsome enemy if you lie. I'm looking into the murder of Noel Armstrong. Some gobshite from Dundalk Garda Station is the SIO. So there's no possibility of finding the culprit.'

'I still don't get what this has to do with me.'

'My dear wee lassie, it has everything to do with you. You're the one that put the finger on Armstrong.'

She opened her mouth to speak and Duane put up his hand. 'Remember what I said. Don't lie to me.'

She closed her mouth and didn't speak.

'The IRA leaks like a sieve. I knew the name of the shooter the day after the murder. He'll never do a day in jail because he has an ironclad alibi. I also know that they tortured Armstrong to get a confession out of him and that a part of that confession had to be about strangling your friend Bridget Kelly and that poor Eastern European woman. So, you can understand that I also know the name of the person who set the whole train in motion.'

She finished her drink. 'My turn, a pint?'

Duane nodded. 'Don't run.'

'I've no intention.' She went to the bar and returned with two drinks.

'Don't think that shopping Armstrong to the IRA didn't cross Wilson's mind. He wanted justice for those women just like you did. But he didn't have your emotional involvement.'

'What happens now?'

'Armstrong was a scumbag murderer who probably got what he deserved, but we're not the ones who make that decision. I want your word that this is the last time you'll cross that line.' He sipped his drink.

'You have it.'

'I researched you. You're a clever wee thing who could be making ten times your copper's salary in the private sector. Maybe that's where you should be. Just in case another emotional case comes up.'

'You're not going to turn me in?'

'What purpose would that serve? Did you pervert the course of justice? Probably, but the men who protected Armstrong did a much better job of it than you, and it cost people their lives. Let's say that this time you were more on the side of the angels but only marginally mind you. By the way, Muldoon shopped you. Don't go there again.'

'Ronan always was a piece of shit.'

He nodded and drank. 'I agree. It's been a great pleasure having a drink with such a fine young lady, but I need to be away.'

'You have a hold on me.'

He stood up. 'Only if you cross the line again. Can I drop you somewhere?'

'I think I'll stay for another.'

'We'll not speak of this again.'

As Duane's broad back disappeared through the pub door, she let out a long sigh. Her hand shook as she lifted the glass to her mouth. Had it been worth it? She knew in her heart of hearts that it was. If Duane passed on the intelligence to Wilson, would he bring a charge of perverting the course of justice against her? She assumed he would, and she was quite prepared to answer for her crime if she had to. After all, hadn't she only been upholding a fine tradition of the RUC in colluding with outside elements.

CHAPTER TWENTY-ONE

W ilson closed up the office at seven o'clock. Reid would already be at the apartment, no doubt luxuriating in a bath and hopefully removing the stench of dealing with dead bodies. It had been a week since she had spent the evening in her own apartment and it was getting near that time when they would have to discuss the logic of maintaining two residences. Wilson had been down that road with Kate McCann and he decided if that conversation were necessary, it would have to be initiated by Reid. He stopped at their favourite Indian takeaway and collected the meal that Reid had already ordered. He had no idea what was in the large plastic bag he picked up, but he assumed from the weight that Reid and he were not eating alone. The animated conversation he heard when he opened the door told him that his powers of detection were still fully operational. The only downside to his pride in being right was that he recognised the dulcet Galway tones of Jack Duane.

'Dinner has arrived.' He plonked the plastic bag on the kitchen table. 'I wasn't aware that we were entertaining.'

'I think Jack was a bit nervous about begging a meal from you,' Reid said. 'So he took the easy route and asked me.'

'I don't see Jack being nervous, period.' Wilson shook hands with Duane. 'In town on business?'

'Pleasure,' Duane said.

Wilson went to Reid, kissed her on the lips and then moved to his improvised bar, where he poured himself a large whiskey. 'Now why don't I believe that?'

'God's truth.' Duane made the sign of the cross. 'This beautiful woman has been filling me in on your adventures in California, and I was offering my condolences on the death of her mother.'

'Are you going to tell me what you're doing in Belfast or not?' Wilson said.

'Or not.' Duane sipped his drink.

Reid had opened the plastic bag and placed the contents in the centre of the dining table. 'Jack has brought some nice red wine and we should begin while the food is still hot.'

'How long are you here for?' Wilson asked Duane as soon as they were settled at the table.

'A day or two.'

'For God's sake, Jack, do I have to drag it out of you?'

'I'm briefing the minister and the boys in Castlereagh on the progress in the investigation into Armstrong's death.' Duane forked some chicken tandoori into his mouth.

'And how is it going?' Wilson asked.

Duane looked at Reid.

She frowned. 'Don't worry, I'm used to it.'

'We have a fair idea who the trigger man was but he's got an alibi that we probably can't break.' Duane continued eating.

'Any idea of how the IRA got on to Armstrong?' Wilson asked.

'Apparently they've been looking for a mole for some time, and there were a lot of people in the organisation who bore Armstrong a certain amount of ill will.'

'So, was it a coincidence that we were investigating him at the time for the Spalvis murder?'

'It appears so.'

'Don't bullshit me, Jack.' Wilson hadn't yet started eating.

'We have the best contacts in the IRA.' Duane put down his knife and fork. 'That's what they say. Armstrong had pissed off a lot of people in his time, and they were looking for a chance to nail him. His murder will stay on the books but don't expect a result, that's the message from Dublin. Enough business, the professor is getting bored and the case is already yesterday's news.' He turned to Reid. 'If I had a fine house in California, I wouldn't be sitting with a cold north wind blowing up my you know what.'

'That thought had crossed my mind,' Reid said.

Wilson looked at her and she looked back. He'd been right. Belfast was no longer the only option for her.

'You're not eating, Ian,' she said.

'Sorry.' He delved into the foil dishes.

When the meal was over Wilson and Duane cleared up the dishes while Reid made a strategic withdrawal. Wilson poured two whiskies and he and Duane sat before the picture window looking out over the city.

'How is she really doing?' Duane asked.

'Grieving but getting there. They'd gotten close by the end.' He was thinking of his own mother. Nova Scotia was four hours behind Belfast, and he made up his mind to call her as soon as Duane left.

'You two are good together. Pity about the business you're in. What's with this Royce killing?'

'On the surface it looks drug-related. A couple of months ago we found a man in the boot of a burned-out BMW over at Helen's Bay. We haven't been able to identify the body, but we think he was a low-level pusher.'

'Sounds like a turf war. We're having one in Dublin at the moment that's already left fourteen people dead, and apparently there's a list with fifteen other names on it. I hope for your sake that there's some other motive for the killing.'

Wilson hoped that for his sake there was any other motive than the one he was thinking about.

'I'm thinking of asking your boss out.' Duane finished his drink and stood up. 'Do you think she'll accept?'

'Are you serious? She's ten years older than you.'

Duane moved to the door. 'I'm totally serious.'

CHAPTER TWENTY-TWO

F ormer RUC detective James Gibbons walked out of the
Orange Lodge 26 directly behind CS Robert Rodgers,
the head of Special Branch. He had spent several days mulling
over the conversation he'd had with Peter Davidson. He'd liked
Davidson, who was one of the boys back in the day, but all that
had changed with the advent of the PSNI. The RUC was
there to protect the Protestant people of Ulster. The new force
had tossed that sacred duty aside. Gibbons had stayed on in
the lodge even though he wasn't feeling the best. The drink
and the fags eventually catch up with everyone, but he was
sure that he had a few more years in him yet. He wasn't happy
with the pain in his chest and the shortness of breath he'd been
experiencing lately. He'd go to the doctor tomorrow. His mind
was focussed on his health when he realised that he had gone
to the lodge so that he could have a word with his lodge
brother. He owed Davidson nothing. And he didn't like the
idea of coppers keeping an eye on each other. There was no
telling where that could lead. He'd been trying to have a quiet
word with Rodgers all evening, but the big man had been in
demand. Every time Rodgers was alone someone else beat
Gibbons to the punch. The meeting had broken up, and this

was his last chance to catch the man before he buggered off home. Gibbons tried to catch his breath as he accelerated his pace to catch up with Rodgers. 'Bobby,' he called.

Rodgers turned and looked behind him. The smile faded from his face. It was that old fart Gibbons. The stupid old bastard was always harping back to the days they had 'served' together. 'How are ye, Jamsie,' Rodgers said over his shoulder and started to walk away.

'Bobby, it's important.' Gibbons voice was a croak.

Rodgers stopped. He needed to be away. He'd arranged to meet his girlfriend for a drink before heading off home to the wife. He turned to look at Gibbons. The poor old bastard didn't look well, he was as pale as a ghost. He walked back.

'Ye don't look too well, Jamsie. Are ye okay?'

'Aye, just a bit of angina, I'll be all right when I catch my breath. I have something important to tell ye.'

'Take it easy, man.'

'That young pup Peter Davidson is asking about one of your boys.'

Rodgers smiled. The only Peter Davidson he knew was nearly old as Gibbons. The old boy must be going strange. 'Is that right?'

'Aye, it is.' Gibbons was struggling to remember the name Davidson had given him. Suddenly it came to him. 'Some fella called Simon Jackson.'

'Is that so. You're a good man, Jamsie. Tell me about Davidson and this Simon Jackson.'

Gibbons looked into Rodgers face and it seemed to get wavy all of a sudden. The pain in his chest was so intense that he couldn't speak. He tried to move his mouth but had lost control. His feet turned to jelly and he would have fallen if Rodgers hadn't caught him. He felt himself being lowered to the ground. The pain in his chest was the only thing he could think of as he expired.

'Get a doctor, for God's sake,' Rodgers shouted. 'What

about Davidson and Jackson,' he shouted to the stricken man. 'Stay with me, Jamsie. Try to keep your eyes open, man.' It was no use; Gibbons' eyes had rolled up into his head and he had the vacant look of the dead. He put his finger to the prone man's neck but couldn't feel a pulse. The old bastard was gone. Rodgers stood up and found their lodge brothers were surrounding them. Why in God's name would Davidson want to know about Jackson? Peter Davidson was still working at the Murder Squad. And as far as he knew Jackson hadn't killed anyone lately, although with Jackson you never really knew. As he started walking away he could hear the sound of an ambulance's siren heading in their direction. If there were a way to kill a person twice, he would have throttled Gibbons for not giving the full information before he died. Davidson was looking into Jackson. They were going to have to do something about that.

CHAPTER TWENTY-THREE

It was one of those mornings when the run was obligatory. Wilson tore himself away from Reid's warm body. They had made love in the early morning and then fallen into post-coital slumber. But Wilson's dreams didn't permit him easy repose. He seldom had dreams where gothic creatures flew at him causing him to recoil, but last night had been an exception. The only solution was to don his running gear and brave the cold in order to clear his head. There had been some rain overnight, raising the outside temperature by several degrees. Still, as he pounded his way towards the Titanic Centre, his breath turned to vapour when it hit the cold air. It was the kind of weather that gave his gammy leg trouble. He could feel the stiffness in his running style. There were two conflicting thoughts in his head. Although the consequences would be extreme, it would be expedient to believe that the deaths of Duff and Royce were the harbingers of a turf war. But when he thought about the carnage and the collateral deaths that might ensue, it was the last outcome he wanted. He didn't need Jack Duane to point out the potential carnage created by drugged-up murderers wielding Kalashnikovs. He'd read the reports of the drugs war from Dublin, and their northern counterparts were equally vicious. That left the second scenario: the deaths were unconnected and Royce's murder had its genesis in PSNI corruption. Dishonesty was not part of his brief in the organisation and would inevitably mean cooperating with Professional Services, and neither he nor they had a good reputation in that respect. By the time he had reached his turning point at the end of East Twin Road, he had developed a strategy for the investigation. The first line of enquiry would concentrate on discounting the turf war scenario. When that line of enquiry was abandoned, they would switch their concentration to potential corruption within the PSNI. His leg eased out considerably and the route back to the apartment felt easier. Or perhaps it had nothing to do with his leg and more to do with his decision to carry out the investigation methodically. He went straight to the shower and turned the water on as hot as he could stand it. He was washed, shaved and dressed when he entered the living room and saw Reid sitting at the table talking to the computer. He leaned over her shoulder and saw the face of her brother, Peter, on the screen.

'Morning, Peter,' he said. He had no idea what time it was in Australia. 'It looks like I'm on breakfast duty today.'

'Morning, Ian, you're looking good. Steph said you were out on a run.'

'Cold as a witch's tit out there. Sorry, didn't mean to interrupt you and your sister.'

'No worries.'

Wilson walked over to the kitchen, put on the coffee and started to whisk some eggs. Ten minutes later Reid joined him as he was putting the finishing touches to scrambled eggs and smoked salmon.

She kissed his cheek. 'So domesticated. I saw on television that some footballer in the UK only learned to make instant coffee when he was thirty-seven.' She sat at the table while he served her scrambled egg on toast and poured her a cup of coffee. She looked at the plate. 'Not bad, what's with this new

Ian Wilson?' She knew the question of moving in was the elephant in the room, but she wanted him to be the one to address it. Dealing with her mother's illness and death had been traumatic for her. Although she was a medical professional who had worked with death all her professional life, she had been forced to reflect on her own life by closely attending to the death of her mother. She had spent the time asking herself indelicate questions about choices she had made. Now she needed to know what her partner was thinking. That conversation was coming soon and might be cathartic.

'No ulterior motive,' Wilson said. 'What's happening with Peter?' He forked some egg into his mouth.

'I wanted Peter to accept half of the Venice Beach house.' She sipped her coffee. 'It's his inheritance as well as mine, but he turned it down. The hurt runs very deep with him. He wants nothing from his mother, but he has children and they should have something from their grandmother. However, Peter is intractable.'

'You tried your best.' Wilson felt that there was a question in there and it had something to do with Reid's decision not to have children. He looked at her and the feeling that she was hiding something from him was there again. It was subtle and barely noticeable, but it was there. Maybe it had something to do with Peter and the inheritance. He hoped so, but his great fear was that it was going to affect their relationship.

'What did you and Jack get up to when I went to bed?'

'He's going to ask Davis out.'

She laughed. 'You can say what you like about Jack, but there's never a dull moment. Anything else?'

'He thinks that the Royce killing has something to do with a drug turf war.'

'But you don't?'

'I'm not sure.'

'And that's why you didn't sleep well last night.'

'Maybe.'

'I can give you a prescription for some mild sleeping tablets.'

'That's a road I don't want to go down. I'm going to look into the possibility of a turf war. We've had turf wars before when the paramilitaries turned on each other. They're not very pleasant.'

'Nothing that we deal with is pleasant.'

There it was again, he thought, the open door to a more meaningful conversation about where they were going. Why didn't he take it? What was she hiding from him? He took the coward's way out. 'We should head off. I have a briefing in fifteen minutes.'

'Yes,' she started to clear up the plates and stack them in the dishwasher. 'And I have some dead people to cut up.'

He took her in his arms as she turned from the dishwasher. 'It's part of the grieving process.' He kissed her gently.

'Maybe.'

CHAPTER TWENTY-FOUR

The team gathered at the whiteboard for the nine o'clock briefing. Wilson stood in the centre, looking directly at the pictures of Royce as a young PSNI constable and his dead body outside the pub. 'What do we now about Hugh Royce? He was an only child of elderly parents who died when he was still young. He joined the PSNI and was mentored by his DCI. Then he was forced to resign from the job he loved and he was divorced by his wife. After that it's blank. What happened to Royce after he left the force and was divorced? People don't just disappear. He lived somewhere. He made money somewhere. He maybe had a friend somewhere. We are professional investigators. Surely it's not beyond our powers to find out what happened in this man's life that obliged someone to pump three bullets into his body. We need to answer the questions relative to Royce's life if we're going to establish a motive for his murder. And when we establish the motive, we'll be halfway to finding his murderer. Come on, we need results.'

'What about his so-called colleagues in the Drugs Squad?' Browne said. 'If Royce was involved with drugs, they should be able to supply some of the answers.'

'Right,' Wilson said. 'This morning I want Rory to go personally and ask for whatever they have on Royce. I'll ring ahead to Pratley.'

Wilson turned to face the team 'I know it might be a false trail, but we're going to move ahead on the premise that the man in the burned-out BMW was Mickey Duff and that he and Royce are the first victims in a potential drugs turf war. If that hypothesis is correct, the Drugs Squad should have some idea of what's going on.'

'It's just as likely that they're the victims of a vigilante group like Republican Action Against Drugs,' Graham said.

'So far they haven't claimed either death, and they're not usually slow when it comes to claiming credit. Anyway, it doesn't look like their handiwork,' Wilson said. 'They're more sawn-off shotgun than two in the chest and one in the head. But I'm keeping an open mind on that.' He looked round the team. 'Anybody got any ideas on how we can fill in the gap in Royce's CV?'

'There's nothing in the files,' O'Neill said.

'We still have Donaldson,' Browne said. 'Royce was staying at a homeless shelter. He had only a few pounds in his pocket. How did he get the money to buy a car? Maybe the car is still Donaldson's.'

'Or maybe Royce nicked it,' Graham said.

'Rory is right,' Wilson said. 'We need to find out what Royce was doing with Donaldson's car.' He looked at Graham. 'No news on Donaldson?'

Graham shook his head.

'Nothing from the phones?'

'A waste of time, Boss,' Graham said.

'Always remember that someone wanted this man dead pretty badly,' Wilson said. 'If our premise about a drug war is valid, why did they start on two low-level operators like Duff and Royce?'

'What are you going to do, Boss?' Graham asked.

'I'm going to see the man at the top of the tree.'

WILSON LOOKED round the interior of Club 69. It was all dark wood, fancy drapes, an Olympic-sized bar area and the now-obligatory stage with the equally obligatory poles. Davie Best had obviously been watching too much of *The Sopranos*, Wilson thought. At ten o'clock in the morning, the club was empty of clients but full of cleaners clearing up the detritus of last night's revels. Wilson hadn't been invited to the opening of the club, and if he had been, he wouldn't have gone. Maybe he was just old school, but Wilson thought there was a certain charm when the gang leaders spent their days in the back of a pub with their cronies. Like everything in life, the old criminals had been replaced by more business-oriented successors. He had no idea how much money Club 69 took in, but he was sure that it was augmented by whatever portion of Best's drug profits needed laundering. He had phoned ahead and was told that Mr Best could see him at ten o'clock and that Mr Best had a busy day planned so he should try to be on time. It was like making an appointment to see a doctor. Wilson was standing in the centre of the bar area admiring the surroundings when he was approached by a young man in a flash suit and led to an office at the rear. The young man opened the door and stood aside to permit Wilson to enter.

'Mr Wilson, what can I do for you?' Best sat behind a large mahogany desk on which only a computer monitor sat.

'Hello Davie,' Wilson looked round the large room and saw Eddie Hills loitering on a chair in the corner. 'You've come a long way from the day you turned up at the station after being worked over by Sammy Rice and his boys. Now there's a name to conjure with. I wonder where Sammy is today.' He turned and looked at Hills. Best and Hills had become inseparable of late. He would write a note to Intelligence with this observation. 'I'll bet even your closest buddies have no idea.'

Best's expression never changed. 'I'm sure you didn't come here to do a comic turn. This is a strip joint not a music hall.'

Wilson stood in front of Best. 'We're finding dead bodies in and around Belfast that appear to be associated with you. We're beginning to think that it's a bit of a coincidence.'

'I have no idea what you're talking about. None of my associates has died recently.'

'I was thinking of Mickey Duff, who happened to get himself incinerated in a stolen BMW at Helen's Bay. And now we have Hugh Royce, shot to death outside a pub on the Antrim Road.'

Best looked over at Hills. 'Do we know a Mickey Duff or a Hugh Royce?'

'Never heard of them,' Hills said.

'Then it's a coincidence that both Duff and Royce were involved in the drugs trade and you're the largest supplier of drugs in the city.'

'Good God, Mr Wilson, I've a good mind to take a case against you for defamation. Did you hear that, Eddie?'

'Loud and clear,' Hills said. 'Detective Superintendent Wilson accused you of being the largest supplier of drugs in the city.'

'I'm a club owner and a businessman,' Best said. 'I take steps to ensure that nobody sells drugs on the premises. If you hear different, give me the evidence and the person involved won't put their foot inside this club again.'

'You're aware that there's a drugs war going on in Dublin that's already claimed fourteen lives?'

'I read the papers,' Best said.

'I don't want the same thing happening here. In fact, I'm not going to allow it to happen.'

'You're talking to the wrong man.'

'I very much doubt that. Sooner or later we're going to come up with a piece of evidence on the Duff murder.' He turned and looked at Hills. 'And when we do, that chair in the corner is going to be empty.'

'My, my, Mr Wilson, you are in form today,' Best said. 'Defamation of character followed by threats against an innocent man. Have you been drinking? I think it's time you left.'

'You're right; there's a smell in here that turns my stomach. But I'll be back, and when I am you won't be so cocky.' Wilson turned and walked towards the door. He looked at Hills as he passed. 'Be seeing you.'

'That man is turning into a right royal pain in the arse,' Best said when the door closed on Wilson's back.

'Maybe we need to take care of him,' Hills said.

Best sighed. 'It's something we might have to consider.'

CHAPTER TWENTY-FIVE

D CC Royson Jennings had been forced to cancel his staff meeting to accommodate CS Bobby Rodgers. The man was apoplectic and incomprehensible on the telephone. Now he sat before Jennings, telling his story of the demise of Jamsie Gibbons the previous evening.

'The last bloody thing he said was that Peter Davidson was investigating Simon Jackson. Then the stupid old fart croaked before I could get another word out of him.'

'Who was this Gibbons character?' Jennings said. He didn't have the length of service of people like Rodgers who seemed to have been in the force forever. 'I've never heard of him.'

'Before your time. He finished up as an inspector.'

'How the hell did he know that Davidson was investigating Jackson?'

'No idea, the old bastard was breathing his last. I asked him, but it was too late. The question is: why is Davidson investigating Jackson? You're the boss, you're supposed to know what's going on with the rank and file.'

'Yes, like I'm supposed to know what's going on in Special Branch.'

Rodgers took the point. 'What's Davidson working on?'

'There are two investigations underway: the body that was incinerated along with a car in Helen's Bay and the Royce killing a few days ago. The burned body still hasn't been identified and apparently all the forensic evidence was destroyed in the fire. As far as both murders are concerned, the Murder Squad is still faffing around looking for a lead.'

'And Jackson has bugger all to do with either.'

'You're sure of that?' Jennings noticed the intonation in Rodgers' voice.

Rodgers didn't reply.

'But Jackson has been involved in something,' Jennings continued.

'He handled the Carlisle business for us.'

Jennings could feel his sphincter loosen. 'That piece of business has been closed definitively.'

'That's what I thought.'

Jennings steepled his fingers in front of his face. It couldn't be. The coroner had already issued a death by suicide verdict. His first thought was that Wilson was involved somewhere, but he discounted the idea. The man was a liability, but he wasn't stupid enough to launch an unofficial investigation into a death that had already been ruled on by the coroner. Davidson must be acting alone. 'You know Davidson better than me. Why would he be investigating Jackson?'

'I looked up his file and he'll be retiring soon, so I can't see him taking on something like this out of the blue.'

'Is there any possibility that the Carlisle business wasn't totally flawless?'

'None. Jackson is one of my best men. He's former military, you know the type, everything is always by the book.'

'Then why do you look so worried?'

'Because I know Wilson, and if he's involved, we definitely have something to be worried about.'

'Not if, as you say, the operation was sound.'

Rodgers didn't reply.

'What do you suggest we do?' Jennings asked.

'First we have to find out why Davidson is on Jackson's back.'

'So you believe this Gibbons character?'

'Isn't it wise to? I'll pass the message to Jackson and tell him to rein things in for a while. We don't want any more of a problem than we already have. Gibbons' little outburst cost me a good night's sleep.'

'Not like you, Bobby, you'll have to give up the young women, it's heart attack land for a man of your age.'

'Very bloody funny. I have a bad feeling in my water about this. Something isn't right.'

'Maybe your pal Gibbons was hallucinating, maybe Jackson is right and the murder was faultless. The coroner has ruled it a suicide. Maybe we have nothing to worry about. And if we have, maybe we can take care of it.'

Rodgers stood up. 'I believed that until last night. I've never been remorseful for the things that I've done but last night ... ,' his voice tailed off.

'I'll be in touch.' He didn't want to hear about Rodgers' encounter with his ghosts of the past, present or future.

'Aye.' Rodgers turned and exited the office.

Jennings sat back in his chair. He didn't believe in ghosts. He did what he did and that was the end of it. The people who suffered because of decisions he made deserved it. Still, he was going to have to report to Lattimer. The Carlisle affair was far too sensitive for him to handle alone.

PETER DAVIDSON's ears should have been burning but weren't. He was sitting in Clements Café enjoying a coffee and a scone with fresh cream and strawberry jam. He'd phoned Jamsie Gibbons early in the morning and learned the sad news. Jamsie's wife had misunderstood Davidson's relationship with her late husband and related the circumstances of his death. Davidson wasn't so happy to hear that the head of Special Branch had been in attendance at the demise. He assumed that Gibbons was following up on his promise to find out about Jackson. But bringing Rodgers into that quest would not have been the smartest move. He had six months to finish the investigation. They were close to having enough evidence to go upstairs. He looked out at the people hustling along Donegall Square. The bitter northeast wind was still blowing and everyone was wrapped up against it. Irene and he had been talking about the future, and they had decided that as soon as he retired and the insurance business was sorted, they would head for Spain to buy a villa where they could spend their future winters. He was even entertaining thoughts of making Irene the third Mrs Davidson. But in his mind this beautiful future all hinged on him proving that Irene's husband was murdered and the implications for the insurance payout. Gibbons was gone and although Davidson had considered other possibilities for information on Jackson, none of them met the required level of trust. He decided to concentrate on the second phone and that meant a visit to Belfast International Airport.

CHAPTER TWENTY-SIX

DCI George Pratley was in conference when Wilson called requesting a meeting for Rory Browne. As soon as Pratley put the phone down he turned to his number two, DS John Wallace. 'Speak of the devil.' He started to laugh. It was a hell of a coincidence to receive a call from Wilson when he and Wallace were discussing how to frame him.

'What did he want?' Wallace asked.

'He's sending his sergeant over to get a read on the characters in the Belfast drugs trade and to find out what we have on Royce. He's afraid that we might be looking at a turf war like the one they're having in Dublin at the moment.'

'There's precious little chance of a drugs war when Best controls eighty per cent of the market.'

'But he doesn't know that. His other big worry is that some outfit like *Republican Action Against Drugs* is taking out low-level operatives.'

'Those outfits are just protection rackets. The pushers who don't pay up are the ones that get hurt.'

'You're a cynic, John.'

'I don't like it, Guv. This is all down to the Royce killing. We don't need the spotlight shining on us.'

Wallace wasn't the sharpest tool in the chest, but sometimes he hit the nail on the head. Royce had to go. Killing him had been the right decision, but it had put Wilson on their trail and everybody knew that Wilson couldn't be bought, which was his bad luck. 'Where's the rest of the gear that we confiscated on the last bust?'

'I have just over a kilo in my desk.'

'Planting it isn't the problem, but how do we manufacture a reason for the search?'

'What about a driving offence? Then they search his car and they find the gear. It's a lot easier to plant it in his car than in his apartment.'

'We'll need help.'

'Best can give us a civilian for the accident and we'll have some of our uniform pals ready to respond.'

'Let's work on it. I want it to be seamless, no loopholes.'

'I'm on it.'

'And you deal with this Browne guy. Spin him some bullshit about who the major players are.'

Wallace nodded. 'I've heard about Browne. He's a regular at Kremlin.'

'That's interesting.'

'Leave it to me, Guv. I'll make sure he remembers his visit to the Drugs Squad.'

RORY BROWNE WAS cold and tired when he rolled up at Musgrave Street station. He wasn't sleeping well, and during a visit to his parents the previous weekend his mother had expressed concern at the dark circles under his eyes. He'd come out a year after he left college and since then he'd had an awkward relationship with his father. Generations of Browne men had been many things but gay wasn't one of them. Although he was enjoying working with Wilson and the team, he was still ambivalent about his future as a police officer.

Homosexuality might be accepted on paper in the PSNI, but he was aware of the looks he sometimes received from his colleagues. Maybe he was being overly sensitive, but he had accepted that it was bothering him. He checked in with the duty sergeant and asked for DCI Pratley. The sergeant made a phone call and indicated that DS Wallace would be down shortly to speak with him. He sat on a bench facing the reception and tried not to get irritated at the delay.

'DS Browne?'

Browne raised his head and was craning his neck by the time he was looking at the man's face.

'DS Wallace, John to you, the boss is busy so he told me to take care of you.'

'Call me Rory.' Wallace was a big man in every sense of the word. He was at least six inches taller than Browne who was five feet ten. He sported a Viva Zapata moustache and had a three-day growth of beard. His barrel chest was almost bursting through a polo shirt and his thighs stretched his jeans. He wore a thick gold chain round his neck. If Browne didn't know he was a police officer, he would have taken him for a drug dealer, which he assumed was intentional.

'Let's do this in the cafeteria,' Wallace said. 'I'll stand you a cup of the worst coffee in Belfast.'

'You obviously haven't been to Tennent Street.' Browne followed him through a door and along a corridor until they reached the cafeteria, where they procured two coffees and sat at an empty table.

'What can I do for you?' Wallace asked when they were settled.

'We're sure that the body in the burned-out car at Helen's Bay is Mickey Duff. My boss is worried that Duff and Royce might be the first casualties in a drugs war. You were in the Drugs Squad at the same time as Royce?'

'I was his sergeant.'

'What did you think of him?'

'Nice guy, at first. Our squad has a lot of contact with drugs and dealers. The drugs are the equivalent of the hookers in Vice. You need to keep your hands off. Royce started to taste the forbidden fruit, and pretty soon he was off his head ninety per cent of the time. Then everything went downhill fast until he left.'

'And after he left?'

'I heard that he was dealing for a while and then nothing. I was sorry to hear that he'd been topped.'

Browne looked across the cafeteria and saw a group of men looking in their direction. He thought he saw them laughing. I'm becoming paranoid, he thought, and put the scene from his mind.

Wallace looked over his shoulder at the group and winked out of sight of Browne.

'What about the idea of a turf war?' Browne asked.

Wallace turned back, a smile still on his face that exposed two rows of small teeth. He brushed back his long black hair with his hand. 'We've got the Chinese, the Russians, the East Europeans and the locals all distributing. We have contacts with all of them, and so far we haven't heard anything about a turf war, but it's possible.'

Browne looked at the table of men again. One of them made a comment to his colleagues that sent them into loud guffaws.

'Checking out the talent?' Wallace asked.

'What did you say?

'Word around is that you're a pansy.'

'I think you should be careful what you say. I have a good mind to report you.' He could feel his cheeks burning

'What for? I was only making a remark I would have made to a man checking out a group of women.'

Browne stood up. He contemplated throwing the remnants of his coffee at Wallace, but he knew that would get him nowhere. 'I'm going to remember you.'

'That's your prerogative. It's just locker-room talk as the man said.'

Browne didn't start breathing properly until he reached the street. He knew he should expect to meet people like Wallace. Homophobia had been institutionalised in the police force for many years, and people like Wallace weren't about to change. He had two choices: he could quit or he could remain and fight the prejudice. He hadn't made up his mind which way to go.

CHAPTER TWENTY-SEVEN

After leaving Davie Best's club, Wilson returned to the station. He'd learned nothing from Best and had probably managed to put him and Hills on their guard. If the turf war scenario proved correct, Best would be right at the centre of it. That would mean Duff and Royce had to be working for the opposition. Whoever that was. Best had amalgamated two drug operations and was the acknowledged major drug player in the city. And yet neither he nor any of his associates had been arrested or jailed. He was still pondering that fact when he sat behind his desk and saw a folder lying on his computer keyboard. He opened it and found a note on the front from O'Neill indicating that the file contained all she could find on the death of DC Colin Payne. Wilson sifted through the twenty pages in the folder. There were newspaper articles, statements from Payne's aunt and the first responders, and the autopsy and inquest reports. He started with the newspaper articles and worked his way through the rest of the papers. Payne reported one of his colleagues for corruption and a few weeks later he was dead. That was one hell of a coincidence and Wilson didn't believe in coincidences. There was a phone number for Payne's aunt at the end of her statement. He picked up the phone and dialled the number.

'Hello.' The voice was female and frail.

'Mrs Bagnell?' Wilson asked.

'Aye.'

'I'm Detective Superintendent Ian Wilson, I'm looking into the death of your nephew Colin and I was wondering whether I could visit you.'

'You can surely, I've been waiting for someone to do something since that boy died. I've been on to the local peelers for years but sure they don't take a blind bit of notice of an old woman.'

'Would it be okay if I came down now?'

'Aye, I'm always here.' She gave him an address in Bally-ward close to Castlewellan.

Wilson took the A1 from Belfast to the Castlewellan exit at which point he put the address of the Bagnell farm into his mobile phone. The disembodied computer voice led him to the Bann Road and brought him directly to his destination. The farmhouse was a neat, whitewashed two-storey house with a red door offset to the right and a single-storey extension built on the gable end. The area in front of the house was tarmacked and he noted the absence of animals in the vicinity as he drove in. He was pleased to see that he wouldn't require his rubber boots.

Wilson knocked on the door and an older lady wearing a housecoat opened it. He took out his warrant card and offered it to her.

She took a quick look. 'Get you inside before we both get our death of cold.' She closed the door behind him and walked slowly towards the rear of the house.

Wilson trailed behind her noting she had curvature of her spine. There was no way she was operating the farm. They entered a large country kitchen at the rear. The room was warm due to the presence of a solid fuel range. A rough wooden table already set with cups and saucers sat at the centre of the room.

'Sit you down,' Bagnell said. 'I gave you an hour from Belfast and I just put the kettle down.' She placed a plate with three slices of fruitcake in front of Wilson. 'Detective superintendent you said on the phone.'

'Yes.'

'And you're interested in Colin's death?'

'I am.'

She let out a sigh. 'I've never believed that the boy fell into a slurry tank. He'd worked on this farm every summer since he was a wain.' She poured hot water into the teapot and carried it to the table.

'What do you think happened?' Wilson asked.

'Someone killed him of course. Colin wasn't his usual self that weekend.' She poured them both a cup of tea. 'He was out of sorts, nervous, edgy. Something was bothering him, but he didn't want to talk about it.'

Wilson sipped his tea. 'A couple of weeks before he died he'd accused one of his colleagues of corruption and the man was forced to resign.'

'That might have been it. Colin was a sensitive boy, wouldn't hurt a fly.'

'Were you here when the accident occurred?'

'No, I was away to Castlewellan on a fool's errand. When I got back he had already passed. Faith, it was a horrible business. I have no children and I wanted Colin to have the farm. He wasn't fit for the police. He was a good God-fearing Protestant.'

'Was there anything else out of place that weekend?'

She thought for a moment. 'Nothing that I can think of. It's all mixed up in my mind now, the ambulance, the police cars and all that business with the coroner. It almost did away with me.'

'Did Colin come here every weekend?'

'Aye, every weekend as regular as clockwork.'

'He had a bedroom here?'

'Aye, since he was small.'

'Do you still have all his things in it?'

'I do, kept it just as he left it.' She stood up with difficulty and saw him watching her. 'I've sold most of the land. There's only twenty acres left, it and the house are with an estate agent. When it's sold, I'll be off to the old people's home.' She started to move towards the front of the house and beckoned him to follow. When they reached the stairs leading to the second floor, she stopped. 'I'll not go up with you. It's the small box room at the end of the landing.'

Wilson climbed the stairs and moved along the short corridor to the room at the end. He pushed the door open and entered. The walls were covered in old football posters that must have been there since Payne was a boy. There was a single bed against the back wall and a wooden wardrobe just inside the door. Wilson slipped on his latex gloves and went to the wardrobe. There were two work jackets and three pairs of old jeans on hangers. He searched through the pockets but found nothing of interest. They were obviously work clothes that were left permanently at the farmhouse. He pulled open the drawer at the base of the wardrobe and rifled through the shirts and underwear that it contained. He moved to the bed and looked underneath. He withdrew a battered leather suit-case and put it on top of the bed. He slipped the catches and raised the lid. He examined the old football programmes, school reports and photos of schoolboy football teams inside. He looked at the faces of the young boys but didn't recognise Payne among them. He turned over one of the photos. On the rear was the legend 'Down High School Junior Football Team 2004–2005'. He took out a photo of a stern-faced older man dressed in Orange Order regalia. Slowly he sifted through the memorabilia of Payne 's early life. Then he closed the suitcase and returned it to where he had found it. He looked up at the posters on the wall and noticed that one of them was askew. He reached out to straighten it and a sheaf of papers tumbled from behind and landed on the bed. They were photocopies of entries to the kind of notebook that all police officers are obliged to carry and keep up to date. There were approximately twenty A4 sheets, each covering two pages of notes. Wilson bundled up the sheets and then checked the other posters, but there was nothing behind them. He left the room and went downstairs. Mrs Bagnell had returned to the kitchen and was pouring a second cup of tea when Wilson entered.

'I found some papers that I'd like to look at back at the station.' Wilson sat and put the photocopies on the table.

Bagnell looked at him. 'Was my nephew killed for what's in those papers?'

'I have no idea.'

'But he didn't just fall into a slurry tank?'

'I don't think so.'

'I knew it.' A smile broke out on her face. 'I told the peelers in Downpatrick that Colin wouldn't make that mistake. All they said was that better men than him had died in similar circumstances. Will you get the bastard that killed that poor wee boy?' There were tears in the corners of her eyes.

'I don't know, but I'm certainly going to try.'

She put her hand on his arm. 'I can't ask any more than that.'

Wilson stood. 'I'll bring back these papers when I'm finished with them.'

'Keep them, I've no use for them.'

'There's an old suitcase under his bed containing old photos. Would you like me to get it for you?'

She looked round the kitchen. 'It'll soon all be gone. It's a sad fact of life, superintendent, but whoever buys the place will probably dump everything that's in it, including the old photos, in a skip. There's nobody left who cares anyway.' She started to rise.

He placed a hand on her shoulder. 'Stay where you are, I can see myself out.'

'If you manage to find Colin's killer, I'd appreciate it if you come and tell me. He was like a son to me.'

'I'll certainly try.'

When he went outside, he turned and looked at the old house. There was a lot of history in there. Some was happy and some sad. The voices of generations had resonated around its walls. But to him, it was simply the scene of a heinous crime.

CHAPTER TWENTY-EIGHT

Peter Davidson arrived at Belfast International and went straight to the security office. The door had the logo of an international company that specialises in airport security. Davidson knocked and a middle-aged man dressed in a black uniform and kitted out like a regular police officer, complete with body cam and two-way radio, opened the door. Davidson showed his warrant card and was invited into the office.

'Michael Johnson, head security guard,' the man said as soon as they were in the office. 'What can I do for you?'

'I want to enquire about a piece of lost property,' Davidson said.

'If you lost it on a plane, you'll have to contact the handling agent.'

'No, it's not mine and it wouldn't have been lost on a plane. In fact, we think that it might have been dumped.'

'What exactly are we talking about? You're a detective, so I suspected you wouldn't be here about a simple piece of lost property.'

'I'm working a murder case. We have information that a mobile call was made to the airport and immediately after, the phone went dead and the number has never been used since.'

'If it was dumped in one of the waste bins in the concourse, you're probably out of luck. A lot of the guys simply tie up the plastic bags as they come out of the bins and put them straight into the dumpsters. You wouldn't believe the kinds of things that people put in the bins and the cleaners don't usually fancy a rummage. Of course, if they copped a mobile phone it would be straight into their pocket.' He sat down behind a desk and hit a few keys on the computer. 'You have the time and date?'

Davidson reeled off the date and the time of the last call to the phone.

Johnson scrolled down with the mouse. 'Nothing in the concourse, not so unexpected, I'm afraid. Let's try the Causeway Lounge.'

'The Causeway Lounge?'

'That's where the business class and VIP passengers hang out while they wait for their flights.' He looked at Davidson. He didn't think that there were many policemen who had the necessary cash to travel business class, much like himself. 'You may be in luck. The cleaners in the business lounge are a little more careful because if a business passenger remembers leaving something in the lounge, and if they've disappeared it so to speak, we have to investigate. That can cost someone their job.' He looked up from his computer and smiled. 'Today's your lucky day. It just so happens a mobile phone was found in the lounge that day.'

'Where is it now?'

Johnson referred to the computer. 'Nobody claimed it so it should be here someplace.' He went to a locker at the back of the office and used a key from his belt to open the metal door. He searched inside and came up with a bog standard mobile phone. 'Not exactly the model most of our business-class passengers favour.'

Davidson took out a plastic evidence bag from his pocket and held it out. Johnson dropped the phone into the bag.

'You're going to find at least a dozen prints on that phone.' Johnson sat back down at his desk and produced a small receipt book. 'You have to sign for it.' He wrote in the book and then handed Davidson the pen.

Davidson signed the page and took the duplicate copy, which he dropped into the evidence bag with the phone. He put the bag in his jacket pocket and held out his hand. 'Thanks a lot.'

Johnson shook. 'Glad to be of assistance.'

As Davidson walked back through the concourse, he could almost feel the heat of the phone in his pocket. This phone had been used only once to receive news of Jackie Carlisle's demise. Whoever owned it had probably ordered Carlisle's murder. And now he had possession of that phone. Things were getting very scary indeed.

CHAPTER TWENTY-NINE

Wilson drove back to the station from Castlewellan. He was painting himself into a corner. The more he learned about Royce, and in particular about Payne, the more he felt their deaths were about what was happening within the PSNI's Drugs Squad. That put him in a difficult position with Yvonne Davis and his own team. If the killings were related to corruption, Davis would insist that he bring in Professional Services, but he didn't want to do that without more evidence. He had no idea how far the corruption might go. The more evidence he collected the more he felt he had to move the whole investigation upstairs. Also, he didn't like keeping his theory from Browne and the rest of the team. He shouldn't be the only one carrying the ball, in case whoever had arranged Payne's death would turn their attention to him. As soon as he arrived at the station, he handed over Payne's photocopies to O'Neill with a request to make additional copies and a secure digital copy. Then he went into his office and collapsed into his chair. He was being forced to peel back the layers of what was turning out to be a very rotten onion. Why couldn't the Royce case have been a simple murder? A case of thieves falling out. Why the hell hadn't Republican Action Against Drugs called in and claimed the killing? What had happened to common-place murder? Had spouses stopped killing their partners? He made a mental note to ask God to send him a simple murder case that could be solved by forensic work and good old skills of deduction.

He was contemplating heading home when his phone rang. 'We're wanted in Castlereagh, be outside in five minutes.' Davis's voice was business-like. He supposed that the visit to HQ was inevitable. McDevitt had been trumpeting on in the *Chronicle* about an impending turf war in Belfast with rivers of blood running in the streets. The population had been down that road before, and there had been mutterings from the religious and community leaders that the PSNI should be doing everything to avoid McDevitt's version of the approaching apocalypse. Somebody at HQ, and that probably meant DCC Jennings, had got the message and decided that the troops needed some additional motivation.

THEY SAT in the back seat of Davis's car. 'Is there anything I should know?' Davis asked as they pulled away from the station.

Wilson almost lost control and laughed. There was so much that he was keeping from her that it was ridiculous. He comforted himself with the thought that it was for her own good, but at the same time he longed to return to the good old days when he shared everything with Donald Spence and vice versa. But Davis wasn't Spence, who had been formed in the cauldron of sectarian violence. And while Spence had topped out at chief superintendent, Davis still had a chair waiting for her in HQ. 'No, ma'am, you're up to date on the current investigations.'

She didn't look convinced. Jennings was like a giant octopus with its tentacles wrapped round the PSNI. She had to steel herself every time she entered his office. And being associated with Wilson certainly didn't help. Jennings would dig up every bit of rumour and innuendo on Wilson and use it against the both of them. They passed the rest of the trip in silence.

JENNINGS WAS SEATED behind his desk when they entered. Although he had a 'soft' suite within his large office, he preferred to have his officers sit directly in front of him like errant schoolchildren.

On entering, Wilson looked to see whether there was any sign of the 'Greek chorus' – those senior officers and acolytes of the DCC who were usually invited to his office to witness ritual humiliations. Thankfully, Jennings was alone.

Jennings motioned to the two chairs directly facing him while continuing to concentrate on the documents on his desk. Wilson and Davis took their seats and waited patiently for their boss to finish his important task.

'This Royce business,' Jennings closed the file he had been working on and put it aside, 'where are we on it?'

Davis looked at Wilson, who took it as a sign to speak. 'We're following a definite line of enquiry.'

'Which is?' Jennings asked.

'We are making a connection between the man found in the burned-out car in Helen's Bay and the murder of Hugh Royce. We're sure that the man at Helen's Bay was Michael Duff, a mid-level pusher. We have information that Royce was also involved in some way in the drugs trade in the city. It might be, as is suggested in the *Chronicle*, the start of a turf war. Drugs have been flooding the city over the past few years and the profits accruing to the gangs have been rising.'

'Is this your theory or your friend McDevitt's?' Jennings asked Wilson.

'Mine.'

'What is the disposition of your team?'

Wilson looked puzzled. 'We work as a team. The only one with a general function is DC O'Neill because of her computer skills. The other members of the team carry out tasks that are assigned on a daily basis as the investigation evolves.'

Jennings remained silent for a moment then stared at Wilson. 'For example, what is DC Davidson working on at the moment?'

Wilson could feel Jennings' eyes on him. There are no coincidences, he thought. 'DC Davidson is doing background checks on Royce and his associates. We're building a picture of the man and trying to establish what he's been up to since he left the force.'

'And Graham?'

'Concentrating on locating the owner of the car that was found at the murder scene and dealing with the responses to the request for information from the public.'

'Davidson is retiring soon?'

'In six months.'

'He should be winding down,' Jennings said.

'We're investigating two murders,' Wilson said. 'We need everybody that we have and a few others if you have any to spare.'

Jennings frowned. 'I would love to assist, but it's not possible under the present budget regime.' He picked up the file he had set aside and opened it. 'You may leave.'

As soon as they were outside Jennings' office, Davis gripped Wilson by the arm. 'What was that about?'

'Motivating the troops by showing leadership and concern?'

'Quit the bullshit, Ian. There was something going on in there that I wasn't part of. And it's probably something that I should be aware of.'

Wilson walked towards the lift. He knows that Davidson has been digging around, he thought. But how does he know?

Maybe it was time to pull Davidson off the Carlisle investigation.

Davis followed Wilson into the lift and they descended in silence. The car was waiting outside and they took their seats in the rear. Davis tapped her driver on the shoulder. 'Alex, why don't you take a toilet break.'

The driver got out of the car.

'Are you going to tell me?' Davis said.

'There's nothing to tell.'

'You have a touch of chivalry about you that could be charming if it wasn't inappropriate. You can't protect me by telling me that nothing went on up there. Jennings passed you a message and it concerns Davidson.'

'I don't think that he's going to replace Peter when he retires.'

'Good, but not good enough, what's Davidson working on?

'He's investigating a murder.'

'Whose murder?'

'Jackie Carlisle's.'

Davis's face went white. 'Jackie Carlisle was murdered? I thought he committed suicide.'

'We have enough evidence to prove that he was murdered.'

'Why the hell didn't you tell me?'

'Because we weren't sure, and because whoever murdered him is very dangerous, and they think they've gotten away with it.'

'We need to formalise it.'

'No, we don't. We need to keep it low key.'

'But Jennings knows about it.'

'I don't think so. His antennae may have picked something up, but he's still not sure.'

She sat back in her seat. 'Do you think that he's involved somewhere?'

'Whoever had Carlisle murdered has clout. Jennings is a

dogsbody for the good and the great in this province. When the proverbial hits the fan, he's their go-to guy.'

'Holy God, Ian, what have you got us into?'

'You know nothing. Let me continue, and when I have enough evidence, we'll go upstairs, all the way upstairs.'

Davis leaned forward and sounded the horn. The driver returned, sat behind the wheel and drove away.

'Drink?' Wilson said after several minutes silence.

'Not tonight, I have a date.'

Jack Duane, Wilson thought, you silver-tongued bastard.

CHAPTER THIRTY

Davis may not have needed a drink but Wilson definitely did. He left his car at the station and texted Reid to meet him in the Crown when she was through with work. The meeting with Jennings had rattled him. Up to that point, he was sure that the Carlisle investigation was under the radar, but obviously Davidson had slipped up somewhere along the line, or perhaps someone had talked. Whatever the reason, it was clear that Jennings had been alerted that Davidson was up to something. Wilson was equally sure that Jennings had no idea what the 'something' might be, because if he had been, there would have been a volcanic reaction. The Castlereagh meeting had been a fishing expedition. At the very least, Wilson and Davidson had a limited time in which to dig up credible evidence of a crime. They were nearly there, but so much of what they had was circumstantial and open to being refuted. He sat in the snug cradling a pint of Guinness and pondering what they could do now. Perhaps Davidson was not yet completely compromised. Wilson needed to have a word with him as soon as possible to find out how word of the investigation might have leaked out. He was still deep in thought when Reid pushed open the door. She bent, kissed him and sat close.

'Your text sounded ominous,' she said. 'You're getting a bit old for making a night of it.'

'Don't worry, this and a couple more will do the trick.'

'Make mine a double gin and tonic'.

He pushed the bell to summon the barman and ordered the drinks.

'Bad day at the office?' she asked.

He explained about his trip to Castlewellan and the meeting with Jennings.

The drinks arrived and he paid.

She sipped her drink. She could see that her partner was on edge. He was handling more cases than humanly possible and now there was another one on the horizon. 'For God's sake, Ian, can't you let sleeping dogs lie? Are you so always on the job that you see murder in every death? Dozens of people die every year in agricultural accidents.'

'That's what the murderer was counting on. It was just a regular farmyard accident. Guy slips and falls into a slurry tank. It doesn't matter that he's twenty-seven and as fit as a fiddle.'

'It happens. People drown in six inches of water. It's not an everyday occurrence, but it does happen.'

'I've been through the post-mortem report and the minutes of the coroner's inquest. They went for the easy option. But there are a few points that bother me. He wasn't overcome by gas. Why didn't he just get his head out of the slurry?'

'His airway could have been blocked.'

He took a slug of his pint. It was a possibility. 'Okay, I'll accept the coroner's verdict if you'll go over the autopsy. The paper I have is only a summary. You can pull up the complete report and if you say that Colin Payne died an accidental death, then I'll accept it. Agreed?'

'Agreed. Let's finish up our drinks and head home. We could both do with the early night.'

Wilson knew that there would be no early night for him. His mind was racing and he needed one more drink to slow it down. 'After one more.' He pushed the bell.

'I'm done,' she said. 'I assume I'm driving us home.'

The barman appeared and Wilson ordered a Guinness. 'It appears that Jack was serious about dating Davis.'

'You're kidding.'

'I wish I was. Davis told me that she had a date tonight and, being a detective, I put two and two together.'

'And you probably got six. Well, they're two consenting adults.'

'Don't get me wrong. The best of luck to them, but somehow I just can't see Jack and Davis as a pair.'

'Stranger things have happened.'

The barman put the pint in front of Wilson, who put his hand in his pocket to pay.

'It's paid,' the barman said.

'By who?'

'Bloke standing at the bar, said your next drink was on him.'

Wilson rose from his seat and joined the barman at the door. 'Which one?'

The barman's eye examined the patrons at the bar. 'He's gone.'

'Describe him?'

'Ordinary sort of bloke, nice coat though.'

Wilson handed the barman back the pint. 'Thanks, but I've changed my mind.' He put his hand out and helped Reid to stand. 'That early night sounds good after all.'

He ushered Reid towards the open door. So George Pratley had decided to play silly buggers with him. If that's the way it was going to be, bring it on.

CHAPTER THIRTY-ONE

The team had assembled for the morning briefing. Wilson had slept fitfully. He felt like an amateur juggler trying to keep all the balls in the air while being scared that one of them was about to hit the ground. 'Okay,' he said. 'Let's start with Harry, where are we on the response to the public for information?'

'I'm compiling a report,' Graham said. 'It'll make grim reading. We followed up on a dozen calls, the rest were cranks. None of the followed-up calls panned out.'

Wilson turned to O'Neill. 'Nothing new on the missing years?'

She shook her head. 'Royce dropped off the radar. Maybe he left the country. You want me to try Interpol?'

'No,' Wilson said. 'What about the Drugs Squad?'

'I visited our friends in the Drugs Squad yesterday,' Browne said. 'I'm obviously too low level for DCI Pratley so I got his sergeant, a guy named John Wallace. I think they thought that I'd just joined the force last week. I got the snow job. This is what we do and this is how we do it. I asked about how Royce got on with the rest of the team. Wallace was a DS during Royce's time. There were no problems until the corruption was exposed. It appears some drugs disappeared on their way to the lock-up and Royce was a user. Wallace knew nothing about Royce's life after he left the force.'

'Did you believe him?' Wilson asked.

'No, and I didn't like him either. There was something about him.' Yes, he was a homophobe.

'Siobhan, get me what you can on Wallace.'

'Yes, Boss.' O'Neill wrote in her notebook.

'By the way, the owner of O'Reilly's has been on,' Browne said. 'Wants to know when he can reopen.'

'Check with Forensics,' Wilson said. 'If they're through, give him a call and tell him he's good to go.' He looked up at the board. 'We've got to fill in the gaps in Royce's life. He must have friends. Maybe he has a woman somewhere who knows him. We've got to hit on everyone we know. It's a shoe-leather job.' He looked at Browne. 'You and Harry have to pound the pavements. For God's sake this guy wasn't living in a bubble. He interacted with someone. Find them. Now I want you to be very quiet for a while, because I'm going to tell you a story about where I was yesterday.' He told them about the farm outside Castlewellan and the death of DC Colin Payne. He told them why Payne was important to their case and that he suspected murder. When he was finished, he found himself looking into four stunned faces.

'When will we know whether it was murder?' Graham asked.

'Reid is looking at the result of the post-mortem. If she says it's clear, there is no case. On the other hand ... '

'It'll be a four-year-old case,' Graham said. 'There'll be no forensic evidence and we'll have a hell of a job establishing a timeline, but I can see where you're going on the motive.'

'Someone thought they were very clever coming up with the agricultural accident scenario,' Wilson said. 'And in a way they were, the pathologist and the coroner both bought it.'

'They're not going to like this upstairs,' Davidson said. 'If you're right, there's a possibility that Professional Service leaked information on the complainant. That means that they've been compromised as well as the Drugs Squad. Right now you're standing on the bank looking out over a river of shit wondering whether you want to wade in. But the river of shit is not the real problem. The real problem is how deep the shit is.'

'For now, we do nothing,' Wilson said. 'Reid promised to look at the post-mortem today. By this evening, we should know whether we require waders. In the meantime, we keep pushing on filling in the gaps in Royce's life. Get to it.' He turned to Davidson. 'Peter, in my office.'

As soon as they entered his office, Wilson closed the door behind Davidson. 'Sit down, Peter.'

Davidson sat and withdrew a plastic evidence bag from his pocket and placed it on the desk.

'Is that what I think it is?' Wilson asked.

'It may be. This phone was binned in the airport business lounge on the day the phone call was made from Hillsborough. There's no SIM, just the phone.'

Wilson picked up the evidence bag and examined the phone inside. It was a cheap throwaway. If it was the phone that received the call from outside Carlisle's house, it probably belonged to whoever organised the hit. And if that was the case, there was a chance that their fingerprints were on the phone. 'You've done a hell of a good job, Peter.'

Davidson smiled, praise from Wilson was praise indeed.

'That's the good news,' Wilson said. 'The bad news is that I was called to Castlereagh last evening by Jennings. He expressed an interest in what you're working on at the moment.'

The smile faded from Davidson's face.

'I don't think he knows what you're investigating,' Wilson said. 'But his interest is ominous. I think someone might have leaked.'

'Jamsie Gibbons?' Davidson said. 'Gibbons dropped dead two days ago, but I had asked him to get me details on Jackson.'

'For God's sake, Peter, Jamsie was a well-known alcoholic who'd sell his soul for a drink.'

'It was all I could come up with, Boss. I was desperate.'

'Who might he have told?'

'I have no idea.'

'And what might he have told them? That you were looking for information on Jackson?'

'Probably.'

'Jennings might know that you're looking into Jackson then, but he has no idea why. We're going to have to work at making sure he doesn't find out.'

'Carlisle's neighbour returned last night. He called me this morning.'

'Put a couple of photos together and include Jackson's. Get him to identify the man in the white coat outside Carlisle's house. If he picks Jackson, take a statement and get him to sign it. There might be enough to bring Jackson in. And be bloody damn careful from now on. If I get even a sniff that Jennings and his crew are on to you, you're off the case. Understood.'

'Understood, Boss.'

Davidson pushed himself out of the chair and left the room. Wilson thought he might have a chequered career but he was a fine detective. He could see Browne hovering about outside his office and motioned him to enter. He felt like a priest in the confessional. 'What's up, Rory?'

Browne explained what had happened in Musgrave Street. 'I'm getting a bit pissed off. I don't know whether the PSNI is for me.'

'An arsehole like Wallace and a few of his hangers-on toss a name about and you want to fold up your tent and slink away. I don't see you as that kind of man.'

'I was back in Coleraine for the weekend and my father hardly spoke a word to me.'

'That's sad. My own father committed suicide when I was seventeen. I blamed my mother and we spent half a lifetime without communicating. Later, I learned that the suicide had nothing to do with her and we've had to rebuild our relationship. I don't usually believe in regrets, but I bitterly regret those lost years. You're a fine detective and I think a fine man. Your sexuality is just part of the picture and the opinion of people like Wallace counts for nothing. I think the Drugs Squad is rotten to the core and if I'm right you might have the occasion to turn the tables on Wallace. Now get out of here and find out where the hell Royce has been for the past two or three years.'

CHAPTER THIRTY-TWO

Professor Stephanie Reid left the lecture room and started back to her office in the mortuary. Most days she enjoyed her job as a pathologist and relished explaining the ins and outs of her speciality to students. Other days she wished she had chosen anaesthesiology. It was neater and a hell of a lot cleaner. This was one of those days. She had instructed her assistant to download the full post-mortem on Colin Payne. Before returning to her office she picked up a cup of coffee and had a chat with a few of her colleagues. She was back on focus by the time she sat down at her computer. Ian was clearly under a lot of pressure, but she wondered whether some of it was self-induced. He was beginning to become murder-prone. She felt that Payne would be a bit of a stretch. He'd been much more laid back when he was away from the job in California. Everybody has a breaking point and Ian wouldn't be the first police officer to lose a sense of reality because of the pressure of work. She brought up the post-mortem file and saw that her predecessor had carried it out. She didn't have much respect for him but that went with the job, everyone thought they were superior to their predecessor and they were definitely a lot smarter than their successor. She started at the beginning and read the detailed examination of the corpse before moving on to the conclusions. Payne had been a fit young man with no sign of any illness; he was a non-smoker and drank in moderation. She brought up the photographs of the body and examined each one in detail. She stopped dead when she saw the photos of Payne's back. There were three contusions and the absence of healing indicated that they were made perimortem. She zoomed in on the bruises and then examined the commentary. There was no mention of the contusions. She sat back in her chair. Her predecessor may not have been the best pathologist in the world, but he wasn't a total idiot. Could he really have missed three areas where significant pressure had been exerted on Payne's back? She hated to admit it, but perhaps Ian wasn't paranoid after all. Examining the photos, she could imagine a scenario where someone had ensured that Payne's upper body was forced into the slurry and kept there. She went through the photographs one by one, concentrating on each. Payne would have been powerful enough to push himself out of the tank, unless he was restrained. Payne had drowned in pig slurry. In many such agricultural accidents the victim is overcome by slurry gas, which contains a high concentration of hydrogen sulphide. There was no sign that Payne had lost consciousness before drowning. Reid was forced to the conclusion that Payne had been forcibly held face down in the slurry until he expired. She shut off her computer and picked up her mobile phone.

'Hi,' Wilson said. 'To what do I owe the pleasure?'

'I hate to start with an apology, but it looks like you were right about Payne. I've examined the photos and there are contusions on his back consistent with him being forcibly held down just before he died. I can't understand how this wasn't noticed during the post-mortem.'

'Maybe it was. The bottom line is that you are willing to go on the record that the pathologist got it wrong in his conclusion to the coroner. Will that be enough to reopen the inquest?'

'It should be, but that will depend on the coroner.'

'We need to get cracking with this right away. Reopening the inquest will be a precursor to launching an enquiry.'

'I'll call the coroner right away. Where are you going with this?'

'Payne was murdered because he reported on corruption in the Drugs Squad. Royce retired because he was instructed to throw himself under the bus. Something happened to Royce in the intervening period, and now he's been murdered. It's all linked. I don't know exactly how yet, but I'm beginning to focus in on some of the personalities.'

'I'll get back to you.' She put the phone down.

Wilson checked out Lucy Kane on the staff list and called her number. 'We need to talk,' he said as soon as she answered.

'We are definitely not going to talk,' she replied.

'I think I can prove that Colin Payne was murdered. And I don't think that you'll like the direction that the investigation into his death is going to take.'

There was a pregnant pause. 'Somewhere offsite and where neither of us are known.'

'Have you been to the Titanic Centre yet?'

She laughed. 'No.'

'It's the safest place to meet. Everyone who goes there is either a tourist, or a schoolchild. I haven't met a native of Belfast who has actually visited it. I'll meet you in The Galley café at four o'clock.'

'I'll be there.'

CHAPTER THIRTY-THREE

'Well?' Rodgers stared across the desk at Jennings.

'I don't know,' Jennings said. 'Wilson almost convinced me that he was telling the truth. But he's a devious bastard, and a consummate liar. What do you have from your side?'

'I passed the message to Jackson, who isn't exactly pissing himself. The Carlisle business was the only possible link with Wilson or Davidson, and as far as Jackson is concerned the operation was as clean as a whistle.'

'I don't like hubris. We both know that no operation is ever as clean as a whistle. There's always a flaw, even in what looks like a perfect plan. Make Jackson go over every aspect of the operation.'

'I already have. Nothing was left to chance. The appointment with the hospice was cancelled, the wife was out and, according to Jackson, Carlisle died with a smile on his face.'

'You know Gibbons. Could the old fool have made the whole thing up?'

'Jamsie was fond of a drink or two, but why should he bother to approach me with a cock and bull story? What was in it for him?'

'How did he know that Davidson was looking into Jackson? Nobody in the force even knows the names of the officers in your service.'

'Don't forget we used Jackson in the operation against Wilson.'

'Not one of your more successful outings. Do you think that Wilson is looking for something on Jackson for revenge? It doesn't really fit with his character.'

'Well, I don't exactly think that Wilson has put Jackson on his Christmas card list.'

'Put a tail on Davidson. Not Jackson, someone else. Let's see where he goes and what he does. Then we can make up our mind what to do about him.'

Rodgers stood up slowly. 'I was against the Carlisle operation. The man was dying anyway.'

Jennings picked up a file. 'But not fast enough.'

PETER DAVIDSON SAT in the conservatory where Jackie Carlisle had taken his last breath. He was finishing his coffee and looking across at Carlisle's widow Irene. He had loved quite a few women in his lifetime, and he had been honest enough to realise that in many cases the love he professed was simply lust. Things were different with Irene. Maybe it was because he was older now and a lot wiser, but what had started off as a piece of opportunism when Irene had come on to him had, over the months that they had been intimate, grown into the most genuine love that he was capable of. Every time he looked at her he felt a warm glow in his chest. In a few months, he would be finished with the PSNI. It had been a hell of a ride, a lot of ups but also a lot of downs. The main point was that he had survived. As long as he and Irene were together, there would never be the spectre in his future of the dreaded security job in a shopping mall, or taking the tickets in a car park.

Irene refilled his coffee and offered him another chocolate biscuit. 'Do you really think you have this Jackson fellow?'

'We're close. I'm meeting your neighbour later. If he identifies Jackson, Wilson is going to haul the bastard in and confront him. Whatever way that interview goes, there's sufficient evidence to prove that Jackie's death was murder. Then you can go back to the insurance company and get them to review the file.'

Irene cuddled up to him. 'You're the smartest detective in the whole world.'

Davidson knew that certainly wasn't true, but he wasn't about to disabuse Irene of her opinion.

She picked up a brochure from the table. 'I can't wait to get away from this cold country.' She flicked through the pages. 'What do you think of this one?'

Davidson looked at the advertisement for a three-bedroomed villa with swimming pool in Tenerife. A few short months ago, this would have been a dream. 'I love it.'

She kissed him on the cheek. 'We're going to buy it as soon as the money comes in from the insurance. Then we're going to move there and spend the winter in the sun.'

'You're not going to keep this place?' They'd never really discussed what was going to happen to the Hillsborough house. Davidson assumed it was Irene's to dispose of as she wished. It was worth in the high seven hundred thousands, leaving plenty of change after the villa was purchased.

She cuddled closer. 'This house will go to my son when I die. It's already arranged.' She saw the look on his face. 'Don't worry, you'll be on the deed of the Spanish house.'

If I last that long, Davidson thought. Although he and Irene were getting on like a house on fire in and out of the bedroom, it would be her name on the insurance cheque. At that point, he would have served his purpose, and she would be well within her rights to show him the door. In that event, he would probably be grateful for the security job in the nearest shopping centre. But that was in the future and it might never happen. He finished up his coffee and turned to give her a hug. 'I love you, Irene.'

'And I love you, Peter. You're ten times the man that Jackie Carlisle was. I spent most of my life as an appendage to that egomaniac. What a bloody waste. You've given me more joy in the few months that we've been together than I had in the previous twenty years. I can't wait to get away together and start a new life.'

He held her close. He wanted so much for it to be true.

WHEN DAVIDSON LEFT Irene's house, he didn't notice the nondescript young man loitering at the end of the road. He crossed to the neighbour's house and rang the bell. When the door was answered he took his warrant card and showed it. 'Mr Cooney, DC Davidson.'

Recognition came into Cooney's face. 'I remember, you're looking into Jackie's Carlisle's death.'

'That's right, sir.'

'What the hell do you want now?'

'I'd like to show you some photos. Perhaps you can identify the man in the white jacket.'

'Then I suppose you'd better come inside.'

They went into the living room and sat on the couch. 'Can I offer you something to drink?' Cooney asked.

'Nothing for me, thanks.' Davidson took four passport-sized photographs out of his pocket and laid them side by side on the coffee table. 'Do you recognise any of these men?'

Cooney stared at the photos moving them sideways after he examined each one. 'This one here.' He tapped the photo of Simon Jackson. 'This is the guy wearing the white jacket who went into the house.'

Davidson took out an A4 pad from his briefcase. 'I wonder would you please write out a short statement for me to that effect and sign it. I'd also like you to sign and date the back of the photo that you've identified.'

Cooney sighed as he took the pad and pen. 'Will this end up in court? I'm very busy at the moment.'

'Hard to say, sir, depends where we go from here.' That's what Davidson loved about Joe Citizens. They enjoyed nattering on about what they would do in a crime situation, but when the chips were down and they were sitting in court looking at some beast covered in tattoos, they generally had an urgent need to visit the toilet. Not that Davidson blamed them. During his time in the force, he had met the worst of the worst, men and women who killed and maimed in the name some ideology from the Middle Ages. And in their midst were the psychopaths taking advantage of a free pass to the blood-bath. He watched as Cooney signed the back of Jackson's photo, and then carefully wrote his short statement.

'That should cover it.' Cooney handed back the pad and pen.

Davidson read the statement. It would probably be enough to bring Jackson in. 'Very good, sir, this will do for the present. I'll get this typed up and I'll be back to have it signed.' He stood.

'You mean we're not finished?'

'Just one more signature on the typed-up version, we'll try to be quick so that we cause the minimum disruption.' He slipped the pad into his briefcase and returned the photos to his jacket pocket.

They walked to the front door together and Davidson walked back to his unmarked police car. He looked across the road at the Carlisle house and pondered returning to visit the lovely Irene but decided it was best to go back to the station instead.

As his car drove down the street, a man came out of the shadows and walked up to the Cooney house. He took out a notebook and wrote the house number down then went to a car parked down the road and sat into the passenger seat.

CHAPTER THIRTY-FOUR

Wilson had been wrestling with the problem of Hugh Royce's whereabouts over the past three years. While he believed that people could go off grid, Ulster was not an easy place in which to do it. Dealing with the bureaucracy doesn't make it easy for a start, and disappearing among a population of 1.8 million souls takes some doing. How had Royce managed the almost impossible? He could think of one man who might have the answer to that question and he had met him in the company of Jock McDevitt. Reluctant as he was to involve the reporter from the *Chronicle*, he had no option.

'And how is my best friend today?' McDevitt said when he answered the phone. He was in the newsroom writing up his piece for the morning edition. 'Want to hear my lead for tomorrow's paper?'

'Not really, I need another one-on-one with Mouse,' Wilson said.

'I see you're not in the mood for small talk today. I'm afraid that the one-on-one isn't going to happen. I'm sorry, Ian, but I'm not about to put contacts I've cultivated for years at risk.

Mouse was emphatic when I dropped him off. You got to ask your questions, and you got your answers.'

'What if the questions weren't the right ones?'

'This isn't a drawn cup-tie, there are no replays. Mouse has no problem slipping me a few titbits, but he has no desire to become a police snitch. And I pay better.'

'I'm not laughing. My back is to the wall on this Royce killing. The guy is a ghost. He retires from the PSNI, divorces his wife, hits the junkie trail and disappears. I need to find out where he disappeared to.'

'It might be as simple as Kathmandu.'

'In which case I'm screwed. You give me Mouse, and I'll give you a scoop, how's that?'

'A bit like tying a carrot in front of a donkey's face that he's never going to get. I'll tell you what, I'll ask Mouse the question for you. And you still owe me this scoop of yours.'

Wilson thought for a minute. He certainly wasn't going to get any help from his friends in the Drugs Squad. McDevitt's proposal was probably the best deal on the table. 'Okay, I need to know where Royce has been for the past three years. How soon will you be back to me?'

'I'm putting the piece for tomorrow to bed. I'll contact Mouse when I'm through. What about a drink this evening at the Crown, seven o'clock?'

'I'll be there.'

'THAT'S THE PLAN.' Pratley sat back and smiled at Jennings. He'd outlined his plan for fitting up Wilson. It involved a car crash, the planting of drugs in Wilson's car and the responding officers finding them. 'The frame is perfect. The bastard will never get out of jail.'

'That's because with a hair-brained scheme like that, the bastard will never be put in jail. That kind of frame would be all right to run on your criminal friends who have a track record with drugs. Wilson, on the other hand, is a squeaky-clean police officer who has never been involved in either handling or using drugs. However, we don't need to get Wilson into jail, we just need him to be preoccupied with a personal problem for a while. I think I've come up with something that might have the desired effect. In contrast to your flight of fancy, it's simple and it might actually work.' And thankfully it doesn't include any input from Pratley and his crew, he thought. 'Listen and learn.'

CHAPTER THIRTY-FIVE

The Galley café is located in the atrium of the Titanic Centre in East Belfast. Wilson ran past the place most mornings, but he had never visited the exhibition. In the same way, he supposed, that there were many Romans who had never visited the Coliseum. At ten minutes to four, he was seated at a table enjoying a black coffee and a chocolate cake that was off the scale in calorie content. Kane arrived and bought her own coffee.

'I got your message,' Wilson said when she sat down.

'I don't know what you're talking about.' She sipped her mint tea.

'I followed up on Payne's death. I paid a visit to the farm in Ballyward and spoke to his aunt. She was pretty adamant that his death wasn't an accident. Apparently, she's been complaining for years, but nobody was taking a blind bit of notice. I left the place convinced that she had a point.'

'Good for you, and how does this affect Professional Services?'

'I'm coming to that. I asked Professor Reid at the Royal to review the initial post-mortem. She's convinced that Payne was murdered. There are bruises on his back that are consis-

tent with him being forcibly held down in the slurry tank.
She's going to contact the coroner and ask to have the inquest
reopened.'

Kane sipped her tea and looked at Wilson over the top of
the cup. She'd heard a lot of rumours about him. It was said
that he only needed the sniff of a murder to get on the trail.
She was aware of that reputation when she sent him the
cutting from the newspaper. 'That must be comforting for his
aunt.'

'There are lots of questions surrounding the murder,
specifically who put the pressure on Payne's back. But that's
going to be my business. However, there is an issue of the
possible involvement of Professional Services in the murder.
How did the killer know that Payne was the whistle-blower?
The only answer I can come up with is that your unit must
have had a giant leak in it. You were supposed to have been the
only ones who knew Payne's identity. I assume that it was
never mentioned in the interview with Royce.'

'You assume right. Although the PSNI Code of Ethics
gives no guarantee of confidentiality to an officer reporting
misconduct in the service, we do everything possible to maintain confidentiality where the issues are serious. In this case,
all documents relating to Royce were marked 'sensitive' and
had a restricted circulation. Also, the computer files relating to
the case were encrypted and password protected.'

'But someone found out that Payne was the source of the
accusations against Royce and by extension the Drugs Squad.'

'It would appear so.'

'Do you think that your unit is leak-proof?'

She shook her head.

'Anyone in particular?'

'I think we're done here.' She started to rise and he put his
hand on her arm.

'I think I know who's behind Payne's death. I think that
Royce was involved in corruption, but he wasn't alone. I'm

going to bring this whole mess to light, and when I do I'm going to get the name of the person who leaked Payne's name and I'm going to put him or her in the dock as an accessory.' He took his hand from her arm and she stood up.

'Good luck.' She turned on her heel and walked away.

He went to the counter and ordered another coffee. He'd hoped that she might be more open to helping him. But she had probably already crossed a line by sending him the newspaper article. A lot of PSNI colleagues were going to be trapped in the net he was planning to cast. Some of them would be in the Drugs Squad, some would be in Professional Services and some might even be in Castlereagh. It was a risky road that he was going down but wasn't it always.

CHAPTER THIRTY-SIX

Wilson called into the station and learned that there was nothing new in the Royce investigation. There was a copy of an email from Reid to the coroner in which she made an excellent case for having the inquest on Payne reopened. It was written in such a way that the coroner would have difficulty in refusing. He thanked God daily that he had someone like Reid in his corner. There was no point to an evening briefing and the team drifted off between five and six. Wilson was anxious to meet McDevitt, so as soon as the squad room was empty, he left. McDevitt was ensconced in Wilson's snug when he arrived and looked like he'd been there for some time. 'You owe me fifty quid,' McDevitt said as soon as Wilson sat down.

'Cheap at twice the price.' Wilson put a fifty-pound note on the table and McDevitt scooped it up. 'Your royalty cheque didn't arrive this month?'

'Sales are down.' McDevitt finished his pint and pushed the bell to summon the barman. 'My agent tells me that we're losing traction.'

'That doesn't sound too good.'

The barman stuck his head in and McDevitt placed the order.

'Apparently it's not,' McDevitt said. 'I'm drowning my sorrows, sort of.'

'Wait until the film comes out. Anyway, most book sales are paperback these days.'

The drinks arrived and McDevitt paid. They picked up their glasses, toasted each other and drank.

'Enough of the foreplay,' Wilson said. 'I assume the fifty quid was for Mouse. Did he come through?'

'Used to be a fiver in the old days.' McDevitt took a drink.

Wilson put on a hard face. 'Don't play with me, Jock. What have you got?'

'You're not going to be happy.' McDevitt moved his hands in a circle over the table as though he was cradling a crystal ball. 'I see fifty quid flying away for no result.'

Wilson was beginning to wish he'd arrived two drinks earlier. But when McDevitt was playing the crazy leprechaun, it was as well to play along. 'Where was Royce living?'

'Mouse hasn't a clue. He hadn't seen Royce in years before he saw him in Donegall Square. That's what aroused his interest.'

'That's not what I wanted to hear.'

'I know, but like Mouse said, he's not a psychic. He's certain that Royce wasn't in Belfast. One day Royce was wandering around central Belfast, the next day he wasn't'.

'Is that what I get for fifty quid?'

'Don't you think you got your fifty quid's worth at the Black Mountain.'

Wilson nodded, finished his drink and pushed the bell. Reid arrived at the same time as the barman and Wilson expanded the order to include her.

'You look great.' McDevitt toasted her with a glass containing the dregs of his Guinness. 'The tan hasn't faded yet. Either that or you're boosting it on a sun bed. But there's no doubt that California suited you. I thought the both of you might have stayed on. At least you would have avoided the shite weather.'

'I think he's been here since four o'clock,' Wilson said. 'He's drowning his sorrows because his book is losing traction.'

'Poor old Jock.' Reid leaned down and kissed him on the cheek. 'Wait until the film comes out.'

'That's what yer man said.' McDevitt turned to Wilson. 'I may be a bit in my cups, but I'm not forgetting the scoop.'

'All in good time,' Wilson said.

The barman arrived with the drinks and Wilson paid him. He put a pint in front of McDevitt. 'One for the road.'

McDevitt picked up the pint and looked at it. 'I was looking forward to a session, but I can see that you love birds want to be away.'

'I'm bushed,' Reid said. 'And I'm away to Coleraine first thing in the morning to give a speech at the university that I haven't written yet.' She sipped a gin and tonic.

'So, you're going to piss off and leave old Jock to get drunk on his own.'

'No,' Wilson said. 'We're going to piss off and put old Jock into a taxi that will take him home.

'And why the hell am I going there?'

CHAPTER THIRTY-SEVEN

The duty sergeant pulled Wilson aside as soon as he arrived at the station. He pointed at a small man sitting alone on a bench in the reception area. 'He's been here since seven-thirty, waiting to see Harry, but I think you might deal with him.'

'One of the phone calls?' Wilson asked.

'I don't think so. Something to do with the Volkswagen Polo.'

Wilson walked across to the man. 'DS Wilson, I hear you want to speak with DC Graham. We work together.'

The man stood and barely reached Wilson's shoulder. 'My name's Tom Donaldson and I think you boys are holdin' on to my car.'

'We've been looking for you.' Wilson looked back at the duty sergeant. 'One tea and one coffee in room one.' He turned back to Donaldson. 'Please follow me.'

They sat in the interview room facing each other.

'Where have you been?' Wilson asked.

'Five days in Tenerife tryin' to get out of this terrible weather, I came back to find no car and this business card in the door.' He tossed Graham's card on the table.

'You own a Volkswagen Polo with this registration number.' Wilson gave the number of the car from O'Reilly's car park.

'I do surely. I loaned it to a friend of mine and he was supposed to leave it outside my house when he was finished with it and post the key in the letter box.'

'And would this friend be Hugh Royce?'

'He would indeed.'

'When did you arrive back in Belfast?'

'Last night.'

'Then you aren't aware that Hugh Royce is dead.'

'Holy God, no.'

'He was murdered four days ago.'

'Murdered you say.' Donaldson put his head in his hands. 'Who would murder poor Hugh? He was a harmless wee git.'

'But he was your friend.'

'He was.

'Where did you meet him?'

'As the social workers say, I have a history of substance abuse. A couple of years ago I attended a church meeting where Richard Pearson was speaking. At the time I was doin' a bottle of vodka a day. Something clicked in my head. I suppose I was inspired by him and his message. Anyway, he convinced me that I could turn my life around. I followed him to his commune on Rathlin Island. That's where I met Hugh.'

Wilson remembered the books in the locker in the homeless shelter. 'What was Hugh doing there?'

'Whatever he was asked to do, just like everybody else. Richard was all about renewal. Everybody at the commune had a problem, and they were there to learn how to deal with it. When I finally realised that I didn't need drugs and booze anymore, it was time to leave.'

'And Hugh was still there?'

'He was like part of the furniture.'

'And you didn't see him again?'

'Not until he visited me just before I left on holiday. He called on me just as I was about to leave. I offered him the keys to my house, but he said he'd made another arrangement. He took the car keys though. It was bloody cold and I think he didn't have much money. We had a cup of tea and then I was away to the airport.'

'Did he tell you why he was back in Belfast?'

'He said he had some unfinished business, but he didn't say what it was.'

'Do you know of any reason why someone would want to kill him?'

'Everyone in Rathlin had something in their past that they were trying to come to grips with. Most people think that substance abuse is the answer to their problem whereas in reality it becomes the problem. I never found out what Hugh was trying to forget.'

'Our forensic people have your car,' Wilson said. 'I'll see that it's returned to you by lunchtime.'

'Do you have any idea who killed Hugh?'

'We're following a line of enquiry.'

'I hope you get the bastard.'

'So do I.'

CHAPTER THIRTY-EIGHT

Wilson was thinking about a trip to Rathlin Island as he ushered Donaldson out of the station. He was about to head for the squad room when he got a nod from the duty sergeant and a finger pointing upwards indicated that he was required in the chief super's office.

Wilson knocked on Davis's door and pushed it in. 'Good morning, ma'am.'

'What have you done now?'

Although Davis was frowning, Wilson had the impression that her real mood wasn't so heavy. He was wondering whether it had anything to do with Jack Duane. 'I'm as innocent as a new-born babe. Who says that I've done something?'

She stood up and picked up her cap. 'We've received an urgent call from HQ. Our presence is required by the DCC, and I don't think it's to discuss the weather. Any idea what may be up?'

Wilson held the door open for her. 'With the DCC you never know.'

'I have a very bad feeling about this,' she said as she passed him.

'Strange, so do I.'

·   ·   ·

THEIR SENSE of apprehension was confirmed when they entered Jennings' office and found Assistant Chief Constable Clive Nicholson in attendance. It certainly wasn't going to be a 'tea and biscuits' meeting. They took their seats directly facing Jennings. There was to be no morning greeting either. The silence in the room was deafening and ominous.

Jennings shuffled some papers on his desk before taking up a buff-coloured file. He showed it to Wilson. 'Detective super-intendent, do you have any idea what this is?'

Wilson doubted he had ever seen the file. 'No, sir.'

'I received this file late last evening. It's the conclusions on the investigation by the Garda Síochána into the murder of Noel Armstrong. Assistant Commissioner Nolan sent it to me personally. It has also been sent to the minister. It makes very interesting reading. The gardaí have been very thorough in their investigation.' Jennings paused and laid the file in front of him.

'Are you aware of what happened to Minister Armstrong?' He removed a photograph from the file and placed it on the table in front of Wilson and Davis.

They both looked at Armstrong's dead naked and bruised body. 'He was tortured and then shot,' he continued. 'The gardaí have identified the perpetrators of this vile act. They have been interviewed and all of them have ironclad alibis. The gardaí have concluded that they will probably never be brought to trial.'

Wilson, who had heard all this from Duane, had no idea where Jennings was going.

Jennings tapped the file. 'One section of the report covers the issue of how the IRA got wind of the fact that Armstrong was possibly a tout as well as a murderer. I'm sure it's of interest to you that they have concluded that the PSNI was the most likely source of that information.'

Wilson could feel the storm clouds gathering over his head. What in God's name had Duane done to him.

'I was reminded,' Jennings continued, 'of a meeting in this office when you requested me to let you arrest the minister for questioning in the murder of Rasa Spalvis. Suddenly two and two made four. You felt yourself baulked in pursuing Armstrong, and in order to serve your twisted version of justice you consigned this man to his death without judge or jury.'

Wilson knew there was no point in responding. He looked across at Davis and saw that her face was white.

'Detective Superintendent Wilson, you are suspended from duty pending an internal investigation into whether you were responsible for leaking information to a terrorist organisation in breach of the PSNI Code of Ethics Article 3, Privacy and Confidentiality. Would you please surrender you warrant card to ACC Nicholson.'

Wilson withdrew his warrant card and handed it to Nicholson.

'You will surrender your weapon to Chief Superintendent Davis immediately. You are not to return to your office, and I have given instructions that it is only to be opened by the investigating officer and or his assistant. A senior officer is being supplied by an outside police force, in this case from Scottish Police. He will arrive in Belfast tomorrow. Your suspension is valid until the result of the investigation into your conduct has been completed, at which time suitable administrative action will be taken. Do you have anything to say?'

Davis put her hand on Wilson's arm indicating that he should remain silent.

'This is bullshit,' Wilson said. 'And it will be proven to be so. In the meantime, you are seriously compromising two murder investigations.'

'You may leave,' Jennings said. 'CS Davis will make suitable arrangements in relation to the management of your squad to ensure that there will be no disruption of the investigations underway.'

Davis and Wilson stood together and walked to the door. As soon as they were outside, Davis turned to face Wilson. 'There's no truth in it, is there Ian?'

'No, ma'am. Not that the idea didn't cross my mind. I wasn't happy with Armstrong escaping justice for two murders he committed and others that he may have had a hand in, but I certainly didn't leak any element of the investigation to anyone.'

They started walking towards the lift. 'What are we going to do?' Davis asked.

'We're not going to panic. DS Browne is a good man and a decent detective. Put in a DCI or DI who will give him free rein until I'm cleared.'

They stepped into the lift. 'I don't trust Jennings,' Davis said. 'He must have something more than the Garda Síochána's report. What if you're not cleared?'

'I don't trust him myself. They can't frame me for this one because I didn't do it.' Who was he kidding? Jennings would do everything in his power to influence the investigating officer.

They exited the building and climbed into her car. 'What are you going to do?' she asked.

'Drop me off at the station and I'll pick up my car. My weapon is at home. I'll drop it off when I get a chance.' He saw the look on her face. 'Don't worry, I'm not going to shoot Jennings. The guy from Scottish Police won't be here until tomorrow, and I haven't had a day off in I don't know how long. I was thinking of visiting Rathlin.'

'Rathlin Island? In this weather?'

'Beggars can't be choosers.'

CHAPTER THIRTY-NINE

On the way back to the station, Wilson looked up Rathlin Ferries and sent a text to Duane that read 'What the F##k have you done to me?' Then he called Reid and told her what had happened in Jennings' office. The explosion on the line was clearly heard by Davis and the driver, and both were suitably shocked to hear a lady use such language. He placated her as best he could and told her that he was taking the day off and heading for the north coast. He'd explain everything when they met in the evening. He picked up his car and headed off immediately on the M2 north towards the Antrim coast. His destination was fifty-five miles and a good hour and ten minutes from central Belfast travelling within the speed limit. Since the ferry left at eleven o'clock and he pulled away from the station just before ten, he had little respect for the speed limit. As soon as the investigating officer arrived from Scotland, he would be totally occupied with establishing his innocence. If he failed, it would be the end of his career in the PSNI. There was a mountain of evidence of collusion between the RUC and Loyalist paramilitaries, but most of the police officers responsible lived to claim their pensions without serving a day in jail. But the PSNI was a new start, and he had no doubt that Jennings would go the full distance in implementing the Ethical Code Article 3. He was on the outskirts of Belfast when his phone rang. He slipped it into the hands-free set and pressed the green button.

'Is it true, Boss?' Browne's voice was strained. 'You've been suspended.'

'It's true.'

'The chief super has put me in charge until she appoints someone else. We're all shocked here. They blocked your office, nothing and nobody in or out until the bloke arrives to investigate. What will I do?'

'What you've been trained to do. Keep pushing the cases forward. You're not a schoolboy, you're an experienced DS and you have to behave like one.'

'Where are you, Boss?'

'I'm having a day out.' He broke the connection.

Just before Ballymena his phone rang again. He saw the caller ID and took the call.

'I just heard,' Duane said. 'That idiot Nolan jumped the gun. We were supposed to discuss the final draft before the report went to Belfast and unfortunately I wasn't in Dublin.'

'At least Davis has a smile on her face.'

'Consenting adults, Ian, don't worry, we know you had nothing to do with leaking information, especially to the IRA. As a good Prod, it's not in your DNA. But I'll bet you thought about it.'

Wilson didn't reply.

'They took your warrant card and gun?' Duane asked.

'I'm on suspension, what do you think?'

'I'm going to Belfast this afternoon, I'll drop in.'

'Don't bother, with friends like you who needs enemies.'

'Just remember, I am your friend. I had no hand in what happened and if I can put things right, I will.'

'I might hold you to that.' Wilson broke the connection.

Maybe Jennings had him this time. All he needed was for

some IRA man to come forward and swear that it was him that had leaked the information. And there were plenty of people in Belfast who would be celebrating when his career was dumped into the toilet. The only real hope was that the guy coming from the Scottish Police was a proper copper by Wilson's definition.

BALLYCASTLE IS a small town located on the northern coast of County Antrim. Its main claim to fame is as the setting for the annual Auld Lammas Fair, a Northern Irish institution. Wilson dispensed with sightseeing and drove directly to the harbour, parked his car and was the last passenger to board the ferry to Rathlin Island. The accommodation on board the small ferry was basic but the crossing took only half an hour or so to arrive in Church Bay. The sun was shining on Rathlin, but there was still a bitterly cold northeast wind blowing. Wilson made his way up from the quay to McCuaig's Bar.

'What can I do for ye?' the barman said as Wilson strode up to the bar.

'A hot black coffee, please.'

'You off to the bird conservancy?' The barman turned and started making a coffee.

'Not today.'

'Didn't think you looked like a twitcher.'

'What do I look like?'

The barman looked over his shoulder at Wilson. 'I'd say you look like a peeler. And I hope that you're here on holiday.'

'I'm here to look someone up.'

The barman placed a coffee on the bar in front of Wilson. 'Since there are only just over one hundred of us on the island, I can probably help you.'

'Fella called Richard Pearson.' Wilson sipped the coffee that was thankfully piping hot.

The barman smiled. 'I thought for a minute that you were

talkin' about a local. I hope you're goin' to drag him back to the mainland where he belongs.'

'He's not popular?'

'We're a funny crowd here. Tightknit doesn't even come close to describin' us.'

'Therefore, he's not popular.'

'He keeps himself to himself and that's how it should be.'

'Where can I find him?' Wilson sipped his coffee, which was sending a stream of heat through his body.

'Turn right outside the door and head back past the harbour and the Manor House, then take a right turn just past the Water Shed café. After about half a mile, you'll come to a couple of stone cottages set in from the road. That's Pearson's place. What's he done?'

'Nothing that I know of.' Wilson finished his coffee and paid.

'We have fresh fish and chips for lunch.'

'Thanks, I'll be back.' He wondered how these places survived the winter.

The walk along the Rathlin coast was spectacular and he was sorry when the cottages described by the barman came into view. He could see how a place like Rathlin could bewitch someone. He hadn't thought about Jennings and his problem since he put his foot on the island. He opened the cast-iron entrance gate and walked into a rough stone area that formed a courtyard between two large cottages set in an L-shape. Just beyond the cottages he saw a young man working in a vegetable garden. He went to the largest cottage and rapped on the door. There was a noise inside and a few moments later a young woman appeared.

'Good afternoon,' Wilson said. 'I'm looking for Richard Pearson.'

'Wait here, I'll get him for you.'

The cottages were freshly whitewashed and the stone courtyard was clean. There were two bicycles leaning against the wall of the smaller cottage. Wilson was still looking round when the door opened wider.

'Hi, I'm Richard Pearson. Delores tells me that you're looking for me.'

The accent was certainly not Northern Irish and possibly not even Irish at all. There was a distinct American twang.

'I'm Detective Superintendent Ian Wilson of the PSNI. I was wondering whether I could have a word with you.' The man in the doorway was just under six feet and cadaverous. His cheekbones and nose stood out of his pale thin face. His hair was grey and pulled back into a ponytail that hung halfway down his back. A pair of dark eyes stared at Wilson.

'May I see your warrant card?'

Wilson smiled. 'I don't appear to have it on me.'

'Then come back when you do,' Pearson said, closing the door.

'I'm not here in relation to you or anyone on the island,' Wilson said. 'I want to talk about Hugh Royce. He was murdered in Belfast four days ago.'

The door opened again. 'You'd better come inside.'

Wilson entered and the door closed behind him. He found himself in a very large country kitchen with a table running almost the length of the room. There were ten chairs on each side of the table and two larger chairs at the head and foot.

'Please sit,' Pearson said, indicating a chair beside the top of the table. 'Can we offer you a herbal tea?'

Wilson sat. 'No thank you.'

Pearson sat at the head of the table. 'How was Hugh killed?'

'You don't have radio or TV here?'

'It's available on the island but we choose not to have it.'

'He was shot.'

'Poor Hugh, he'd come such a long way.'

'How long had you known him?'

The young woman deposited a cup of tea in front of Pearson. 'Are you sure you don't want a tea, it's very refreshing and made from herbs we collect on the island.'

Wilson shook his head.

'Hugh came to us just over two years ago. He was heavily addicted to heroin and had heard about our work here with drug addicts. We took care of him through his withdrawal. His suffering was great, but Hugh found God here and that meant that he found strength.'

'That's what you do here, rehabilitate drug users?'

'It's a place of prayer and contemplation. People come here for many reasons. Each one has his or her own demon. We try to help them in any way we can.'

'How long did Hugh stay?'

'He only left about six days ago.'

'Why?'

'He had some sins on his soul that he had been unable to excise.'

'Did he tell you what they were?'

Pearson remained silent and drank his tea.

'You're not a Catholic priest so there's no problem about the confidentiality of the confessional,' Wilson said. He had come expecting to meet a charlatan, but he felt that Pearson believed in what he was doing. In any event, nothing that Pearson was doing would be of interest to the PSNI. 'We only want to find the man who killed Hugh. There's nothing that you can say that will harm him now.'

The young woman came and took Pearson's cup away. He thanked her and turned to Wilson. 'Hugh was a good man who had been forced to do things that he didn't agree with. He lived a life that was false and ultimately felt responsible for the death of one of his colleagues. That knowledge sent him on a spiral of drugs and despair until one day he woke up and tried to end his life. He didn't succeed and by chance when he woke up he saw an article describing our work here. He arrived on Rathlin the next day and stayed.'

'We found no trace of him receiving welfare payments. How did he pay?'

'We don't ask for payment. But Hugh contributed from time to time in cash.'

'How did he come by it?'

'I didn't ask.'

'How did he intend to excise his sins?'

'He didn't say. I think he had a plan but obviously it didn't work. He talked about working with some very unscrupulous people. We begged him to reconsider his proposed action. Hugh was very happy here. Have you any idea what will happen to his body?'

'I don't rightly know. We haven't been able to find any direct relations and his former wife is unlikely to want to deal with the funeral arrangements.'

'Over the last years, we've been Hugh's family. If it's all right, we'd like to take care of the funeral arrangements. Hugh's ashes will be incorporated into a tree that will be planted on the island. I think he would have liked that.'

'I'll see what can be done.'

While Pearson had been talking, Wilson noticed a number of people entering the room and standing away from their conversation.

'Would you like to join us for lunch?' Pearson asked. 'But I should warn you we're all vegans here.'

'No thanks,' Wilson remembered the contents of Royce's stomach. Maybe not all vegans, he thought. He stood up and extended his hand. 'Thanks for your help. I'll be in touch about the disposition of the body.'

Pearson took his hand and shook. 'Fish and chips in McCuaig's?'

'Washed down with a pint of Guinness.'

They both laughed.

CHAPTER FORTY

Siobhan O'Neill's first reaction on hearing about Wilson's suspension was to run immediately to the chief super's office and admit that it was her who leaked the information on Armstrong. She was on her way when she had to divert to the ladies' toilets, where she threw up everything she had eaten that morning. Sitting on the toilet seat to recover, she took time to go through what might happen if she confessed. Talk in the office was that Wilson was being framed by the DCC. Nobody knew why. If O'Neill confessed, perhaps it would be seen as an act of loyalty and an attempt to have Wilson immediately reinstated. That might be the spin HQ would put on it. On the other hand, maybe she would be believed. Then there would be an investigation and in order to validate her claim she would be obliged to name names. That would put Ronan Muldoon in the frame and he might be charged with aiding and abetting a murder. She knew that she owed the bastard nothing. After all, he had given her up to Duane. But he might not be the only one to go down. She would do time for perverting the course of justice or for a more serious charge. Still, owning up was the right thing to do. Her phone rang and she opened the call.

'It's DCI Duane, where are you?'

'I'm in the ladies, having tossed by breakfast. You've heard about the boss?'

'Yes, and right now I don't want you to do anything stupid like admitting your guilt.'

'I can't let the boss go down for something that I did.'

'Noble sentiments, but Wilson isn't going down. We both know that he's innocent and that's going to be the result of the investigation. You have to hold your nerve and let this thing play out.'

'Easier said than done.'

'You fall on your sword and you might just succeed in dragging Wilson down with you.'

'What do you mean?'

'Nobody's going to believe that you leaked information all on your own. It'll just be spun that you were ordered by Wilson to leak. I'm working on a scenario where there was no leak, but it's going to take a bit of time. So, no rash moves. Get back to work and act naturally.' The line went dead.

O'Neill stood up and exited the stall. Thankfully she had been alone in the toilet. She walked to the washbasin and ran the cold water, sloshing it with cupped hands onto her pale face. She looked in the mirror. She was a state. She sloshed more water until she started to feel better. She'd known when she'd entered the Muldoon house that she was crossing a line and might one day have to pay a price for doing so. She was still prepared to accept whatever came. She would wait and see how things played out, but there was no way she was going to let Wilson take the rap for something she did.

CHAPTER FORTY-ONE

'Where are you?' Reid's voice was strained.

'In McCuaig's Bar in Rathlin enjoying their best fish and chips and a pint of Guinness.'

'Sometimes I wonder about you, Ian. Jennings is trying to end your career and you're sitting on your fat arse in a pub on Rathlin scoffing fish and chips and skulling pints. Get your arse in gear or you're handing your head on a plate to Jennings.'

'There's method in my madness. The investigating officer doesn't arrive in Belfast until tomorrow. There's nothing I can do until he arrives. So calm down.'

'Calm down he says. I want to rip that rotten little bastard's throat out.'

'So do I, but we'd have to join a long line.'

'Tell me, why Rathlin?'

'Royce was part of a commune here run by a guy called Richard Pearson. I thought the guy might have been a con artist, but he appears genuine enough. All the people in the commune have problems that they're working through. Royce was wracked with guilt for something he did and went to Belfast to sort things out.'

'It all sounds very 1960s. Doesn't this Pearson fellow know that communes had their day when Jim Jones dished out the Kool-Aid in Jonestown? Royce should have understood that there's nothing dodgier than a reformed lowlife. Maybe in his case it was the reformation that got him killed.'

'I tend to concur.' He popped a piece of fish into his mouth and chewed.

'You're still bloody eating. The next time you go on an enforced holiday you might think about taking me along.'

'You're always too busy.'

'Apropos of which, I just got off the phone with the coroner. I'd be understating it if I said that he was apoplectic. He came up with a dozen reason why he shouldn't reopen the inquest on Colin Payne.'

'And you came up with a dozen reasons why he should. How did you end up?'

'He's agreed to reopen the inquest.'

'Great, that should put the cat among the pigeons with respect to our friends in the Drugs Squad.'

'Do you enjoy playing with fire?'

'Something is rotten in the Drugs Squad and it's led to two deaths. And I don't like people thinking that they've gotten away with murder.'

'And that's all you've got to worry about? You've been suspended from duty indefinitely and your career is on the line, and you're sitting in a bar on Rathlin Island eating fish and chips and swilling Guinness. I've heard of sang-froid but you take the biscuit.'

Wilson looked at his watch. 'I have fifteen minutes to make the three o'clock ferry. I'll be back in Belfast by five and I need to have a talk with McDevitt.'

'You're crazy, Ian, but I love you.'

'I love you too and let's try to keep it that way.'

He finished his meal and paid at the bar. 'You were right

about the fish and chips. I don't know whether I'll be back, but I've enjoyed the trip.'

The barman counted the money and saw that he'd been left a generous tip. 'That's a first for a peeler,' he said, pocketing the change.

CHAPTER FORTY-TWO

D S Browne was leading the evening briefing and to his mind he was making a hash of it. He'd been called to the chief super's office in the early afternoon and informed that since there was no senior officer available to take over the Murder Squad, the chief super would be handling the management herself. Which meant that he would be reporting directly to her for the foreseeable future. Some people might see that as an opportunity to shine, Browne saw it as an opportunity to screw up in a very major way. The atmosphere in the squad room was subdued. Browne stood in front of the whiteboard. No information had been added during the day. He looked at O'Neill. 'Where are we on the CCTV from Traffic?'

'They sent over a disk this evening and I've just started working on it. The system looks old and the images are a bit grainy, but I'll go through it tomorrow.'

Browne turned to Graham. 'Anything on your side, Harry?'

'I've rechecked all the calls we received after the appeal. Ninety per cent were from whack-jobs and the other ten per cent were genuine but turned out to be cases of mistaken identity. It's just about closed itself down.'

'Anyone got an idea as to how we can progress this investigation?' Browne was becoming desperate.

'The CCTV seems like the only avenue,' Graham said. If the boss doesn't return soon, he thought, we are in major trouble. It wasn't the sergeant's fault. He didn't have the SIO experience.

'Okay,' Browne said. 'We start again in the morning.' He glanced across at Wilson's office, which was locked and had crime scene tape across the doors and windows. How he wished to see that bulky body sitting behind the desk.

WILSON ARRIVED BACK in Belfast at five o'clock after an uneventful journey from Ballycastle. He was just entering the outskirts of the city when his mobile phone rang.

'Boss, it's Moira, I just heard.'

'Where are you?'

'Back in Belfast. I started in Vice last week. One of the sergeants there has been suspended.'

'Why the hell didn't you contact me immediately?'

'Reintegration hasn't been as smooth as I hoped. My family are threatening to disown me for coming back.'

'It didn't work out?'

'If it had, I wouldn't be here.'

'I'm just coming into the city. Are you in Musgrave Street?'

'Yes.'

Although he felt like a drink, it was too early. He had set up a meeting with McDevitt for seven o'clock at his apartment and he couldn't think of a better way to spend the next two hours than with Moira McElvaney. 'Are you up for afternoon tea at the Europa.'

'What the hell has happened to the Crown?'

'Nothing, I'll meet you in the lobby of the Europa in fifteen minutes.'

Moira was sitting on a couch in the lobby when Wilson arrived. She looked good but a little drawn. Her red hair was tied back and her cheeks were rosy from the cold. He rushed across and hugged her. To the casual onlooker they would appear to be lovers. He eased her back into her seat.

He looked round. 'Brendan?' He asked as he sat down beside her.

'It didn't work out.' She looked away and round the lobby. 'This isn't exactly one of your hangouts, unless things have changed.'

'I'm sorry about Brendan, he's a nice guy. I'm keeping a low profile since this morning. I doubt that I'll run into any coppers here, aside from you. Let's have some coffee and you can tell me all about being back.'

An hour later, they had updated each other on their lives. Moira hadn't reacted as well as he had expected to the news that Reid was a fixture in his life. Otherwise it had been a nice cosy chat.

'Can I help, Boss?' Moira asked.

'You didn't ask me if I was guilty.'

'I don't have to. It's not you, but that doesn't mean that Jennings won't fit you up for it.'

'Stranger things have happened.'

'What's it about? Why now?'

'I think it's about a murder case we're handling.' He saw the light in her eyes. She had turned out to be a naturally talented detective and would be a total waste in Vice. He told her about the body in the boot of the burned-out BMW and the Royce murder. He also told her about Reid and the reopening of the inquest on Payne. He could see the disappointment in her face that she was not part of the investigating team.

'Jennings is involved somehow,' she said.

'He's always involved somehow. The question is finding

out where and how. I think Niccolò Machiavelli could have taken lessons from Royson Jennings.'

'Can I do anything?'

'I'm going to get you back on the squad. I don't know how or when, but I'm going to keep at it until you're back where you belong.' He was thinking how much he'd love to have her in the squad right now. Browne was a good copper, but he wasn't a patch on Moira.

The wall clock in the lobby said six-thirty. 'I'm meeting Jock McDevitt in half an hour. The guy who's going to look into the allegation against me is arriving tomorrow morning, so I suppose I'll be busy most of the day.'

'You have my number from the call I made earlier today.'

Wilson stood up. 'It's great to see you again. I was bloody annoyed with myself that I allowed you to escape. It's not going to happen again.' He hugged her and started for the door of the hotel.

She watched him leave and felt that a part of her was missing. She knew that she had been right to return to Belfast. Now she needed her old job back.

CHAPTER FORTY-THREE

'Sorry,' Jock McDevitt put a mock-up of the following day's *Chronicle* front page on the coffee table in Wilson's apartment. 'Not my doing, the editor was adamant that it's a major story.'

Wilson hadn't made the major headline, which had been reserved for the ongoing impasse between the political parties that was denying the people of Northern Ireland their legislative assembly. But neatly placed beneath the main story was the suspension of a senior police officer for alleged leaking of information to a terrorist organisation. Wilson wasn't named, but he knew that in the tightknit community of Belfast his name was being broadcast in every pub and social gathering in the city. If Jennings succeeded, it wouldn't be just the end of Wilson's PSNI career, he would be branded a pariah amid demands for him to be tried as an accessory to murder.

'No offence taken.' Wilson handed McDevitt a glass of whiskey and cradled one himself.

Reid had disappeared to the bathroom as soon as McDevitt had arrived. She knew that the conversation would be centred on the Payne murder and she didn't want to be part of it. McDevitt had a bad habit of forgetting a promise not to quote people.

'For a man in so much trouble you seem to be remarkably calm.' McDevitt lifted his glass in a toast.

Wilson touched his glass to McDevitt's and drank. 'I didn't leak information and I'm quite sure that the investigation is going to come to that conclusion.' He sat down facing McDevitt.

'You wouldn't be the first innocent person to be found guilty.'

'Let's just say that I'm confident. There's no proof that anyone leaked anything to the IRA. Anyway, my current diffi-culties are not the reason I invited you here. I'm going to give you that scoop I promised you.'

McDevitt sat up attentively and put his phone on the table between them.

Wilson picked up the phone and checked that it was off before putting it in his pocket. 'No recording. Don't you have one of those spiral reporter's notebooks that Clark Kent uses.'

McDevitt bent and removed a spiral notebook from the messenger bag at his feet.

'Now you look like a real reporter. Three years ago, a young detective constable from the Drugs Squad died in an agricultural accident. He was drowned in a slurry tank on a farm in Ballyward just outside Castlewellan. The man's name was Colin Payne. At the time, it was assumed that he had fallen into the tank, been overcome by fumes and drowned. The coroner gave a verdict of death by misadventure at the inquest.'

'It's happened lots of times.' McDevitt wasn't smelling a story just yet.

'This is the part of the story where I have to depend on your discretion.' Wilson took a sip of his whiskey. 'You can sometimes be discreet?'

McDevitt smiled and nodded.

'Payne had reported one of his colleagues for corruption, and the accused had been induced to resign. I thought that the two events might be connected. So I asked the pathologist, who has absented herself because of her lack of belief in your ability to be discreet, to have a look at the post-mortem results. It's her opinion that Payne was held down and drowned. She has imposed on the coroner to reopen the inquest.'

'With a view to a revised verdict of murder, don't you have enough on your plate?'

'There's someone out there who thinks they've gotten away with murder. I want them to know that they haven't.'

'Won't they cut and run?'

'I don't think they can.'

'You canny bastard, you already have a suspect, but you're not going to tell Jock who it is.'

'No, I'm not.'

'I won't run it tomorrow to give me a chance to make some checks on the story. Whose farm was it?'

'Payne's aunt, her name is Agnes Bagnell.'

McDevitt was writing furiously in his notebook. 'Kindly old lady, scones and tea, life destroyed by the death of her nephew. I see a very nice human-interest piece on the side.'

'But apply discretion.'

'I'll look the word up in the dictionary when I get home. You're a devious one, Ian. Using your partner and old Jock to flush out your suspect.'

'Is that what I'm doing?' Wilson sipped his drink.

CHAPTER FORTY-FOUR

Jack Duane was within an ace of punching his boss. They were in Chief Superintendent Nolan's office in Harcourt Street in Dublin. Nolan was refusing point-blank to retract the statement on a possible information leak from the PSNI in the report to Belfast.

'Don't be getting ahead of yourself, Jack,' Nolan said. 'The report that goes to Belfast is the one that I decide to send, not the one you want to sanitise. And I'm not about to lose face by retracting it. Even the dogs in the street know that the buggers have been leaking to terrorists since their organisation was founded.'

'We have no proof that anyone leaked information from the PSNI.'

'What about the fella we have on the Command Council? Didn't he more or less swear to it.'

'No, he didn't. I was dealing with the Armstrong investigation. It's in everyone's interest that it dies a death. The man had been working for the Brits for years. They'd just done a messy job of clearing up the murder of a prostitute that he'd committed. Armstrong was a liability and he was becoming a bigger liability as time went on. There's a bloody good chance that it was MI5 that leaked the information. Are you going to put that in your damn report?'

'You're trying to make me think that I was a bit hasty with the report. Why don't we blame Uncle Tom Cobley and all?'

'You were too fucking hasty. That arsehole Jennings has started a witch-hunt on the basis of a report from us. How do you think that's going to play with the people upstairs?'

'Is there any other way out that doesn't involve retracting the report? We'll look like a crowd of bunnies if we tell them the report isn't accurate.'

Duane was pleased to see that the penny had finally dropped. 'Maybe you should give Jennings a call and tell him that the report was only a draft and a leak from the PSNI was only one of the scenarios that we were considering. Another scenario is that the leak came from MI5 because they were fed up covering up for a murderer. That should raise a few hackles in Belfast and London.'

'Whichever way you spin it, we're going to lose face. I'll have to clear it with the commissioner.'

Duane could see a door closing right in front of him. The commissioner was already in hot water with his minister on a local matter, so there was no way Nolan was going to be given the green light to embarrass the gardaí further. He'd given it his best shot and he'd failed. At least he could embarrass Nolan with the commissioner. 'Go ahead and see what he says'. Duane left Nolan's office before he said something he knew he'd regret later. They had dropped Wilson in it and try as he might he wasn't going to be able to pull him out. The other option was to let O'Neill stand up and take the blame, but that would ruin the young woman's life. It was a doomsday scenario that would only be employed if Wilson couldn't extricate himself. He went back to his office and took out his phone. He'd promised Wilson that he was going to put things right and he had failed. Failure didn't sit well with Jack Duane.

CHAPTER FORTY-FIVE

W ilson woke at seven and looked out at the weather. The cold snap was over and it had rained overnight. Conditions were not perfect, but he had to clear his head and the best medicine for that was a run to the Titanic Centre and back. He put on his running gear and headed out while it was still dark. There were black clouds approaching the city from the Black Mountain and he'd be lucky to make it back before the rain started in earnest. He pounded his way along the still wet streets. The phone call from Duane had been disappointing but not unexpected. In his experience, once the genie is out of the bottle it's damn hard to get it back inside without creating further damage. To add insult to injury, he had thought that someone on the team had been responsible for leaking the information that Armstrong was a tout to the IRA. The sad fact was that the Intelligence Service knew that Armstrong murdered women and they still protected him. Maybe someone should be investigating that, but he doubted it was going to happen. Bridget Kelly and Rasa Spalvis were only prostitutes who didn't merit having their killer brought to justice. Marie O'Neill had been right after all: prostitutes don't count. In the meantime, McDevitt was onside with his little ploy to stir the pot of shit that was the PSNI Drugs Squad. Wilson might not be there to see the results, but he would ensure that Browne had enough evidence to push the case forward. He looked up at the sky. The man who would decide his future would be taking off from Glasgow soon. Wilson's first meeting with the investigator was scheduled for ten o'clock at Musgrave Street station. He turned for home just as the rain started. He was soaking wet within five minutes, but somehow it felt good. There was an important day ahead and he wanted to be on top form.

His breakfast was on the table as soon as he exited the shower. 'This is service.' He sat at the breakfast bar.

'It's a big day. You'll need to be properly fortified.'

'I love you Stephanie Reid.'

'And I love you.'

'Then when are you going to tell me what's bothering you?'

'Something's bothering me?'

'They don't call me a detective for nothing.'

'Doesn't this bullshit with Jennings not bother you? Do you really need to be harassed like this?'

'Of course it bothers me and I certainly don't need it. But I'm not in control. I can only change the things that I control.'

'But aren't you fed up fighting them?'

'Where's all this coming from?'

'I've been offered a job at the UCLA Medical Center.'

'How long have you been keeping this news to yourself?'

'Since we got back. I met the director socially and he was impressed with my CV. I can start whenever I like, but the offer isn't indefinite.'

'Why didn't you tell me?'

'I know that your heart and soul are in Belfast, but I was waiting until they shat on you again. And it didn't take too long.'

'What have you decided?'

'That we should both decide. I'm not going to drag you with me only for you to be unhappy. If we make this move, we make it together.'

Wilson saw that neither of them had eaten. 'Would the move be good for your career?'

'Who knows? The job's the same, the weather is better and my partner won't be put at risk of jail by his employers. I'm beginning to think that Belfast sucks.'

He stood up and picked her up from her seat and held her. 'You're one hell of a woman, and I will never stand in your way. I'm not going to run away. Jennings would use that as an admission of guilt and he would pursue me. Let's put UCLA on the back burner.' He saw the look of disappointment on her face. 'But I'll be thinking about it.'

CHAPTER FORTY-SIX

Wilson arrived at Musgrave Street station at ten minutes to the appointed time.

The duty sergeant nodded to him. 'Morning, sir.' He held up a visitor's lanyard. 'Sorry, I've been told that you have to wear one of these.'

Wilson took the lanyard and put it on. It was one more humiliation ordered, no doubt, by Jennings.

'We're all with you, sir,' the duty sergeant continued. 'The Protestant police officer who would give information to the IRA hasn't been born. They're waiting for you in Interview Room 1.' He pointed to a door on the right.

Wilson didn't bother to remind the sergeant that he'd spent four years in the station.

He pushed open the door of the interview room and saw two women sitting at the table. One of them was DS Lucy Kane. The second was a slight woman with short blonde hair who looked to be in her late forties. They stood when he entered.

'Please join us, Detective Superintendent Wilson,' the blonde woman said. 'I'm Detective Superintendent Fiona

Russell.' She held out her hand. 'And this is DS Lucy Kane of your own Professional Services.'

Wilson shook her hand. 'Ian Wilson, pleased to meet you. DS Kane and I have already met.'

'Please take a seat,' Russell said.

Wilson sat opposite the women. Russell had a bird-like appearance with a pale angular face and the body of a committed runner. There was not a pick of excess flesh on her frame. She was attractive rather than pretty.

'I work for Professional Standards in Edinburgh,' Russell said. 'You probably know they call us the 'Complaints' because we're constantly asking people to complain about police officers. We're about as popular with our colleagues as your Professional Services are with you.'

Wilson looked at the tape recorder on the table and saw that it hadn't been turned on. Before the real business began there was going to be a 'meet and greet' session. He sat quietly. This wasn't his gig and he knew the rules, he would speak only when spoken to.

'I remember seeing you play at Murrayfield against Scotland,' she continued, 'must have been nearly eighteen years ago. You haven't changed much.'

'Only twenty kilos heavier and my hair isn't fair anymore.'

'I don't believe the twenty kilos and my husband was all a-twitter when he heard I was coming to interview you. He's a big fan. It must have hurt to give up playing.'

'It was my own fault. I didn't heed them when they said stay away from the bomb. I left myself no choice.'

'Before we start I want to tell you that I take no pleasure in investigating my fellow officers. We do a very difficult job under extreme pressure. If we're honest with each other, we may be able to get this unpleasant business over with quickly. Already this morning we've picked up your computer and ordered a log of all your phone calls and text messages. I know that is intrusive, but I can assure you that no details that are not relevant to this enquiry will go beyond Lucy and me. We have also obtained a copy of the murder book relevant to the Rasa Spalvis murder investigation.' She picked up the file in front of her and nodded at Kane, who switched on the tape recorder.

Wilson watched as Kane did the preliminaries. He had been advised to take along a representative from the Police Federation of Northern Ireland, but he had declined. He identified himself for the tape and then sat back.

'You are the head of the PSNI Murder Squad and you were the SIO on the Rasa Spalvis murder investigation?' Russell said.

'Yes.'

'Would you please take us through the investigation from the moment the body was found.'

Wilson began with the dog-walker and Redburn Country Park and spoke for over an hour as he walked Russell and Kane through the investigation. He segued into the Kelly investigation to the extent that it was relevant to the search for Rasa Spalvis's murderer.

'At what point did Noel Armstrong become a person of interest?'

Wilson thought for a few minutes. 'There isn't really a 'Eureka' moment in a murder investigation. Suspicions develop slowly. I always look on an investigation as a process. You keep teasing out the evidence until it points in a certain direction. I could say that I was convinced that he was involved when his alibi for the Kelly murder was shown to be manufactured by ... ' he stopped short. There was no way he was putting on record the allegation made by Margaret Whiticker.

'You came to the conclusion that Noel Armstrong was being assisted in the commission of murder?' Russell asked.

'There was evidence that his crimes were being covered up and I concluded that those covering up the crimes had an interest in maintaining him in his position in the government.'

'And it was common knowledge that he had been a member of the IRA?'

'Yes.'

'So it could have been the IRA covering up his crimes. Apparently, they have done so in other cases.'

'It could have been. The IRA don't cover up crimes, they just give the criminals an escape route. Whoever covered up for Armstrong interfered with police evidence, faked alibis and suborned perjury. There was credible, but uncorroborated, evidence that a senior police officer was involved.'

'Why didn't you bring that evidence forward?'

'Because of the mental condition of the witness, her evidence would never have held up. And the powers that be would never have permitted a story that a Sinn Féin minister in the Northern Ireland Assembly was an agent of the Security Services.'

'And yet you considered the evidence of this mentally unstable witness credible.'

'In the light of the depth of the cover-up, yes.'

'So, you came to the conclusion that Noel Armstrong should be arrested and interviewed as the prime suspect in the Rasa Spalvis case?'

'Yes.'

'And why didn't that happen?'

'My chief superintendent insisted, probably quite rightly, that we should have HQ approval before bringing a government minister in for interview. We took our suspicions to the deputy chief constable, who refused point-blank to allow us to interview Armstrong. He would only allow an interview when the evidence against Armstrong was irrefutable.'

'Did that frustrate you?'

'Of course it frustrated me.'

'You and your team had worked day and night to find a

murderer. You were sure that you had your man and he was about to escape for the second time. That must have offended your sense of justice, which I have concluded is part of what makes you such a good detective.'

Wilson could see where she was going so he remained silent.

'You wanted Armstrong to pay for his crimes,' Russell said.

'In front of a judge and jury.'

'So, you never thought of giving the IRA the information that formed the basis for your theory that he was reporting to the Security Services.'

'I thought of many ways that Noel Armstrong might be brought to justice.'

'And leaking information to the IRA was one of them?'

'Perhaps.'

'Yes or no.'

'Yes.'

'Do you think that the information that Noel Armstrong was working for the Security Services came from the PSNI?'

'That question I cannot answer.'

'Okay, do you think that the information that Noel Armstrong was working for the Security Services came from your squad?'

'No, I don't.'

'Do you have an alternative scenario as to how the information on Noel Armstrong reached the IRA?

'Armstrong had murdered two women during sexual encounters. We had identified him as a prime suspect and his mentors knew that we were getting close. He was an asset that was quickly becoming an embarrassment. I can imagine that his handlers were becoming worried, not only that he would be exposed, but also that their role in covering up his crimes would be exposed. They could have dealt with him themselves, but how much safer and smarter to have the IRA do it for them.'

Fiona Russell had rarely seen a better performance. Wilson had an answer for every question. If he had leaked the information to the IRA, he would have covered his tracks. 'We'll leave it there for this morning.' She nodded at Kane, who did the closing remarks and gave the time before switching off the machine.

'We'll examine your computer and the phone logs this afternoon. I'll arrange interviews with your team for tomorrow morning and we'll finalise the investigation with a second interview tomorrow afternoon. I think I should be ready to report to the deputy chief constable tomorrow evening.'

'I'm currently handling two murder investigations and might be adding another in the next few days. I'd like to get back to my job.'

'That depends on whether I can clear you.'

'Of course,' Wilson said. He stood up and left.

'What do you think?' Russell asked when the door of the interview room closed.

'It was all very plausible,' Kane said.

'Was Armstrong guilty of murder?'

'Who knows.'

CHAPTER FORTY-SEVEN

P eter Davidson hadn't bothered to turn up at the station. The morning was cold and wet, and Irene's bed was warm and cosy. Nothing was going to happen until Wilson proved himself innocent and Jennings uncoiled his scaly body from round him. If the briefing the previous evening was anything to go by, Browne was not yet ready to be entrusted with an investigation. The Royce case had hit the buffers, and he could see that Browne was floundering. Depending on how long Wilson was going to be sidelined, it would be up to Graham and him to keep the ship on course. It was after ten when he smelt the bacon frying in the kitchen and roused himself from the bed. He'd attended a retirement party recently where the retiree broke down and cried. When he was asked why, he said his wife didn't want him at home. Davidson was looking forward to having days with absolutely nothing to do but lie in the sunshine by the pool knocking back Pina Coladas. But that was several months away. After breakfast, he would skip across the road and get Cooney's signature on the piece of paper that would allow them to drag Simon Jackson to the station. Wilson would break him, and when he did, the whole dirty business about Jackie Carlisle's death would come out.

As soon as he had finished his breakfast, Davidson crossed the road to the Cooney house and was obliged to stand at the door while old man Cooney read the typed statement and signed it. He'd put out a request to the mobile phone manufacturer concerning the phone found in the VIP lounge. Soon he would know where it was bought and that would close the investigation for him. He walked away from the house feeling rather pleased with himself. In fact, he was so pleased that he didn't notice the man who exited a car down the street and made his way up Cooney's drive.

Cooney cursed when he heard the bell ring. He'd just signed the bloody statement and that wretched detective fellow was back at the door. He was preparing his broadside when he opened the door to a fresh-faced young man. 'Not today,' he prepared to close the door but the young man stuck a warrant card in his face.

'Sorry to bother you, sir,' the young man said.

Cooney held the door. He hadn't realised that the warrant card was no longer visible and neither had the young man introduced himself by name. 'What now?'

'My colleague who was here a moment ago, DC Davidson, I hope that his business with you was concluded satisfactorily.'

'Yes, it was,' Cooney attempted to close the door again but the young man's foot was stopping him.

'What exactly was his business?'

'For God's sake, don't you people talk to one another. I was signing a statement about the fellow I saw outside Carlisle's house the day he died.'

The young man looked down the street, but Davidson had already disappeared. 'Thank you, sir, you won't be bothered again.'

The foot was no longer blocking the door and Cooney took the opportunity to slam it shut. 'What a bunch of idiots,' he said under his breath.

CHAPTER FORTY-EIGHT

Siobhan O'Neill was having a bad day. And it wasn't just because she was fighting down a feeling of dread about dropping her boss in the proverbial. She had been sleeping badly and was awakened at three o'clock in the morning by a call from her mother's care home. Her mother had taken a 'turn,' which could have meant anything, and she should get to the home as quickly as possible. By the time she arrived, the 'turn' was over and her mother was sleeping peacefully. The on-call doctor informed her that her mother had had a mini-stroke and they wouldn't know the full impact until they examined her. Given that she no longer communicated anyway, and that she had no idea where she was or who her daughter was, estimating the effect of the stoke was not going to be easy. When her mother had first been diagnosed with early dementia, she had immediately accepted that her future was going to be dominated by her mother's condition. She accepted that recognition would gradually slip away and that her mother would, with each passing day, retreat into her own private world. What she found difficult was that the mental disintegration was accompanied by a physical degeneration that rendered her mother incapable of making a cup of tea or feeding herself. And now they were rapidly approaching the other aspect that she had accepted, her mother's death. Although she had somehow dragged herself to work, her mind was still half in the care home. The other half was at Musgrave Street station, where the rumour mill had it that Wilson was being interviewed. She looked across at Browne and Graham and they looked to be in a similar subdued mood. They were like children whose parents had disappeared for a surprise holiday and left them to fend for themselves. The over-riding feeling was 'what do we do now?'

She withdrew the disk with the traffic CCTV from its plastic sleeve and inserted it into her computer. She looked at DS Browne and saw that he was looking at her. Did he suspect that she had leaked the information on Armstrong? She would follow Duane's advice and let the situation play out. She had already decided that if Wilson was about to go down, she would stand up and admit her guilt. She understood Duane's point that HQ would continue to point the finger at him, but she wouldn't be able to live with herself if he paid for her sin. She turned on her computer and brought up the CCTV file. Searching the grainy images was boring but maybe that was what she needed.

CHAPTER FORTY-NINE

Rory Browne was tired of asking himself 'What would the boss do?' Deep inside he knew that he was no Ian Wilson. But he was the SIO and he had to develop his own lines of enquiry. It was easier said than done. The Royce investigation had ground to a halt. Forensics had come up with nothing. There was no physical evidence. The gun was a dead end. They hadn't come up with a motive for the killing, and he had no idea how Royce's former career as a PSNI officer fitted into the jigsaw. There was no prime suspect; in fact, there were no suspects at all. And yet someone wanted Royce dead. Somehow he was going to have to develop a motive. The atmosphere in the squad room resembled a morgue. A tangible air of despondency hung over the place. O'Neill looked like someone had just kicked her favourite dog. Graham's normally cheery face wore an unaccustomed frown. And Davidson hadn't even bothered to turn up. It was a sign of the times. Browne glanced at his watch. It was almost twelve o'clock. He picked up the murder book and started to look at what little evidence there was, beginning with the finding of the body.

His phone rang and he saw Wilson's ID on the screen.

'Boss.'

'I'm thinking of having a coffee in The Galley café at the Titanic Centre,' Wilson said. 'Would you and Harry like to join me?'

'Fifteen minutes.' Browne signalled to Graham that they were on their way.

WILSON WAS GETTING to like the coffee at The Galley. He had no doubt that Jennings and the gang at HQ wouldn't appreciate him contacting his team while on suspension, but that wasn't going to stop him, and as long as they didn't find out, what harm could it do. He was sitting at one of the tables in the Atrium when Browne and Graham approached.

'Not banged up yet, Boss?' Graham said, as he pulled up a chair.

'Before your behind gets used to that chair,' Wilson said, 'three black coffees please.'

'Come on, Boss,' Graham said. 'I'm a married man with three kids. Every penny counts.'

Wilson handed over a ten-pound note. 'And bring back the change mind.'

'How did it go?' Browne asked.

'The way it always goes. There was a certain amount of shadow-boxing, but I get the impression that Superintendent Russell is a pretty serious person. She'll look at the evidence and make her mind up.'

'She?'

'Yes, our friend from Edinburgh is a woman, and a pretty smart one if I'm not mistaken.'

'A woman won't suit Jennings,' Browne said.

Wilson smiled. He would bet a month's pay that Jennings had been counting on a lodge brother being the investigating officer. Count one for the good guys.

Graham returned and distributed the coffees. Then dropped a series of coins on the table. 'What's the story?'

Wilson sipped his coffee. 'I don't think Russell will be influenced by Jennings. The fact that she's a woman means that there'll be no special handshake. I was a little worried about that aspect until I walked into the interview room at Musgrave Street. I think she'll give me a fair shake and it's as much as I can ask for under the circumstances.'

'You're not being replaced,' Browne said. 'Davis has nobody available, so I have to report to her directly. I'm floundering, Boss. There are no lines of enquiry.'

'That's why I've asked you and Harry here.' Wilson looked at the two expectant faces and realised that if he had a major fault it was keeping a lot of his cards too close to his chest. He was the one who was continually rabbiting on about the importance of the team when in reality he was a bit of a grandstander. 'I haven't been exactly up front with you guys.'

Over the next hour, and another coffee, he told them about Royce's retirement and the link to Colin Payne who died in an agricultural accident that wasn't. He explained Reid's part in getting the inquest reopened, and he disclosed his meeting with Mouse and Donaldson. Finally, he told them about his trip to Rathlin and his meeting with Pearson. When he was finished, he didn't like the look on their faces.

'You didn't trust us,' Browne said.

'Of course I do.' Wilson knew that the words sounded empty in the light of his behaviour. If there were a course on leadership, his conduct wouldn't be held up as a paragon.

'That was quite a lot to keep to yourself all the same,' Graham said. 'We've been thinking that we're a group of dopes because we can't generate lines of enquiry while you've been sitting on all this stuff.'

'In a way I was just trying to connect the dots. Rory's visit to the Drugs Squad was a part of that process.'

'You've connected some of the dots?' Browne asked.

'Enough to keep us moving forward. McDevitt will be writing an article in tomorrow's *Chronicle* about the reopening of the inquest into Payne's death. That should stir things up among the murdering bastards. They've been sitting pretty since the initial inquest concluded that the death was an accident. A conclusion of unlawful killing will open the whole can of worms, and those who have been sleeping well in their beds will be having sleepless nights instead. When things begin to fall apart, we'll be around.'

'What about Royce?' Graham said. 'Maybe he murdered Payne because he was fingered by him.'

'On the surface of it, I don't think so. I think Royce was a patsy, or maybe he just drew the short straw. In any case, his retirement ended the investigation into corruption in the Drugs Squad, which was the objective of the exercise. Royce discovered God in Rathlin, and it looks like his involvement in Payne's death weighed on his conscience. Maybe he returned to Belfast to put things right.'

'It was good that you could use your connection with the professor to get the coroner to reopen the inquest,' Graham said. 'A former PSNI officer who retired from the force under the cloud of corruption wouldn't have had a snowball's chance in hell of getting a new inquest. And without a new inquest, no crime and no murder.'

'You're right, Harry. I've been thinking about that. Unfortunately, Royce isn't here to tell us what his plan was, but I have a feeling that he had one. He was happy on Rathlin, and he would have stayed there indefinitely if he didn't feel he had something important to do.'

'Where do we go from here?' Browne asked.

'Professional Services won't give us any details of what they were investigating,' Wilson said, 'so we have to assume that it has something to do with stealing and reselling drugs, or maybe the unit was in cahoots with the drug runners or pushers. It could be any of those.'

'How are we going to find out?' Graham said. 'Drugs are not our area of expertise.'

'And I wouldn't bet on any help from Pratley or Wallace,' Browne said. 'I wouldn't trust that Wallace guy as far as I could throw him.'

Wilson looked at Graham. 'Go back to the shelter tomorrow and go through that place with a fine-toothed comb. If Royce was on a crusade to put things right, he would have had some evidence. In the meantime, get the team to do a bit of investigating into our friends in the Drugs Squad. McDevitt's story will appear tomorrow morning. Let's see if they react.'

'What are you going to do, Boss?' Graham asked.

'I'm going home and I'll probably spend the afternoon watching westerns,' Wilson said. 'In case you hadn't heard, I'm on suspension.'

Browne stood. 'I have to pay a call. Two coffees is my limit.'

Wilson waited until he was through the toilet door. 'Moira's back.'

'No way,' Graham said.

'She's in Vice at the moment, but I have to work out a way to get her back in the squad.'

'What does that mean for Rory?'

'I don't know, but she's too good at what she does to waste her time picking up Toms and Johns.'

They both looked up as the toilet door opened and Browne reappeared.

'Good luck with that, Boss.'

CHAPTER FIFTY

R ussell and Kane spent the afternoon going through
Wilson's computer and examining call logs from both
his mobile phone and his landlines. It was the kind of tedious
investigative work that was the bread and butter of Professional Services. Russell was pleased that her younger colleague
was competent, thorough and possessed computer skills that
she could only dream of. They made a good team. By the end
of the evening, they had managed to clear Wilson's computer
and his phone logs. Russell was a twenty-year veteran of the
'Complaints' and as soon as she had read Wilson's personnel
file she had formed an initial opinion that he was innocent. If
he weren't, it wouldn't be the first time that her intuition let
her down. The interview and the examination of his computer
and phone logs only confirmed her initial impression. But this
was Northern Ireland and there were political overtones to
every aspect of life. Over lunch, Kane had clued her in on the
internal politics that might be affecting their investigation.
Despite his success, the hierarchy, or at least some elements of
it, didn't like Wilson. Although Kane didn't say it outright,
Russell had the impression that the rank and file felt the allega-

tion had been a put-up job by the DCC. Russell would have to
walk carefully. An innocent conclusion might not be univer-
sally popular. But that wasn't her problem. So far there wasn't
an iota of direct evidence that Wilson had leaked information.
She was turning over the last pages of the murder book when
she came to a photo of the whiteboard that had been taken
before it was dismantled. Most of Wilson's case against
Armstrong was there for all to see. She noted the handwritten
word 'tout' beside Armstrong's photo. Anyone with access to
the Murder Squad's room could have seen that whiteboard.
She supposed that meant most of the staff of the station. And
what of Wilson's hypothesis that the security services had
leaked the information to avoid embarrassment? It was as
reasonable as the information coming from the PSNI. From
what she had learned from Kane, Armstrong wouldn't be the
first person thrown to the wolves in the history of the province.
She looked at her watch and nodded at Kane. It was time to
interview the chief super.

DAVIS GREETED the two investigators warmly, made the introductions and ushered them to the 'soft' section of her office,
where tea and coffee had been laid out. She allowed Kane to
play mother. It was the first time in her career when there was
a serious subject under discussion where all the participants
were female.

Russell waited until Kane finished before putting her
mobile phone on the coffee table. 'I'm afraid this has to be a
formal recorded interview.'

'I'm in your hands,' Davis said.

'During the Spalvis case, were you in close consultation
with DS Wilson?' Russell asked.

'Yes, we had a debriefing most evenings.'

'So, you were aware of the direction of the investigation?'

'In the main, yes.'

'What do you mean by 'in the main'?'

'As the chief superintendent of the station I try to give direction and pass on messages from HQ. I do not carry out investigations myself. Of necessity, I am informed of the general direction of the investigation but not of every specific piece of information.'

'At what point did you become aware that Minister Noel Armstrong was a prime suspect?'

'When Wilson established that the alibi he provided for the Bridget Kelly murder was suborned.'

'Are you aware of the name of the police officer who suborned this alibi?'

'I am informed but with the added proviso that the witness is unreliable and in any case is resident outside the United Kingdom.'

'But this witness was also the source of the information that the alibi was false.'

'The witness provided the alibi.'

'And Wilson used this information to establish Armstrong as the prime suspect?'

'Armstrong's fingerprint was found at the Kelly apartment and the file on the murder mysteriously disappeared. Wilson suspected high-level collusion aimed at protecting Armstrong. Therefore, he was a credible suspect.'

'And you fully supported Wilson's conclusion?'

'Yes.'

'Then you went together to seek the permission of the DCC to have Armstrong interviewed under caution?'

'Yes, it was the next logical step.'

'Was DS Wilson upset when the DCC refused to allow Armstrong to be interviewed?'

'During the meeting he didn't appear to be.'

'And afterwards, did he express any frustration at the DCC's decision?'

'I don't think so.'

'Did the DCC's decision kill the investigation?'

'Not in Wilson's mind, he would have continued to look for evidence against Armstrong.'

'I take it that you don't believe that DS Wilson leaked information to the IRA that would lead them to suspect Armstrong of being a mole, and thereby leading to his death.'

'You can take that as a fact.'

Russell realised that no one had touched the tea. She picked up her cup and sipped. 'I also take it that you get on well with DS Wilson.'

'We are colleagues and I respect him as a fellow officer.'

'Thank you, chief superintendent.' Russell leaned over and switched off the recording.

'When do you think the investigation will be concluded?' Davis asked. 'I need Wilson back as soon as possible. We've a heavy workload in this station.'

'We'll interview the team tomorrow.' Russell drank the rest of her tea. 'Of course, it would be an advantage to interview someone from the IRA, but we'll probably have to stick to the evidence we have.'

'Evidence from that quarter might be very unreliable indeed,' Davis said. 'Look at Wilson's record. Is there anything there that is consistent with the allegation that's been made against him?'

Russell remained silent.

'Are you free for dinner?' Davis asked. 'Don't worry, we won't talk about the investigation.'

'I've already refused a dinner invitation from the DCC,' Russell said. 'I think tonight it's going to be room service.'

Davis smiled. Very professional, she thought.

They stood together and shook hands.

'What did you think?' Russell asked Kane as they walked towards the lift.

'She's a high-flier who the rumour mill says is headed for

the top. She's not the sort to tie her colours to the mast for a lost cause. But the DCC isn't going to forget that she's not on his side.'

CHAPTER FIFTY-ONE

The Special Operation Branch of the PSNI, most commonly known as Special Branch, is located in the Castlereagh complex, one of the most fortified buildings in Europe. The occupants of the complex are supposedly the safest citizens in Northern Ireland. The head of Special Branch, Robert Rodgers, would not describe his situation that day as safe. In fact, the man who gloried in the nickname of 'Black Bob' on account of the number of black operations he'd run was decidedly uneasy. It wasn't a feeling he was used to. He was supposed to be the one that made other people anxious. Although he'd never attended university, he had read every book on psychology he could get his hands on. With the arrival of the Internet, he'd studied the Stanford prison experiment and other experimental studies involving influence and fear. Black Bob had long ago accepted that chief superintendent was as high as he was going. Unlike his friend Jennings, he had no desire to grasp the brass ring. He was happy running black ops and being allied to the strongest power in the province, the Circle. The source of Rodgers' unease was sitting directly in front of him. Sergeant Simon Jackson was one of the Branch's top operatives. A former member of Military

Intelligence, Jackson had a range of skills that Rodgers frequently called on. Up to now, Jackson had performed each of his operations with military precision. However, it was beginning to look like something had gone wrong with the operation to murder Jackie Carlisle. And there were a lot of people who would not like their pleasant lives disturbed by the possibility that their involvement in Carlisle's death might be exposed.

'Young Leslie here has been following Davidson since Jamsie spluttered out the fact that he was looking for information on you.' Rodgers was looking directly at Jackson, 'What he's come up with is interesting.' He turned, looked at Leslie and nodded.

The young man shuffled nervously. 'Davidson is shacked up with Carlisle's widow. He's at the house morning, noon and night.' He tossed a series of photos on the desk showing Davidson and Irene Carlisle in clinches in the conservatory. 'It's obvious he's shagging her.'

'So fucking what?' Jackson said. He was lounging in his chair. 'Davidson as a detective isn't worth the full of my arse of boiled snow. He's a bummed-out old has-been, or never-was would be more accurate.'

Rodgers looked at Leslie. 'Continue.'

'Over the past few days, Davidson has been twice to a house across the road from Carlisle that's owned by a guy called Cooney. After his second visit, I followed up with Cooney and apparently Davidson has a statement identifying a man he saw entering the Carlisle house on the day of his death.'

'And you think that man is me,' Jackson said.

'It was you,' Rodgers said. 'But how did Davidson find out that you were involved? To have Cooney identify you, Davidson had to show him pictures. Why was one of those a picture of you?'

Jackson was sitting more erect. 'I see what you're getting at, chief. Maybe this has something to do with Wilson.'

'Or maybe Davidson is acting on his own,' Rodgers said. 'I've been doing some checking and it appears that Carlisle had a hefty insurance policy. The coroner's verdict of suicide voided that policy and cost Carlisle's widow a cool half a million pounds. Davidson shagging her could be based on a quid pro quo of him proving that her husband was murdered.'

'That operation was watertight,' Jackson said. 'I was in and out in a couple of minutes and Carlisle died with a smile on his face. I get pulled in and there'll be a dozen guys who'll swear I was somewhere else. They have nothing.'

'Wrong,' Rodgers said. 'They have your name, and we don't know where they got it.'

Jackson was thinking back over the Carlisle killing. It had gone completely to plan. 'I'd like to know that too. I'm not scared of Davidson playing at detective to get into Carlisle's widow's pants. But I don't like to think that Wilson is behind this somehow.'

'He's got his own problems at the moment,' Rodgers said.

Jackson leaned forward. 'Wilson is going to be a thorn in our sides until he's put six feet under, and even then I'd make sure to drive a stake through his heart before he's planted.'

'We know that we have a problem,' Rodgers said. 'How are we going to solve it?'

'Leave Leslie on the case,' Jackson said. 'Sooner or later Davidson will give up, or Carlisle's widow will realise that she's turned to the wrong man.'

Rodgers nodded. That solution didn't dispel his unease. It was a holding pattern and he didn't like sitting on his hands when his gut told him that action was needed.

CHAPTER FIFTY-TWO

A stone's throw from Rodgers' office, Royson Jennings was in conference with his closest ally, ACC Nicholson. 'That bloody woman refused my invitation to dinner.' Jennings had met Russell earlier that morning. He knew better than to try to influence her at their first meeting. 'I bet that Wilson has her eating out of his hand. Why in God's name did they send a woman?'

'I thought that she came across very professionally.' Nicholson didn't look his boss in the eye, he was never comfortable when offering an opinion that was not in line with the DCC's.

'I don't give a damn about her professionalism. I want her to find the allegation proven.' Jennings had started having misgivings as soon as he had met Russell. It wasn't just that women tended to respond positively to Wilson, it was the fact that she wasn't looking to him for guidance. He disliked people who put forward the idea that their opinion had the same validity as his. 'What has she been up to today?'

'I have no idea.'

'I thought you'd given her someone from Professional Services to help her.'

'I did, a young woman called Lucy Kane.'

'A woman, you gave her a woman as an assistant. So now two women are investigating whether Wilson is guilty of leaking information to the IRA. Are you out of your bloody mind?'

'I didn't know at the time that Russell was a woman.'

'I suppose the name Fiona might have been an indication.'

Nicholson said nothing. He often wondered why Jennings was fixated with bringing Wilson down. He rather liked the man himself and no one could doubt Wilson's record. But his own colours were firmly attached to Jennings' mast and his opinions normally reflected those of his mentor. 'Perhaps we were a little hasty in bringing the allegation. There's no doubt that the IRA had the information that Armstrong was a tout, but Nolan might have been a little out of order to suggest that someone in the PSNI passed along that information.'

'Don't be a bloody fool. Wilson was the one who worked out that Armstrong was working for British Intelligence. He had to be involved.' Jennings realised that he was trying to convince himself. Once again he had let his emotions rule his head in an effort to get rid of Wilson. He had jumped when he should have waited to see whether concrete evidence could be found, or perhaps manufactured. 'Leave me.' He dismissed Nicholson with a wave of his hand. He needed to be alone to think.

CHAPTER FIFTY-THREE

Wilson watched the final credits of the *Wild Bunch* roll up the screen. Peckinpah's classic was one of his favourites, but Reid wasn't into the genre so it had become a sneaky watch. He'd seen it so often that he could almost quote the dialogue from memory. The advantage of this level of familiarity is that while he was watching, a large portion of his brain was concentrating on something else entirely. And he had plenty on his mind. Some would say too much. There was nothing he could do about Russell's investigation. But he could do something about Royce and especially about Payne. The young detective constable had been murdered and justice needed to be served. The problem was he wouldn't be able to do it alone. Under normal circumstances he should go to his superior, but he had the feeling that Davis would insist on moving up the line and that meant Jennings. The morning edition of the *Chronicle* would launch another round of invective from HQ. McDevitt would protect his source, but even a deaf, dumb and blind man would know that he was somewhere behind Reid's re-examination of the post-mortem and the request that the coroner reopen the inquest. There was only one place he could go for help and that was right to the top. When the chief constable had given him command of the Murder Squad, he'd said that he would always be available to help. Wilson was about to put that to the test. He took out the card with Norman Baird's personal mobile number on it and called. It was answered quickly.

'Chief Constable Baird.'

'Ian Wilson, we have to talk.'

There was a moment's silence on the phone. 'Does this concern your current situation?'

'No, it's a totally unrelated matter.'

'I hear you were something of a rugby player.'

'So they tell me.'

'My son is playing in the School's Cup semi-final at the Kingspan Stadium tomorrow afternoon. I thought you might be attending.'

'I was definitely planning to go,' Wilson lied.

'Good, if you're in the Grand Stand then I'll probably see you there.'

Wilson put the phone away. He was about to either make the greatest mistake of his life or solve two murders. If he were right about who the murderers were, it would shake the PSNI to its foundations. But there was a long way to go before that happened.

He eased back in his chair. There was a third problem. Reid was no longer happy in Belfast. Perhaps it was the weather, or maybe the job had lost its lustre, or maybe the curse that invaded his relationships with women had struck again. The thought that he and Reid would no longer be together was painful for him. One way or another he was going to hold on to her. She was on her way home and he decided to play house-partner by setting the table for dinner. Neither of them was a great cook so dinner generally consisted of some kind of protein and salad, either that or they got a takeaway. He felt the small bulge about his belt. The morning run was going to have to be a more regular event. He was putting knives and forks on the table when the intercom went. He picked up the receiver.

'Don't put the phone down.'

'Jack, I'm really not in the humour tonight.'

'Let me up. I won't stay long.'

Wilson pushed the button releasing the door downstairs. Duane didn't stop being a friend just because of Nolan's memo.

'Nothing I could do,' Duane said as he entered the apartment. 'Nolan's a cantankerous old bastard. His pride wouldn't let him say that he made a mistake.'

'I've met a few cantankerous bastards in my time,' Wilson said. 'The problem is I believe he's probably right. Someone leaked information on Armstrong and although justice was served in a perverse way, it wasn't the right thing to do. Have you eaten?'

'No, but I have an arrangement for later.'

'Davis?'

'A gentleman doesn't say.'

Wilson started laughing. Duane looked more like a pirate or a highwayman than a gentleman.

'How did it go today?'

'The investigator from Scotland is Superintendent Fiona Russell. She seems professional and independent. It's more than I expected.'

'I think we might all be wrong about who leaked the information. My contacts in the IRA tell me that they've been on to Armstrong for some time. He pissed off a lot of people when he was heading the 'nutting squad'. Some of them wanted revenge.'

'I'd like to believe that.'

'I'm just passing on the message. Did you surrender your weapon?'

Wilson nodded.

Duane took a gun from his pocket and held it out. 'I think you should take this.'

'No way. I don't do unofficial.'

Duane put the gun back in his pocket. 'It's your funeral. I have one other piece of news. I don't know whether you've already heard, there was a meeting on a yacht in the south of France last week involving one of our heavies from Dublin. The subject was a hit on a police officer in Belfast. The enquiry was preliminary, but our information is that the hitman in question was receptive. We've passed the information along to your Intelligence people.'

'What's that got to do with me?'

'We don't have a name, but I wanted to give you a heads-up. If anything more comes of it, I'll get back to you. I have to go and I'm sorry again for landing you in the shit.'

'No harm done, yet.'

Wilson closed the door of the apartment. Duane wasn't the type of individual to share information unless there was a good reason. Perhaps he'd already shaken the tree with the investigation into the Drugs Squad. But they'd only just started on the Drugs Squad and the meeting with the hitman had been last week. Maybe it had nothing to do with him, but then again, it might.

CHAPTER FIFTY-FOUR

Siobhan O'Neill stood in the locked toilet cubicle taking deep breaths. It wasn't working. She lifted the toilet lid just in time to send a stream of vomit into the bowl. She quickly flushed it away. So much for the calming effects of the full Ulster breakfast. Replacing the lid, she sat down. She was about to be first up for interview with DS Russell. She'd spent the evening using visualisation techniques to imagine what the interview would be like and how it would go. She knew that the woman leading the investigation into the leak was an experienced operator. The smallest slip would be picked up, and then either she, or Wilson, would be in real trouble. She tried deep breathing again. She was due downstairs in ten minutes and needed the panic in her mind to recede. The breathing exercise gradually began to have the desired effect. She had nothing to worry about as long as she held her nerve. She took out a roll of mints and popped two into her mouth.

Fiona Russell was sitting in the interview room at the station. She'd spent the evening replaying the interviews with Wilson and Davis and re-reading the murder book. It all appeared above board. Wilson and his boss had been calm and betrayed no signs of either lying or nervousness. She had reviewed their personnel files as she listened again to a recording of their evidence, and both were distinguished officers with impeccable records. There was little likelihood that they would throw away their careers, especially by cooperating with a terrorist organisation. But stranger things had happened and everybody has their breaking point. The main issue that nagged at her was the fact that there was no direct evidence that any information had been leaked. She had asked for and received the Garda Síochána memo relating to the investigation into Armstrong's murder. It was very clear that the IRA had murdered him after torturing him into admitting his guilt for both betraying them and murdering two young women. The accusation of the involvement of the PSNI was an assertion of the SIO and completed without any evidentiary basis. In her experience, the existence of a crime was the necessary basis for an investigation. And to her mind there was no proof that a crime had been committed. Why then had there been a rush to put a senior officer under investigation? Wilson's record was certainly one of a detective who had the habit of upsetting his superiors. However, he got results by doing so. There was something fishy about this whole investigation. The sooner she was finished and back in Edinburgh the better.

DS Kane entered the interview room carrying a briefcase in one hand and balancing a cardboard tray containing three cups in the other. She dropped her briefcase on the floor and laid the tray down gently on the table. 'I sent out for these, take my word for it, the coffee in the cafeteria here is undrinkable.' She put her hand in her jacket pocket and produced mini capsules of milk and sachets of sugar, which she scattered on the table beside the tray.

'Siobhan O'Neill is up first.' Russell lifted up a file. 'A very interesting CV.'

'Not your run-of-the-mill copper.' Kane took one of the

cups off the tray and dumped a sachet of sugar into it. 'People with those kind of computer skills can earn a fortune in the private sector.'

'Then what the hell is she doing in the police?' Russell took one of the coffees, removed the lid and sipped. It almost scalded her lips.

'Apparently it has something to do with her mother, Alzheimer's.'

'Let's have her in then,' Russell said.

'Is this the first time you've been interviewed by the Complaints?' Russell asked when they were seated and the preliminaries had been observed. It was obvious that the young woman was nervous. She'd turned down the offer of the third coffee. Russell decided that she'd snare it later. She hadn't seen her bed until two o'clock in the morning

O'Neill coughed. 'Yes.'

'Why don't you tell us what you do on the team?'

O'Neill described the various tasks she performed for the squad.

'So, you're the brains of the outfit?'

O'Neill laughed. 'I wish, I'm more the general factotum.'

'You never go out on an investigation?'

'Not so far. I only joined the squad recently. I think that they're breaking me in gently.'

'Did you know Noel Armstrong?' Russell had been clued in on the names issue in Northern Ireland. O'Neill was almost exclusively a Catholic name.

'Only to vote for.'

'Do you have any connections with the IRA?'

'No, I'm not from a politically active family. My father died from cancer when my sister and I were young. Until recently I've been taking care of my mother at home. She's just moved into a care home.'

'I suppose that would have been checked before you joined the PSNI?'

'I'm not sure, but I suppose so.'

'What was your role on the Armstrong investigation?' Russell asked.

'I maintained the murder book, collated all the interview reports and took care of the whiteboard.'

Russell flicked through the murder book, it was exemplary. She turned to the photograph of the whiteboard at the end of the book. 'Was it you who wrote the word 'tout' on the board?'

'No. I added the information on the victim as it was developed. The minister was presented as a suspect and I assume the boss or someone else wrote 'tout'.'

'Thanks for your help,' Russell said and nodded at Kane who closed the interview and knocked off the tape recorder. 'Off the record, do you think DS Wilson would leak information to the IRA?'

O'Neill was breathing a sigh of relief internally. 'If he did, it would go against everything that he believes in. He's one of the most ethical people I've ever met.'

'On a more personal note, with your level of computer skills, why did you join the police?'

'I wanted to contribute to creating a better society. Making money isn't what I'm about. All the money in the world can't make my mother better.'

CHAPTER FIFTY-FIVE

Harry Graham was on his hands and knees testing the floorboards of the homeless shelter on the Malone Road. He had already spent two hours searching every nook and cranny for the mysterious evidence that Wilson felt had to be present. It really was way beyond looking for a needle in a haystack, at least there you knew there was actually a needle. Sometimes Wilson's intuition led to a mountain of effort for zero result. There were no loose floorboards in the dormitory and the locker had no secret compartments. He had found no papers, no photographs, no USBs, in effect nothing. Graham needed to get a move on. He had never heard of the Pareto Principle but as a twenty-year veteran of the force, he knew instinctively that eighty per cent of what they did led nowhere and the other twenty per cent managed to trap the criminal. As he tested the floorboards close to the bed Royce had been allotted, he had already fixed in his mind that he was involved in an eighty per cent activity.

It was almost time for his interview with DS Russell. He didn't like Professional Services or whatever they called it in Scotland. No copper likes to have his professionalism questioned. But it would be naïve to think that there weren't some bad apples in the force. He was aware that his old friend Davidson had been lucky to hold onto his job after an internal investigation. And the boss had come close once or twice. This time the allegation against Wilson was a serious one. If it succeeded, it might mean jail time and there were a lot of people at HQ who would be dancing a jig if that happened. There was no point continuing, the shelter didn't hold the missing evidence. Another one of Wilson's intuitions bites the dust. Graham left the shelter and strode to his car. He took his phone out of his pocket; it was time to give Wilson the bad news.

CHAPTER FIFTY-SIX

Davidson was in the lobby of the Merchant Hotel in Skipper Street. He looked up at the magnificent chandelier above his head and then at the marble floor beneath his feet and wondered who the hell had the money to pay for a stay in a place like this. Maybe when Irene got her half-a-million-pound cheque they might spend a night in this pleasure dome. He walked over to the concierge's desk and waited behind a couple enquiring about restaurants for lunch. When they were finished, he stepped forward and produced his warrant card. 'Detective Constable Davidson, I'd like to speak to whoever manages the concierge desk.'

The young lady manning the desk disappeared through a door behind her and returned some minutes later with a thin young man dressed in a dark suit.

'May I see your warrant card please?' The accent was French.

Davidson presented the card again.

'My name is Jacques Micheux, and I am the deputy manager in charge of the concierge desk. Do you mind if we speak in my office?'

'Not at all,' Davidson said, wondering if every employee in top hotels had to speak with a French accent.

Micheux beckoned Davidson to follow him into the office behind the desk and closed the door. 'How can I help you?'

'We're making an enquiry about a telephone that was purchased by one of your staff,' Davidson said. 'The mobile was purchased at the O2 shop in Victoria Square on March 21st, 2016.'

'And you know it was a member of our staff how?'

'Because the buyer said that he was buying the phone for a client of the hotel. O2 detail all purchases.' Davidson showed him a copy of the bill signed by the member of staff.

Micheux walked to a cupboard and pulled out a ledger marked '2016'. He flicked through to the date in question and he ran his finger along the entries. 'Ah! There it is.' He turned the book round and pointed at the entry.

'May I have a copy of that page?' Davidson said.

'It is most unusual.'

'It's in connection with a murder enquiry. It would be awkward for the hotel if we had to obtain a warrant.'

Micheux let out a deep sigh and moved to a copying machine in the corner of his room. He copied the page and handed Davidson the A4 sheet.

Davidson checked the sheet before folding it and putting it in his jacket. 'Thank you.' He opened the door and left. Outside he went immediately to the hotel lobby, took out his mobile phone and called Wilson. 'Boss, I'm at the Merchant Hotel following up on the phone found at Belfast International. You'll never guess who purchased it.'

As soon as Davidson left the lobby, DC Leslie stood up from one of the chairs and made his way to the concierge desk. He produced his warrant card and the girl went into the office at the rear.

Micheux exited the office red-faced. It was raining policemen today.

CHAPTER FIFTY-SEVEN

Wilson's mind lurched when he heard Davidson's latest discovery. Many people put their head in the lion's mouth as part of a circus act, but they had assured themselves beforehand that the lion was well fed. He had just woken up to the fact that his head was firmly in place in the lion's mouth, and it was a lion that was always hungry. When he needed sleep most it just wouldn't come. He finally slept but woke two hours later completely awake. He forced himself to stay in bed and slept fitfully for the rest of the night. When he finally clambered out of bed at seven o'clock, he was more tired than that when he'd lain down. Although he didn't want to, he completed his run and ran the shower as hot as he could bear.

Reid was in the kitchen fixing scrambled eggs when he entered. 'I've left a prescription on the table for a mild sleeping pill,' she said when he sat down at the breakfast bar. 'You look like you-know-what warmed up.'

'Ladies don't speak like that.'

She put a plate of scrambled eggs on toast in front of him. 'I never claimed to be a lady.' She put her arms round his neck and looked into his face. 'I know you're worried. It's not like you. The one thing that always impressed me is your coolness under pressure.'

'Don't worry about me, I'm only trying to solve a couple of very complicated murders that probably involve members of the organisation I work for.' He shot his head forward and kissed her. 'As long as you stick by me I'm going to work my way out of this mess.'

She moved away without speaking and brought her plate to the table. 'Listen to your doctor and take the pills, a good night's sleep is the basis of health. What's your plan for the day?'

'I thought I'd lie around for the morning watching daytime television and then there's a School's Cup game at Kingspan this afternoon, all in all a busy day ahead. What about you?'

'Same old same old. What's with the School's Cup? Revisiting old glories?'

'Bored.'

The phone rang and Wilson picked it up.

'Seen the *Chronicle* yet,' McDevitt said.

'I haven't had the pleasure,' Wilson said.

'The editor put the Payne story on the front page. I spiced it up a bit but not enough to annoy you. If this doesn't flush the killer out, nothing will. Any idea when the new inquest will be held?'

Wilson put his hand over the mouthpiece. 'Did your coroner friend say when he would reopen the inquest?'

'As soon as he has a slot, could be in days or weeks.'

He relayed the information to McDevitt.

'My article should put a little pressure on him. Gotta fly, crime never rests in this city.'

If you only knew, Wilson thought.

Reid was already putting on her coat and getting ready to leave.

'No point in asking you to join me for a morning of daytime television.'

She turned at the door and blew him a kiss. 'Enjoy.'

He cleaned up the breakfast dishes and made himself a second cup of coffee. Then he took a pad of paper and a pen and sat at the dining table. Royce was the key. He had hidden his disappointment from Graham concerning the search of the homeless shelter. He was certain that Royce didn't come back to Belfast empty-handed. If he was going to put things right, he would have had something concrete. He started to sketch out his ideas on the pad. He had a feeling that daytime TV was going to be shelved.

CHAPTER FIFTY-EIGHT

DCI George Pratley was apoplectic. A copy of the *Chronicle* lay on the desk in front of him with McDevitt's story on the reopening of the Payne inquest facing up. He was pacing up and down behind his desk trying to regain control of his thoughts. His mind was racing. Wallace was standing in the centre of the office in stunned silence. Pratley's stomach had collapsed when he'd read the story and he'd had to make an urgent trip to the toilet.

'What the fuck is going on?' Wallace asked.

'That bastard Wilson is what's going on,' Pratley said. 'Read the bloody story. Somehow or other he found out that Payne was the one who snitched on us. He's had the post-mortem reassessed and the coroner has agreed to reopen the inquest. This time they're going to get it right. I'll bet that Wilson has an idea about what really happened in Ballyward. You don't have to be a genius to know where the investigation is going to go.'

'Then he has the link between Payne and Royce?'

'Maybe, but whatever he has we're in trouble.'

'Shouldn't we turn this situation over to Best and his crew?

We're only the small fry in this operation, but if we go down, so do they.'

'Don't be bloody stupid. If we go down, we'll be the only ones who do. If we run to Best with this, he's going to cut us off like a malignant growth.'

'Then what the hell are we going to do?'

'I think it's a little late to sign a resignation letter and fade away into the sunset. We're in this mire up to our necks.'

'What about Jennings? He knew what we were up to.'

'Are you joking? If we go to Jennings with this we'll be dead by nightfall. Our only hope is that the coroner won't want to admit that he screwed up last time and so continues to maintain a verdict of accidental death.'

'And in the meantime?'

'I don't know about you, but I'm going to get a visa for Belize. When the shit leaves the fan on this one, you are I are going to be covered in it.'

'We should take Wilson out, or put a bomb in the Murder Squad room and take them all out. We could blame it on the IRA.'

Pratley looked at Wallace and shook his head. 'Remind me never to play poker with you. You really know how to up the ante. Get the fuck out and let me think.'

Pratley picked up the *Chronicle*. The Royce story was relegated to page five. He reread the story on page one. The state pathologist had asked to reopen the inquest, but he knew Wilson was behind it. He didn't want to imagine what was happening in the office at the rear of Best's club. The ganglord might be angry enough to stick his Rottweiler on them. This was all on that fucker Royce. Why couldn't he have just stayed on his island and continued praying to his God? Oh no, the bastard had to get pangs of conscience about the drugs, and the money, and Payne's untimely death. Some people could never leave well enough alone. What did the fool think he could accomplish? A disgraced junkie ex-copper, who the hell was going to listen to him? But he'd mentioned having evidence and that's what had sealed his fate. It was all going to shit in a basket.

Royson Jennings was shaken enough to cancel his first two appointments. The article in the *Chronicle* had come out of the blue. When the coroner changed the verdict from accidental death to unlawful killing, as he was sure he would, it would be the beginning of the end for Pratley and Wallace. Wilson had used his bitch of a partner to resurrect Payne. Risen from the grave, Payne's story would put an end to their comfortable arrangement with Best. And there was nothing he could do about it. He slammed his fist on the table. He was the deputy chief constable of the PSNI and he could not get rid of this bloody nuisance. Every time he tried to skewer the bastard, Wilson managed to slip out of the net. He'd spoken to Russell the previous evening and, although she didn't come right out and say it, it was apparent that she had found no evidence of a leak from the PSNI. She was going to turn in her report today and Wilson would be picking up his warrant card and weapon by early evening. Perhaps the only way to get rid of Wilson was to kill him. He was certain he wouldn't be the only one having that thought today.

Peter Davidson was having a lie-in, which he felt he was entitled to. He had done as fine a bit of detective work as he'd seen in his thirty years on the job. He'd developed the line of the investigation from the call to the hospice and he'd identified the two parties who'd shared the line when the Carlisle job was done. He'd be retired soon and it would be good to have a result under his belt before he said his final farewells. He sat up in bed when Irene entered carrying a tray.

'Breakfast,' she declared, waiting for him to get into a

comfortable sitting position. She placed the tray on his lap and climbed into bed beside him. 'You are a clever boy.' She kissed him on the cheek and removed a cup of tea and a piece of toast from the tray.

Davidson smiled. It felt great to be in Irene's good books. He'd informed her the previous evening that they were almost at the end of the road on the investigation and that they would soon be crossing the 't's and dotting the 'i's. He didn't give her any details of the who and the wherefore, and quite honestly Irene didn't give a damn about anything other than proving the crime in order to collect the insurance money. She was not one who wished to be burdened with insignificant details like who had murdered her husband and why. She had been so excited that they were almost there that she immediately decided to celebrate and booked them dinner at the Plough Inn. A fine meal and a classic bottle of red was followed by as fine a romp as Davidson had enjoyed. It had been a perfect night and today there was nothing on the schedule except rest and recuperation.

Yesterday, he'd been the last of the team to be interviewed by Lady Macbeth, as he'd termed DS Russell. He'd had extensive experience of being interviewed by Professional Services and he gave her his version of the facts, which backed up Wilson one hundred per cent. Jennings was obviously getting desperate. There were a lot of coppers in the PSNI who'd sell their grandmothers for a bit of filthy lucre, but Ian Wilson wasn't one of them. He finished his tea and toast and set the tray on the ground before turning towards Irene. He put his hand out and felt her soft full breast. Please don't dump me when you get the money, he thought.

CHAPTER FIFTY-NINE

Wilson was hit by a wave of nostalgia as he walked up the stairs at the back of the Grand Stand at the Kingspan Stadium. There was a buzz of excitement from the supporters of the two schools contesting the semi-final. His father had been part of that excitement when he had made his first appearance for his college in a School's Cup semi-final. He came out from the darkness of the stairs and the green swathe of the playing pitch appeared in front of him. It had changed greatly since the day he had first walked out on its luscious turf. It was a measure of the advances rugby had made in the professional era. Wilson had played on mucky grounds that the young men about to play in front of him would scorn. He made his way slowly to his seat in the centre of the stand. The two teams were already out on the pitch doing their warm up exercises. He seldom attended rugby matches these days. It wasn't because he had fallen out of love with the game – that would never happen, it was because it left him with a feeling of melancholy that something he loved so much had been ripped away from him before he was ready to let it go. The melancholy was akin to the way he felt about his father's suicide, and the way he felt about the lost years without his mother. He settled himself into his seat and looked at the programme. Baird's son was playing at outside centre for Campbell College, one of the big names in Ulster junior rugby. He received several looks and nods from some of the other spectators. He was rather embarrassed to be remembered as the great who had his career cut short because of his own stupidity.

He tried to shake the gloomy feeling off. He wasn't the only person whose career was ended by injury. His thoughts immediately turned to Reid. Knowing her and being part of her life more than made up for everything he'd lost. And now there was a distinct possibility that he might lose her too. There was movement to his left and he saw Baird arriving and being greeted by some notables. The chief constable was wearing a fur-lined sheepskin coat and was sporting a Campbell College scarf. Within minutes of Baird's arrival the game was underway and Wilson's concentration was directed to the playing surface. Twenty minutes into the game, Wilson noticed movement to his left and turned to see Baird making his way towards the rear of the stand and heading down the stairs. Wilson stood and moved to his side, descending the stairs closest to him. The two men met underneath the stand.

'What's the problem?' Baird asked.

Wilson gave a quick run-through on the Royce murder and the connection with Payne's death three years previously. 'I don't have all the proof to hand, but I think Payne was murdered because he was exposing corruption in the Drugs Squad. Royce was the patsy who closed down the Professional Services investigation, but Pratley and Wallace never considered that Royce would later find God and need to atone for Payne's death.'

Baird looked round to see if anyone was listening. 'What an almighty fucking mess. If you're right, this is going to cause one hell of a stink. The politicians will have a fucking field day.'

'Like I said, I don't have all the proof to hand.'

'Don't wind me up. If there's a possibility that you're wrong, tell me now.'

'It's possible, but I don't think I'm wrong.'

'Then we're screwed. What do you need from me?'

'First off, access to the Professional Services investigation into the Drugs Squad.'

'You're assuming that you're going to be cleared on the leaking of information allegation.'

'I didn't do it, and I think DS Russell will confirm that.'

'Professional Services investigations are confidential.'

'I need to see the corruption allegation.'

'I'll arrange it. What else?'

'We keep this on a need to know basis until it breaks.'

'Meaning keep DCC Jennings out of the loop. I don't like creating unofficial channels.'

'It's a delicate situation.'

There was a pause. 'Okay, you have my approval to bypass the DCC. Anything else?'

'Not for the moment.'

'You're about to drop me into the middle of a shit storm.'

'I remember when you were appointed you said you wanted to run a clean ship. You'll be making good on that promise by cleaning out the Drugs Squad.'

'I'm not so sure, but that's another day's work. I also have a request.'

'Fire away.'

'The guy from the sponsors saw you upstairs. He's going to ask you to join the reception after the game, you'll accept. You've still got a lot of fans in the rugby community.'

'Okay.'

'He'll approach you at half-time. And I want an autograph on the programme for my son.'

'He's not a bad wee player. He'll need to bulk up a bit.'

'I'll pass the message along.' Baird turned and headed for the stairs. 'I'll be in touch,' he said over his shoulder.

Wilson watched him leave. His old boss told him that he could trust Baird. He hoped to God that Spence was right.

CHAPTER SIXTY

D S Russell and DS Kane had spent the morning drafting their report on the investigation into the allegation that Wilson had leaked confidential information to the IRA. They had concluded that there was no evidence to support the allegation. They'd had a final meeting with Davis, and Russell had booked herself on the evening flight to Edinburgh. The final act of the investigation was possibly the most difficult, the presentation of the conclusions to the DCC.

Jennings and Nicholson were already present in the office when Russell and Kane entered. After a round of introductions, Russell went through the details of the investigation, starting with the interview with Wilson. She presented the results of the forensic examination of Wilson's computer and her examination of the murder book. Wilson's notebook had been examined and they had established the timeline of his actions during the days preceding the death of Armstrong. His phone logs had been examined and were cleared.

Jennings had anticipated the result, so he remained calm throughout the presentation. He cast the odd glance at Nicholson and had seen the idiot nodding along in agreement. Although he was mad as hell at Wilson escaping yet again, he would have to admit that it was a very comprehensive presentation. Given the lack of any real evidence of Wilson actually sitting down with someone from the IRA, his plan was up shit-creek. However, a more compliant investigator might have been a help. He had no option but to be gracious. 'An excellent piece of work,' he said as soon as Russell had finished. 'I will pass my congratulations and thanks to your superiors.'

'I would like to recognise DS Kane's contribution,' Russell said.

'It will be noted on her file.'

Russell packed up her documents and shoved her files into her briefcase. The man sitting opposite her had tried to fit up one of his own officers. She had no idea why, but she was glad that she had been a part of making sure that it didn't happen. She expelled a long breath as she and Kane walked to the lift. 'Sometimes I hate this job.'

'It's a crap job,' Kane said, smiling. 'But someone has to do it. Being detested by the majority of your colleagues isn't exactly the recipe for happiness at work. Mind you, nobody asked the officers we investigate to break the rules – they did that all on their own.'

'I joined the police because I wanted to make a difference. But after twenty years of misogyny and finding that a large proportion of my colleagues are no better than the criminals they're supposed to be putting away, a lot of my enthusiasm has waned. That man in there made my skin crawl. I'm actually pleased to have thwarted his plan.'

Kane pushed the button summoning the lift. 'I think Wilson got lucky this time. Next time Jennings will be more attentive as to who the investigator is.' The lift arrived and they entered. 'You have a few hours before you have to catch the plane and I think we've earned a drink.'

'That's an excellent idea.'

CHAPTER SIXTY-ONE

Bobby Rodgers, Simon Jackson and DC Leslie were in conference in Rodgers' office. Leslie had reported on Davidson's visit to the Merchant, and the effect of the news on Rodgers and Jackson was clear to see. They looked to be on the point of crapping themselves.

'The rotten old shite,' Jackson said. 'I didn't think he had it in him.'

Rodgers turned to Leslie. 'Good job. Now I need to talk to Simon alone.

Leslie stood and left the room.

'What do we do now?' Rodgers said.

'The first thing is we don't panic,' Jackson said. 'He knows who bought a phone and he has a statement from a neighbour that a guy outside Carlisle's house looks like me. So what?'

'But is that all he knows? And is that all Wilson knows?'

'Let's assume that Davidson is running a private project.'

'No, let's not assume that,' Rodgers cut in. 'Let's assume the worst-case scenario. Let's assume that Wilson knows what Davidson knows. We need to find out exactly what real evidence he has.'

'There's only one way to do that: I'll have to ask him.'

'That will escalate matters considerably.'

'It's the only way. Either that or we sit tight and wait to see what happens. Maybe he can be talked to?'

Rodgers was silent. He'd checked the records, Davidson would be out the door in a couple of months. If he was in the lead on the investigation and wasn't passing what he had to Wilson, there was a chance he could be bought off. Davidson had two ex-wives who were bleeding him dry. Maybe a few thousand quid would be enough to get him off Jackson's back. 'I need to pass this upstairs.'

'That might delay the inevitable.'

'Davidson is a copper, we need to be a bit wary about extreme actions.'

'Like you said before, it's my funeral. But remember, if I go down, then you go down.'

When they met later in the DCC's office, Rodgers thought that Jennings looked like he felt. He wondered what new disaster had befallen his chief. So much so that he questioned whether it was advisable to broach the subject he had come to discuss. He opted to proceed. 'We appear to have a problem.'

Jennings had been examining a spot on his desk and he looked up into Rodgers' face. He was not one to be gracious in defeat. As soon as he'd gotten rid of Russell, Kane and Nicholson he'd had a good old rant, which had culminated in him throwing his desk lamp against the wall. Chief Constable Baird was cutting his power with every day that passed. He had been surrounding himself with his own men and gradually freezing Jennings out. He had to drag his mind back to the possible reason for Rodgers' visit. 'You're not the only one. Tell me.'

'Davidson has been a busy boy over the past few days. He has a statement from a neighbour identifying Simon Jackson as the man he saw going into Jackie Carlisle's house.' Rodgers coughed. 'And he's identified the person who bought the mobile phone Jackson called afterwards. Somehow he got his hands on the phone and traced it to the concierge at the Merchant. They'd logged it.'

'What!' Jennings came to his feet and stared at Rodgers. 'How the hell did he do that? Do you realise what this means?'

'Of course I know what it means.'

Jennings slumped back in his chair. 'A flawless operation you said. We're talking about Davidson here, not Sherlock Holmes. He's managed to put Jackson at the scene of Carlisle's death and he has a name for the owner of the phone Jackson called at the end of the operation. And of course the log from the Merchant. I wouldn't call the operation flawless, would you?'

'No. And I know the consequences.'

'Where do we go from here?'

'Put a stop to the investigation.'

'What investigation? Officially there is no investigation. Wilson says that Davidson is working on the Royce case.'

'I think they may have enough to bring Jackson in.'

'Do you think Jackson will talk?'

'I know he won't. But they might have enough to bring other people in, people who are a lot more important than Jackson.'

'They'd have to come through me before they could do that.'

Rodgers hesitated. 'Or they could go higher.'

The hesitation and the remark struck Jennings to the core. There was a time when if a flea farted in a PSNI station, he got the smell. Now, even Rodgers could see the writing on the wall. A chill ran down his back. 'What do you suggest?'

'If we can't stop the investigation, we have to think of stopping the people.'

Typical Special Branch solution, Jennings thought. PSNI

officers must be in season, so many people want to cull them. He had read the Garda Síochána's intelligence about the meeting in the south of France. He had a very good idea who the participants were and who the target might be. He supposed that he should pass on the intelligence to Wilson. After all, forewarned is forearmed. But he was willing to bet that Jack Duane had already done so. 'I think it's already under consideration.'

'The sooner the better.'

'You're losing your touch, Bob.'

'What do you mean?'

'Time was there'd be no screw-up on an operation like Carlisle.'

'It was a good plan.'

'So good that someone like Davidson could pick it apart. I hope that Jackson does keep his mouth shut when the time comes.'

'That could be the case for a lot of us.'

CHAPTER SIXTY-TWO

Wilson was the star attraction at the Danske Bank reception held in the hospitality area of the stadium. It only went to prove that old legends never really die. He always assumed that when he was compelled to retire that he would fade from people's memories, but that wasn't proving to be the case. He was never seduced by the backslapping that went with fame. He played the game because he loved it and not for any other reason. It was the way his father had brought him up. Still, he had promised Baird to attend. He told his rugby stories and signed whatever pieces of paper were pushed under his nose. It was a performance. The real Ian Wilson wasn't the crocked former player, he was the copper who went to work every day with other coppers. Baird gave him a nod, which he took to mean that he had satisfied the needs of the sponsors and he could start a strategic withdrawal. Outside the stadium, he took a deep breath. He remembered why he didn't go to games any more.

He was moving in the direction of his car when his phone rang. It was Davis transmitting the result of Russell's investigation. He was in the clear, for the moment anyway, and she expected him back at work the following day. Jennings had already sent over his warrant card and she would return his weapon. It was another victory against Jennings and his cronies at HQ. But it would be a short-lived one. Soon Jennings would be back with another attack and perhaps he wouldn't win that battle. Jennings could sustain losses, but he couldn't. One loss and he would be looking for a new job. It was all about power, and Jennings had the power.

His phone rang again and this time it was Reid. The coroner had found a slot the following day and would reopen the inquest on Payne. She would be the only witness in what would be a curtailed session. The outcome wasn't certain, but she was going to give it her best shot. He couldn't ask for more. He told her about his escape from Jennings' clutches and she whooped with joy. They needed to celebrate and there was only one place to do that. He drove into town and found a parking place on Hope Street. McDevitt was sitting in his snug when he pushed in the door.

'Back in the land of the living,' McDevitt said. 'That can mean only one thing, otherwise you'd be hiding your face in your apartment. It won't exactly make the front page but a nice little article inside.'

'You're like one of those bloodsucking creatures that cling to people and won't let go.' He pushed the bell to call the barman.

'I can see that you're in celebratory mood and who better to celebrate with than your best friend? Mine's a pint. I've never been fond of champagne.'

'For the nine hundredth time, you are not my best friend. And I'm going to have a word with the management about letting you into my snug.' Wilson ordered two pints of Guinness and sat down.'

'Our sports reporter saw you at the School's Cup game. Finally coming out of hibernation?'

'I was at a loose end and thought I'd see if there was any talent on the horizon.'

McDevitt took out his phone and showed Wilson a picture of Baird and him under the stand.

Fucking mobile phones, Wilson thought, nowhere is safe.

McDevitt laughed. 'The press is everywhere.'

'Busybodies are everywhere.'

The barman delivered the drinks and Wilson paid.

'Private conference with the big boss, I'm intrigued.' McDevitt touched his glass to Wilson's and drank.

'And you'll have to stay that way.'

'No scoop today then?'

'Be in the coroner's court tomorrow morning.'

'That's a scoop.'

'It will be.'

Reid pushed in the door and frowned when she saw McDevitt.

'We're celebrating,' McDevitt said.

She looked at Wilson.

'He was here already.' He pushed the bell and ordered for Reid.

McDevitt picked up his drink. 'I know when I'm not wanted.' He turned to Wilson. 'The photo has been deleted.'

'You don't have to go,' Reid said.

'It's okay.' McDevitt stood. 'We've already had our little chat, and there's a guy at the bar I want to have a word with.' He left the snug.

'I didn't mean to force him out,' Reid said.

'You didn't force him out. He's becoming sensitive in his old age. He knows that occasionally we need to be alone.'

'What photo was he talking about?'

He told her about his visit to the Kingspan Stadium and being photographed by McDevitt's colleague.

'You're playing a dangerous game, Ian.' Her drink arrived and she took a sip. 'You may have bested Jennings this time, but someday you're going to put your foot in a trap and it'll snap shut.'

'Until then.' He toasted her and finished his drink. 'I'm parked outside so that's my lot, and I've got work in the morning. What do you say to an Indian takeaway and a nice bottle of something?'

She downed her drink in one swallow. 'Lead on, Macduff.'

CHAPTER SIXTY-THREE

Coleville House, the country home of Sir Philip Lattimer, is situated just outside the town of Ballymoney in County Antrim. It had taken Rodgers and Jackson an hour and twenty minutes to drive there from Castlereagh.

'Who is responsible for this disaster?' Lattimer looked from Rodgers to Jackson and back again. His white face had been getting progressively whiter as they told their story. Jackie Carlisle was in his grave and the coroner had already given a verdict of death by suicide. It was a sleeping dog that should definitely be allowed to lie. There was no way that they could allow some peasant of a detective constable to resurrect him. Lattimer rubbed his palms on his trousers and found that he was sweating profusely. Why the hell had these two idiots come to him with this problem?

'It was a clean operation,' Jackson intoned. It was becoming his mantra because it exonerated him.

'It doesn't really matter who is responsible,' Rodgers said. 'What's important now is what we're going to do about it. That's why we've come to see you.'

Lattimer brushed his hand across the short goatee beard he had recently grown. It gave the impression that he was considering the alternatives when in effect he was stalling for time. He was in his element in a board meeting when there was a show of hands and he could row along with the members who had already read the documents they were considering. He looked at the men in front of him. They were men of action and as far as he was concerned they might as well have been aliens from another planet. If he told them to kill this detective constable fellow, they would just ramble off and kill him without considering the consequences. But he was sufficiently alarmed by the information to know that something needed to be done. 'We need more information.' He was delighted that he had come up with a strategy that sounded reasonable but also delayed a decision. 'This Davidson fellow may be acting alone.' He turned to Rodgers. 'You said so yourself. If that turns out to be the case, we have several alternatives. Have you discussed the situation with DCC Jennings? He should be aware of an official investigation.'

'Of course I've discussed it with the DCC and the investigation is unofficial. The Carlisle business is spiralling out of control and we need a decision soon.'

Lattimer was beginning to feel uncomfortable. 'Yes, we'll have a decision soon.' But someone else would have to make it. He needed to get rid of these two imbeciles and place a call to Antibes. Helen would know what to do. She always did.

CHAPTER SIXTY-FOUR

Wilson was sitting on his couch cradling a whiskey. Reid sat close beside him. It was a clear night and the lights of the city were spread out in front of them. He should have been in celebratory mood but he wasn't. Tomorrow he might have another murder case to investigate, a case that would throw a shadow over the PSNI. If his suspicions about the identity of the men who murdered Payne proved correct, there would be a mountain of heat from the press, the public and the politicians. But handling the heat is Baird's job. Somewhere there is a piece of evidence that will put Payne's, and possibly Royce's, killers behind bars. He just needed to locate it.

'Happy to be back at work?' Reid asked.

Wilson sipped his whiskey. 'I was getting used to my life as a free agent.'

'You could decide to say goodbye to the PSNI. Think about it, you could visit Rathlin Island every day or spend your leisure time watching your precious westerns.'

'How did you know I was watching westerns?'

'You left your copy of the *Wild Bunch* in the DVD player.'

'You may get your wish yet. Jennings won't quit until I'm out of the PSNI.'

'If he succeeds, can we run away to Venice Beach? Or maybe we should just pre-empt him and go now.'

'Sounds idyllic.'

'We can make it happen if you want it. I can accept the job at UCLA.'

He saw the excitement in her eyes. 'You really want to do this don't you?'

'You mean do I really want to say goodbye to this crap weather, hospital budget cuts, political stalemate, Brexit and xenophobia, and swap it for sunshine and a sparkling well-equipped new hospital? Yes I do, so I suppose I must be crazy.'

'I thought you loved it here.'

'I do. Or rather I did until I discovered that there was a life somewhere else.'

'You're ignoring the people living on the streets, the panhandling, the guys playing the imaginary pianos in the bus shelters, the drugs and the drive-bys.'

'We're supposed to be celebrating your escape from Jennings. This conversation is just depressing me.'

He held her tight. 'I can't abide the thought of losing you.'

'You're not losing me. Like I said, if we're going, we're going together.'

They sat holding each other in silence, staring out at the lights of the city. Maybe she was right, Wilson was thinking. Perhaps it was time he let someone else clean the sewer.

She looked up at him. Her eyes were glassy and sad. 'I suppose I'll see you in Laganside House tomorrow at ten o'clock.'

He nodded. 'I'm not exactly happy that I'm trying to prove the organisation I work for is corrupt.'

'It's not the organisation, it's some of the people in it.'

'McDevitt has this snitch called Mouse. I met him and he shocked me when he said the PSNI is the largest firm in the city, bigger than Davie Best and all his friends. Now I can see what he was talking about.'

Reid could see that one of the pillars that supported Wilson's ethic was being slowly eroded. There was a hell of a lot of schoolboy in Ian Wilson, and she loved him for it. Most people with the job he had would have become a dyed in the wool cynic, but he still thought the best of people.

'There's someone out there who calls himself 'Mouse'?'

Wilson smiled. 'Small guy, wears a balaclava.'

'I've seen him at funerals walking with all the other mice. Then they shoot their guns in the air. Drink up that whiskey. It's time for bed.'

Wilson drained his glass. 'I thought you'd never ask.'

ON THEIR RETURN to Belfast Rodgers and Jackson had gone to the Stadium Bar on the Shankill Road. 'Fucking tosser,' Jackson said, not for the first time. He was now on his fourth pint of lager and whiskey chaser. 'I hate when they kick the ball to touch and they have no skin in the game.'

'They're in charge,' Rodgers said. He had two more years in the madhouse and then he was off to the villa he owned in Tenerife. Sunshine and golf for the rest of his life, and they could do whatever the fuck they wanted with the province of Ulster. He was sick of the Lattimers and their like with their big houses and their businesses and farms. They had nothing in common with the people on the ground. And they used men like him and Jackson to do their dirty work. Black Bob was sick of being used.

'I have an idea,' Jackson said.

'Simon, I have great respect for you as an operative, but I get very worried when you start having ideas. You're a sergeant because you're good at following orders. We don't pay you to think.'

Jackson was more than a little drunk, but he logged away

his idea in case he forgot later. Rodgers was like the rest of the higher ranks, they thought they had a monopoly on brains. He'd show them.

CHAPTER SIXTY-FIVE

Wilson got a larger than usual nod from the duty sergeant when he arrived at the station. 'Good morning, Boss,' the sergeant said. 'Good to have you back. The lads were right happy with the result.'

The tape had been removed from Wilson's office and he received a cheery wave from O'Neill as he made his way inside. Kate McCann used to call this office his womb. Strange he never thought about Kate these days. He was astonished at how easy it was to excise someone you once loved from your thoughts. Or maybe he was as venal as the rest of mankind. It wasn't a thought that pleased him. He sat behind his desk and turned on his computer. He opened his email file and a flood of unopened messages appeared on the screen. Not today, he thought. He looked into the squad room and saw the team waiting.

'Okay, your bad luck I've been exonerated. Let's see what's new,' he said as he joined them at the whiteboard. 'Okay, Harry, what have you got?'

'We're nowhere on Royce. I came across some interesting titbits on the shelter search but nothing related to Royce. The information phone line has gone silent.'

'Whatever evidence Royce had is still around.'

'Trust me, Boss, no house has ever been examined so thoroughly.'

'The coroner is going to review the verdict on Payne at ten o'clock in Laganside. By lunchtime we might have a new investigation and whatever evidence Royce had will be vital to it.'

'I'd go and get it if I had a clue where it is,' Graham said.

'I know, Harry.' Wilson turned to O'Neill. 'Siobhan, anything from the CCTV?'

O'Neill pointed at a picture. 'This is Royce two hundred metres away from O'Reilly's car park at a quarter to twelve. And this is another vehicle passing the same point fifteen minutes later. It's a Skoda, but the licence plate is false.'

'Any shots of the driver?' Wilson asked.

'None clear,' O'Neill said. 'I've gone through the footage from cameras closer to the city centre, but I haven't been able to pick the Skoda up.'

'Keep at it. See if you can enhance the driver's image. I need to be away. We'll meet again this evening.'

Davidson followed him back to his office. 'Boss, I think we need to put the evidence on the Carlisle case under lock and key.'

'I'm inclined to agree. Take it downstairs and have it put in the evidence locker and make sure that it's locked and we have the only keys. Only you and I can have access.'

'I'm pretty much done, Boss.'

'You've done a great job, Peter. Better than I could have expected. Find something to do around the office.'

'Thanks, Boss.'

'We'll sort something out for you when we have the result of this morning's enquiry. I've got to go.'

CHAPTER SIXTY-SIX

The inquest room at Laganside House was virtually empty when Wilson arrived. He sat at the rear and watched Reid at the front preparing her evidence with the aid of a slide projector. She noticed Wilson and made her way to him.

'Who's the guy with the sour face?' Wilson asked, indicating a man standing guard over the projector.

'The coroner's officer, he's not very pleased with this turn of events.'

'Thinks he did a perfect job the first time round?'

'Exactly.'

'Are we going to win this one?'

'It'll be a close-run thing. They won't want to admit that they made a mistake.'

'We need it badly. I don't think that we'll be able to solve the Royce murder if we don't link it to Payne.' Wilson turned round when the door opened behind him.

George Pratley entered the room, stared at Wilson and then sat nearer the front and on the opposite side of the aisle.

Reid followed his progress. She turned to Wilson. 'If looks could kill, you'd probably be dead.'

He didn't bother to agree. The room was filling up with spectators. He noticed Agnes Bagnell arriving with a group he took to be relatives. Jock McDevitt arrived and took the seat beside Wilson.

The coroner's officer coughed. 'We're about to begin.' Reid squeezed Wilson's hand and made her way to a table to the left of a raised dais at the front of the room.

McDevitt was carrying a copy of the *Chronicle*, which he opened and showed Wilson a two-column article headed 'Senior detective cleared of unprofessional conduct'. 'If that had gone the other way, you would have been front-page news.'

Wilson kept his gaze fixed on Pratley. The coroner arrived and opened the proceedings. He outlined the conclusion of the inquest that had already been held and the reason for the current session. Then he called on Reid to present her evidence.

Wilson knew Reid as his partner, and sometimes it was a shock to see her as the professional pathologist and university professor. She was cool and calm as she presented her opinion on the results of the post-mortem. She didn't belittle the colleague who had given evidence at the original inquest but simply stated why she believed his conclusions were incorrect. Her presentation completed, she sat awaiting questions from the coroner.

'I am loath to change the conclusions of the original inquest,' the coroner said, 'on what appears to be a question of professional difference. You make a compelling case but so did your colleague. You are asking me to adjudicate between the two of you.'

Reid knew it was a big ask for the coroner to revise his earlier decision. It was time to toss Ian into the ring. 'Your honour, Detective Superintendent Ian Wilson is in the audience. I think he might be able to put forward the police perspective on the case.'

'By all means let us here from the detective superintendent,' the coroner said.

Wilson rose from his seat and made his way to the front.
'Thank you, your honour, for giving me the opportunity to
testify. I have been to the farm in Ballyward and I have examined the scene. I have also spoken to Mr Payne's aunt. It is my
opinion that the death was made to look like an accident. It
would have been appropriate for a police investigation to be
launched at the time, but the findings of the initial post-
mortem were never challenged. Of course, the investigation I
have made has been a cursory one and I believe a new verdict
would permit us to instigate a proper enquiry.'

The coroner put down his pen and looked round the room.
'Thank you, superintendent, as you can imagine it is very
painful for me to revisit an inquest at which I presided, and I
cannot say that I am happy to alter a conclusion already
arrived at. I will not give a verdict of unlawful killing on the
evidence presented here today. What I will do, in the interests
of justice and closure for the relatives, is issue an open verdict.
This inquest is closed.'

Wilson turned quickly to look at Pratley, who was already
out of his seat and moving towards the exit.

'Got what you wanted?' McDevitt asked. 'You're a right
shit-stirrer.'

'That boy was dumped into a slurry tank, and someone
kept his head under until he drowned. You're damn right I'm a
shit-stirrer and I'll continue until we put the bastards that did
it away.' He looked to the front of the room where Reid was
putting her papers into her briefcase. He didn't notice Agnes
Bagnell moving towards him.

'Can I shake your hand, superintendent?' she said.

Wilson shook with her.

'Poor Colin didn't deserve to die by drowning in pig shit,'
she said.

'We're going to put that right,' Wilson said.

'I know you are.' There were tears in her eyes.

McDevitt picked up his messenger bag. 'It's always interesting watching you work. When you have the scoop, you know where to come.'

'Satisfied?' Reid linked his arm as they left the court.

'It was the best we could have got. Aside from the marks on his back, we have no real evidence to justify a verdict of unlawful killing. But I don't doubt we'll be back here again.'

'You're a sucker for punishment.'

CHAPTER SIXTY-SEVEN

W hen he entered the squad room, Wilson walked
directly to O'Neill's desk. 'A new case for the whiteboard, DC Colin Payne. Get his photo on the board and any
photos taken in Ballyward at the scene of his death. There's a
post-mortem report on its way from Professor Reid. I'll send
you the report of the coroner's original inquest and anything
else I think appropriate. I want everything you can dig up on
the death.'

'On it, Boss,' O'Neill nodded towards his office. 'You have
a visitor. I told her to wait in reception but that wasn't acceptable. She's only been here ten minutes or so.'

Wilson looked through the glass surround of his office and
smiled. He walked over and entered the office. 'I should have
guessed.'

DS Lucy Kane stood up. 'Good afternoon, sir.'

'I don't like 'sir', you can call me Boss the same as everyone
else. I thought we were done. What's the story?' Wilson
flopped into his chair. 'Take a seat.'

'I'm simply following orders, Boss.' Kane sat facing him.
'My superintendent got an instruction from HQ that you are
to have all the material collected on the investigation into the

corruption in the Drugs Squad.' She nodded at a Xerox box on the floor. 'Apparently, there is to be a joint operation between the Murder Squad and Professional Services. Since this has never happened before, we're in uncharted waters.'

'There has to be a first time for everything. I've just come from the Coroner's Court. They reviewed the Payne inquest and the verdict has been changed to an open verdict. That gives us the green light to investigate the death. So our little bit of subterfuge worked.'

'What little bit of subterfuge?'

'The cutting from the newspaper you sent me.'

'I sent no cutting, Boss. That would be unethical.'

'Have it your way. Do I take it that you've been seconded for the duration?'

'I understand that there's a document to that effect on your email.'

'We've been working on the Royce murder without too much success, but I have a feeling that Royce's demise has its genesis in Payne's murder. We crack one, we crack them both. I want to turn the emphasis of the investigation onto Payne. I've just asked DC O'Neill to make up a whiteboard. Maybe you could assist her by adding the elements of the corruption investigation. You'll give the team a briefing on your investigation at five o'clock this evening. There's a spare desk in the squad room, it's yours.

'For the duration.'

'For the duration.'

He watched her as she stood up and moved into the squad room. He had spent a large part of his life with athletes and he recognised the way they move. He had no idea what her sport was, but he knew that she was good at it. He walked round the desk and picked up the cardboard box. It was going to be an interesting afternoon. He was being given a unique experience, a look into a Professional Services investigation.

CHAPTER SIXTY-EIGHT

George Pratley was a twenty-year veteran of the PSNI and during that time he had never felt fear. All his experience told him that he had nothing to worry about, and yet, as he stopped on Chichester Street to light a cigarette, he couldn't disguise the shake in his hand. He was certain that there was nothing to tie either him or Wallace to Payne's death. They had waited until the old woman left and they were well away by the time she returned. A week ago, Payne had been a death by misadventure; today, there was an open verdict and Ian Wilson was on the case. That was enough to put the willies up even the most hardened criminal. A week ago, he had been safe; now, he was in danger. Everything he'd done had been to preserve the scheme they had set up first with Rice and McGreary and then with Best. Who was he kidding? Payne and Royce had been murdered because they represented a direct threat to him. As soon as he'd left the court, he'd called Jennings. The DCC had refused to take his call. That was a first. Did the little bastard know something he didn't? Maybe they were preparing to throw him to the wolves. If they did, he wouldn't be the only one to go down.

· · ·

Royson Jennings was not in the office to take Pratley's call. He was walking across the lobby of the Fitzwilliam Hotel in Victoria Street, from where he had taken the lift to the sixth floor, marched along the corridor and knocked on the door of room 610. The door was opened by Eddie Hills, who immediately stood aside. Jennings entered and walked into the large bedroom. Davie Best sat at a table that had been set with afternoon tea. A cake-stand stood in the centre of the table beside two cups, a milk jug and a sugar bowl.

Jennings removed his cap and put it on the table. He sat in the free seat without greeting either man.

'Tea?' Best asked. 'Or maybe you'd prefer something from the bar?'

'Tea will be fine. I don't drink alcohol.' Jennings was aware of Hills somewhere behind him.

Best poured tea for them both and pointed at the milk and sugar. 'Help yourself. You've heard the result of the Coroner's Court this morning?'

'Of course.' Jennings had known thirty seconds after the verdict was announced.

'This could seriously alter our business arrangements.'

'How so?'

'Pratley and probably Wallace are fucked. Payne's murder was an amateur job. They should have left it to the professionals.'

'Yes,' Jennings sipped his tea. 'The professionals might have stuffed his body in the boot of a car and set it on fire. That wouldn't have attracted any attention at all.'

'They're going to go down and Pratley knows too much.'

'Pratley won't blab. He knows the consequences.'

'I wouldn't like to bet a million pound on it, and that's the cost of the next shipment.'

'Wilson might not be able to nail him.'

'Killing Payne was stupid, killing Royce was insane and Wilson's no dummy. I'll bet he's already linked both murders.'

'Correction, Payne is simply an open verdict. Murder hasn't been established.'

'I'll bet the investigation started the minute Wilson walked out of the Coroner's Court. One of my guys was there and he saw the look that passed between Wilson and Pratley. Wilson may not be certain yet, but he suspects. We need to have a plan. There's too much at stake.'

'What do you suggest?'

'Don't be so naïve. Pratley has to disappear.'

'To join Sammy Rice, no doubt.'

Best finished his tea in one gulp. 'An interruption in supply is unacceptable.'

'And so is precipitate action. Wilson will have to report to me on the progress of the investigation. If he crosses a red line, I'll be the first to know.'

'And I'll be the second. The British Army taught me to look at all the options. In this case there aren't too many.'

CHAPTER SIXTY-NINE

The team stood before the new whiteboard that was packed with details of Colin Payne. 'Okay, Siobhan,' Wilson said. 'Talk us through it.'

O'Neill stepped forward. 'Colin Payne,' she pointed at a portrait photo of Payne attached to the board. 'Twenty-eight years old, unmarried, joined the PSNI at twenty-four, previously a paramedic first responder, three years on the beat, then made detective and was assigned to the Drugs Squad. A native of Castlewellan, his parents still live there.' She pointed at a second photo showing a slurry tank surrounded by crime scene tape. 'About four years ago he was helping his aunt on her farm at Ballyward, when he apparently fell into a slurry tank and drowned. Every year there are a fair few agricultural accidents, and problems with cleaning slurry tanks rank high among them. The local plod quickly decided that they had such an accident on their hands and behaved accordingly. If there was any forensic evidence at the site, it was quickly destroyed.' There was a photo of police Land Rovers and an ambulance attached to the board. 'There was a post-mortem and the pathologist's conclusions were that Payne had fallen into the tank, been overcome with fumes and drowned. The coroner agreed and issued a verdict of accidental death. The boss somehow made a connection between the death of Hugh Royce and Payne and Professor Reid reviewed the post-mortem and came to the conclusion the Payne was held down, in other words he was murdered.' She pointed at a photograph of Payne's back taken during the first post-mortem. 'A reopened inquest this morning returned an open verdict, which leaves it up to us to prove murder.'

'Very impressive, Siobhan,' Wilson said. 'And I'm sure you're all wondering how I made the connection between Payne and Royce. For the duration of this investigation we are going to be assisted by our colleague DS Lucy Kane from Professional Services.' He noticed the look that passed between Graham and Davidson. 'Lucy will be a member of the team while she is with us and is not here in her capacity with PS. Understood?'

Four heads shook in unison although Graham and Davidson looked sceptical.

'Lucy,' Wilson said. 'If you'd be so kind.'

Kane changed places with O'Neill.

'DC Payne got in touch with Professional Services off his own bat. It's usually difficult to find whistle-blowers. He'd been in the Drugs Squad for just over a year and he'd been taken aback by the number of times well-planned raids were just a little late at the warehouse. He'd also noticed that when they did succeed in locating the drugs, there was never anyone to arrest. The clincher for him was when he was aware that there was a discrepancy between the drugs that were confis-cated in a successful raid and the drugs that were lodged in the station. He was a conscientious officer, so he ignored the peer pressure and came to us. It was obvious that something was up in the squad, but we had no proof concerning who might be involved. We launched an investigation and we were preparing to interview the whole squad when Hugh Royce came forward and more or less confessed. HQ was delighted.

The investigation would have cost maybe half a million pounds and Royce owning up like that was a major saving. He signed the resignation letter and as far as PS was concerned we'd got rid of the bad egg. Payne had his fatal accident a month later.'

'Nobody connected the dots?' Graham asked.

'Everybody was screaming accident. My boss wrote a note at the time to HQ but nothing came of it. Then there was the coroner's verdict. End of story.'

'Let's assume that Royce was involved, but he wasn't the only one,' Wilson said. 'How could someone else know that Payne was the whistle-blower? I assume PS didn't broadcast his name.'

'On the contrary,' Kane said. 'His name was a closely guarded secret.'

'Obviously not closely guarded enough,' Davidson said.

'It still doesn't answer how you connected the two deaths, Boss,' Browne said.

'We knew that Royce had resigned because of possible corruption in the Drugs Squad so I made a request for information on the PS investigation. I was refused, but then I received a copy of a newspaper article on Payne's death anonymously. The article stated that Payne was a DC in the Drugs Squad. That's why I went down to Ballyward.'

'Anonymous?' Davidson said.

'In a plain white envelope with no name attached,' Wilson said. 'I take it where I can get it. I've had a chance to review the PS investigation into the Drugs Squad and Lucy's briefing was perfect.'

'Okay, Boss, so how come PS is working with us,' Graham said. 'I've never seen that before.'

'Above your pay grade, Harry,' Wilson said.

Browne was about to speak.

'And yours too, Rory.'

'Okay, Boss,' Browne said. 'It's great that we have another

case, but it doesn't look like we have much in the way of evidence. There's no forensic material.'

'I never said it was going to be easy. I've already spoken to the aunt, Agnes Bagnell. She was away to Castlewellan at the time Payne died. My guess is that whoever murdered Payne waited until she left. Ballyward is a country area and people there are curious about strangers. We have to go back to basics on this one. We'll need to talk to the first responders and the local uniforms as well as the neighbours. Maybe we'll end up with nothing, but we have to try to stir old memories and hope that something falls out. We'll distribute jobs tomorrow.'

Wilson turned towards his office and was joined by Davidson.

'I need a word, Boss.' Davidson couldn't hold the existence of his relationship with Irene Carlisle to himself any longer.

'It'll have to be later. I'm already late for a meeting upstairs with the chief super.'

'Five minutes, Boss.'

'Later.'

CHAPTER SEVENTY

'Satisfied?' Davis said.

'It's another case, but I think it'll help us crack the Royce murder.' Wilson noted that Davis appeared more relaxed than usual.

'I don't suppose you're going to tell me how you got Professional Services to add themselves to the investigation?'

'No, I'm not.'

'This is going to end badly, like Armstrong.'

'I think so.'

'You can thank your lucky stars that Russell was in charge of the enquiry.'

'I do, maybe I'll drop her a note.'

'I think she would appreciate that. Where are you on the Royce murder?'

'Nowhere, the forensic material is no help. We have a picture of a Skoda with false plates, but we can't identify the driver. It looks like Royce went to O'Reilly's to meet someone. But who the hell makes an appointment for twelve midnight on a lousy winter's evening?'

'The sun has just passed the yardarm so we can safely have a drink.' She reached into her drawer and pulled out a bottle of

Jameson and two glasses. 'I think we can have one and only one.'

'I'm glad to hear it.'

She poured two measures and passed a glass to Wilson. 'Cheers and please try not to get into any more trouble.'

'By the way, what's this business with Jack Duane?'

'Ever hear the phrase "mind your own business". I'm not a sixteen-year-old with my hormones running wild and neither is Jack. And you're not my father.'

Wilson sipped his drink. 'I don't like coincidences and the IRA finding out that Armstrong was a tout was a little too convenient.'

'You think you would have nailed him?'

'I would have tried. I don't believe in summary justice. Even scum like Armstrong deserve their day in court. The ones I'd really like to get are the people who cleaned up after him when he murdered Bridget Kelly.' Jennings had been the one responsible for the false alibi and Wilson was sure that he was also the one who disappeared the original file.

'How are things at home?'

He had to think before he spoke. 'Good, Steph is back at work but still in the grieving process. I think her time in the States unsettled her a bit.'

'Tell me about it. Put me in the Californian sun for a couple of months and it would take wild horses to get me back. I go to bed thinking about walking along a sun-kissed beach. You actually did it.'

'Peter Davidson is leaving soon, we should be thinking about a replacement.'

'You obviously have someone in mind.'

'Moira McElvaney, my old sergeant, she's back from a sabbatical. She's one of the best detectives I've ever worked with. I'd like her back in the squad.'

'Two sergeants and two constables, same number of chiefs

as Indians. Might be a little conflict on the horizon. Where is she now?'

'Vice, she's covering for that asshole Deric Beattie.'

'You mean the one who was anonymously shopped to Professional Services for taking money from the Lithuanian pimp you interviewed in Liverpool?'

'That's him.'

'Any idea who shopped him?'

Wilson shook his head and they both laughed.

'I'll keep her in mind,' Davis said. 'What will Jennings make of it?'

'He'll block it.'

She drained her glass. 'Then we'll have to do something about that.'

CHAPTER SEVENTY-ONE

Wilson sat alone in the snug at the Crown. Reid was working late and would drop by to pick him up on her way home. In anticipation of a few drinks more than usual, he'd left his car at the station. Jennings would know that he had spoken to Margaret Whiticker and he probably surmised that she had revealed his role in covering up the murder of Bridget Kelly. That meant that for the first time Wilson posed an existential threat to him. Jennings was a dangerous foe. He had tried to get rid of Wilson by quasi-fair means and had failed. There was a probability that someday he would try means that weren't at all fair. Wilson looked at the drink on the table. There were days when he felt like getting totally blasted. It was the uphill battle against the 'unseen hand'. Nothing was ever what it seemed in Northern Ireland. There was always something afoot under the table. Since the Assembly was constituted, the politicians had also caught the disease. They had been elected to rule but spent inordinate amounts of time undermining each other. He was tired of knowing who the culprits were and being unable to put them away. But Spence had taught him that it was part of the job. The guilty very often get away with their crimes, even the most heinous of crimes. Ulster wasn't the only place where you could hurl a hand grenade into a crowd of mourners in a graveyard and be considered a hero. Sometimes he wondered whether it was all worth it. Maybe he should have taken up the coaching offers he'd received when he retired. He could have become a pundit, appearing on TV and writing a weekly column for the *Chronicle*. But he knew that wouldn't make him happy.

There was a knock on the door and Moira McElvaney stood in the gap. 'Am I bothering you?'

'Not at all, come in.' He pushed the bell for service. 'Your ears must have been burning this evening.'

She sat. 'Why is that?'

'Peter is retiring in a few months and I was discussing possible replacements with the new chief super. I told her I want you back in the squad.'

'That's why I came home. It took me a while to realise what I was doing here with you was what I wanted. I wouldn't be happy doing anything else.'

'Someday you may regret not taking the option of the husband and the two point four children.'

'Maybe.'

The barman arrived and Wilson ordered for both of them.

'Are you and Reid happy?' she asked.

'Yes, we are. I love her and I hope to God that she loves me.'

'And Kate McCann?'

'That finished a long time ago. She's getting married to some investment banker or entrepreneur from Ballymoney. The announcement was in the *Chronicle* a few months ago. I'm sure her mother is over the moon.'

'And you never think of her?'

'Hardly ever. What about you? It all seemed to be go when you left here with Brendan.'

'Life happened, I never saw myself as a Stepford wife. You remember the film?'

He nodded.

'Brendan is climbing the career ladder at Harvard and I wasn't ready to travel on his coat-tails.'

'It's never the same when you go back. Eric is gone and Peter will be away shortly. We have a new sergeant, Rory Browne. He's young and doesn't have your innate talent for the job. Eric's replacement is a young woman, Siobhan O'Neill, who is a kind of computer whiz-kid. Nobody knows quite what she's doing working for the PSNI.'

'And you and Harry are fixtures. One more for the road?' She pushed the bell.

'Why not, isn't it the Irish curse?'

CHAPTER SEVENTY-TWO

Davidson and Graham were having an after-work pint in the Rex bar on the Shankill Road. They sat in the corner away from the regulars, most of whom knew them.

'I wanted to tell the boss about me and Irene but he was in a hurry upstairs,' Davidson said as soon as they were settled. 'It might affect the validity of the evidence I've collected.'

Graham took a large draught of his Guinness. 'You're a right gobshite, you should have told him sooner. You just didn't want to queer your pitch with the widow.'

'I know, but there was never a good time. I'm glad I'm going to be out of it in a couple of months. It's not the Belfast it used to be. Everybody is rushing around and chasing their tails. Although Rice and McGreary were arseholes, they were our kind of arseholes and we could deal with them. Best and his gang give me the willies. They've been trained to kill and they've seen things in Iraq and Afghanistan. When you look into their eyes all you see is the emptiness.'

'We're getting old. I spend a lot of time worrying about the kids.' Graham took out his wallet and showed Davidson a picture of his three girls. 'They look so angelic. But they haven't grown up yet. The place seems to be swamped with drugs. My eldest tells me that most of the kids in her class have tried cannabis. How are your lot getting on?'

'Never see them,' Davidson said. 'It's the price I pay for not being there for them when they were younger. There are a lot of things I'm sorry for and I'm out of time to put them right. Take my advice and stay close to the kids. It's the only way to keep them out of trouble.' Davidson finished his drink and called for another.

'Hindsight is twenty-twenty. Until they invent time travel we'll just have to live with our mistakes.'

'Irene and I are out of here as soon as the insurance money comes through. We're going somewhere hot.'

Graham was instantly envious. His youngest was eight, if she went to university that meant fourteen more years of supporting her. And the two others. 'Are you going to marry her?'

'Not this time, maybe we'll stay together just the way we are.'

Davidson was fifteen years older than Graham, but they had become good friends through the job. Graham had never seen his friend so happy. He raised his glass. 'To you and Irene, I hope it all works out.'

'So do I. A couple of months ago I was looking at a retirement that involved working security in a shopping mall or doing follow-ups for an insurance investigation firm. Now I'm thinking about sitting by a pool in Spain drinking a gin and tonic. Maybe I'm just caught in a dream.'

'You think the boss can get a result on the Carlisle business?'

'If he can't, then nobody can.' He lowered his voice. 'We have Jackson bang to rights. Special Branch is right in the middle of it. If he can get Jackson to flip, God only knows how far the investigation can go.' The identity of the owner of the second phone was so sensitive that he decided to keep it to himself. 'I'm out of it now. The boss wants me to ease myself out and that's just the way I like it.'

'I wouldn't fancy taking Special Branch on. Those guys are a law unto themselves.'

'Not my problem. Time for another one?'

'I'd love to, but it's a school night and I have to help out with homework.' Graham finished his drink. 'I'm going to miss you, old friend.'

'And I you, Harry.' Davidson stood and they man-hugged.

As Graham left the bar, he took no notice of the man sitting on the bench at the bus stop across the street.

Simon Jackson had a beanie on his head and wore a pair of thick-rimmed glasses that covered much of his face. He had dispensed with Leslie's services and been waiting outside the Tennent Street station. He'd followed Davidson and Graham to the Rex and waited patiently in the bus shelter until Graham left. He needed to know what they had on him. The gnawing at his innards caused by the uncertainty was increasing with every passing day. It was all right for the likes of Rodgers to suggest caution, but it was Jackson who was in the frame for Carlisle's murder. Rodgers and the other principals would slip quietly away. He thought about going into the Rex but good as his disguise was it mightn't pass close examination. He needed to tail Davidson for at least twenty-four hours. A plan was formulating in his mind and he had no intention of discussing it with Rodgers.

CHAPTER SEVENTY-THREE

W ilson immediately blamed McElvaney and Reid for the pounding in his head when he woke up. McElvaney had kept him in the Crown, pumping him for information on the Royce and Payne murders, while Reid had worked later than he could remember. He dragged himself out of bed and after a swift visit to the toilet headed to the kitchen in search of an antidote. He thought about going for a run but immediately dismissed the idea. The pain in his head was stationary and he didn't want to disturb it by bouncing it up and down. He located a vial of tablets that he thought Reid recommended as a hangover cure and tipped a couple into his mouth, washing them down with a glass of water. The events of the previous evening were not totally clear, but he seemed to remember Reid and McElvaney getting on like a house on fire. It was a strange turn of events considering their relationship had begun with such antagonism. Two cups of coffee and some toast and marmalade restored him somewhat but he wasn't looking forward to a difficult day.

WILSON WAS STILL NOT FEELING TOTALLY human when he

saluted the duty sergeant and made his way to the squad room. He picked up a cup of cafeteria coffee and assembled the team at the whiteboard. 'Rory and Harry, draw a car and head for Castlewellan. Give Agnes Bagnell a ring before you head off. She'll introduce you around the neighbours. See if they remember anything about the day of Payne's murder. Specifically, did they see any strangers or unusual cars in the neighbourhood of the Bagnell farm. It's been a while so memories might have dimmed, but it's a close-knit community where people can usually remember the day something like the accident with the slurry tank happened.'

'You fancy someone for this, Boss,' Browne said. 'Why not let us in on the secret?'

'I think that Pratley and possibly Wallace were involved. And they may even have roped in Royce.' He looked at Kane. 'I need you to take another look at the PS interviews with Payne and Royce. I know this is going to be a sore point, but we need to look at the possibility that someone in PS leaked the fact that Payne was the source of the information about the corruption in the Drugs Squad.'

'Siobhan, remember those photocopies I gave you when I came back from Castlewellan.'

'Safe and sound, Boss, I've made the digital record.'

'Good. I want you and Lucy to examine them.' He finished his lukewarm coffee. 'If I'm right about Pratley and Wallace for Payne, and if the two cases are linked, they did Royce as well.'

'Holy God, Boss,' Graham said. 'We're going to stir up a hornet's nest. PSNI officers involved in two murders.'

Everywhere Wilson turned there was evidence of PSNI involvement in crime. Jackson was almost certainly Carlisle's murderer and he was a serving police officer. Now the Drugs Squad was riddled with corruption and killers and even PS appeared to be compromised. They would have to be careful because the ice they were skating on was getting thinner and thinner. 'Find me something I can use to get Pratley and Wallace in here.'

Kane joined him on his walk back to the office. 'I have to meet my chief this morning. I'll find out if anyone remembers Payne referring to his notebook during the interviews.'

'Keep me informed.' He went into his office and sat behind his desk. It was inconceivable that no evidence existed in the deaths of Payne and Royce. There was no such thing as the perfect crime, and Pratley and Wallace were not criminal geniuses. Something that kept circulating in his head was the fact that Royce had left Rathlin and gone to Belfast to put things right. That had to mean that he had some evidence that would accomplish his aim. What the hell was the evidence and where was it? It was highly unlikely for him to take it with him when he met his killer, and Graham had searched the shelter. He took out a pad and started to doodle. If he were Royce, where would he have hidden something that he valued so highly?

CHAPTER SEVENTY-FOUR

B rowne and Graham drove to Castlewellan in silence. They did get on, but there was a tension around Graham being the longer-serving in the squad and Browne being the superior officer. Graham had tried for the sergeant's exam on several occasions, but his mild dyslexia did for him every time. He accepted that he would remain a detective constable. It didn't sit well with his wife, who managed their financial affairs. Money was never discussed in the Graham household, principally because there was never enough of it to discuss. Outside Castlewellan they branched off to the right and headed towards Ballyward. They were obliged to plug in the coordinates of the Bagnell farm into the Satnav otherwise they would have been rambling around the countryside all day. Agnes Bagnell greeted them with tea and scones before they set off on a tour of the neighbours. Given the scarcity of people, neither detective gave good odds to finding the evidence Wilson was looking for. If you were planning to murder someone, Bally-ward was a good place to do it. It was a community of small farmers who were predominantly Protestant and situated close to the border between Northern Ireland and the

Republic. It was not an area renowned for cooperation with the police force of either part of the island. They checked in with several farmhouses between Ballyward and Moneyslane but came up empty.

Agnes Bagnell sat despondently in the rear of the police car. 'There's only a couple of farms between Castlewellan and Ballyward, I suppose we should give them a try.'

'How long were you away from the farm?' Graham asked.

'An hour and a half, maybe.'

'And nobody passed you on your return?' Graham asked

'I don't think so. Not that I remember anyway.'

'If you were away for such a short period, whoever killed your nephew must have been watching for you to leave.'

They had passed the Bagnell farm and were heading east on the Bann Road. About two hundred yards along the road there was a depression on the right-hand side and a small lane leading into a cleared area. A shed was just visible in the clearing.

'What's in there?' Browne asked.

'That's Packie's garage,' she said, 'the locals all use it.'

Graham turned the car into the lane and drove into the depression. The garage consisted of a concrete block shed with a corrugated roof. The two sliding doors in the middle of the building were open. The building was surrounded by motor cars in different stages of decay. He stopped the car and the three of them got out.

A small grey-haired man in his seventies exited from the building. He was wearing a pair of faded blue overalls, heavily stained with oil, and a well-worn pair of stout leather work boots. 'Ah, Agnes, it's you,' the old man said.

'How are you, Packie?' Agnes said. 'These two boys are peelers from Belfast.'

Packie looked from Graham to Browne and didn't seem to like what he saw. 'Peelers you say, now what would the peelers want with the likes of me?'

Browne and Graham showed their warrant cards and introduced themselves.

'Were you around the day that Agnes's nephew had the accident?' Browne asked.

Packie was cleaning his hands with a rag. 'Aye, I remember it well, it was a terrible thing. Mind you, I was at the funeral. We all were.'

'Were you working here that day?' Browne asked.

'Aye, I was.'

'You didn't happen to see anything out of the ordinary?' Browne said.

Packie continued to clean his hands and looked at Agnes, who nodded in return. 'I seen three boys I never seen around here before or since. They was parked at the top of the lane. I thought they was coming here, but they just sat there.'

'Did you approach them?'

'No, it was a fine day and I thought they might be tourists lookin' for Castlewellan Lake. They weren't from here anyways and people around here are brought up to mind their own business.'

'Do you know what they looked like?' Browne asked.

'I passed them on the way out,' Packie said. 'One was an older fella and the other two were about your age.' He pointed at Browne. 'I couldn't say what they looked like, but I could tell they weren't dressed for muck-spreadin'.' He laughed, exposing a mouth of tobacco-stained teeth.

'Thanks,' Browne said and motioned to Graham to follow him as he walked up the short lane to the road. He pointed ahead. The Bagnell farmhouse was clearly visible off to the right. 'It's a perfect place to keep an eye on the farm. Someone with binoculars would have had a great view of the house.' They stood for a while before making their way back.

'Why did you go to Castlewellan that day?' Browne asked Agnes.

'On a fool's errand. I was selling land at the time and the

agent called me and said he'd had some interest, but the boy who wanted to view was lost and I agreed to meet him at Mulholland's bar. When I got there the place was empty.'

Browne turned to look at Packie. 'What sort of a car were they driving?'

'I think it was a Skoda.'

Graham and Browne looked at each other.

Packie had done his civil duty and so started moving in the direction of the shed. 'I need to get back to work. Take care, Agnes.'

They walked back to the car. 'Packie had a fancy for me when he was younger,' Agnes said before climbing into the back of the car. 'Of course, he was a much finer man back then.'

They continued along the road, stopping at two other farmhouses and enquiring about the Skoda, but nobody had seen it. It was time to call a halt and they returned Agnes to her house before heading back to Belfast.

'It wasn't a total failure,' Browne said as they turned onto the main road.

'But it wasn't a total success either,' Graham said. 'We're no closer to finding the owner of that bloody Skoda.'

CHAPTER SEVENTY-FIVE

By mid-afternoon Wilson's hangover was almost gone and he decided to stretch his legs and check on his team's progress. O'Neill and Kane were at their desks.

'I've had a preliminary look at the notes you found in Ballyward,' O'Neill told him. 'Payne was all over the corruption. He's got the times and dates of operations and the results, and he'd also checked the drugs in the lock-up and found the missing weight. He put the finger on Royce as a user.'

'It would be better if we had the original notebook rather than photocopied pages,' Wilson said.

'I know, Boss. I've already called his parents and there was no notebook in the effects they received.'

'Why am I not surprised?' Wilson said. He turned to Kane, 'Anything to report?'

'I floated the idea with my chief that someone in our group leaked Payne's name. He looked like he was about to have a seizure on the spot. He asked whether Baird was aware, but I wasn't able to answer.' She saw that Wilson was looking inscrutable. 'Okay, so he does.'

'I never said that.'

'Anyway, I also checked whether we had Payne's notebook and we don't.'

'I have a feeling that we're never going to find it. The photocopies are gold but getting them admitted might be a stretch. But that's going to be the DPP's problem. We'll use them to sweat Pratley and Wallace, if we ever get that far. Take a look at them from your angle and see if there's anything you can add.'

Wilson returned to his office and spent the rest of the afternoon re-examining the murder book. When he had finished, the nagging feeling that he was missing something was still present. There's a time in every investigation when the tide turns and the criminal's errors begin to appear. At the morning briefing, he'd thought that they had reached that point but now he doubted it.

The evening briefing went through the day's progress. O'Neill and Kane summarised the content of the photocopies. Browne and Graham relayed the news concerning the Skoda and the ploy to get Agnes Bagnell away from the farm so that Payne would be alone.

The team were standing at the whiteboard and staring at Wilson, waiting for him to come up with some incisive comment. Perversely, he was looking to them to come up with a piece of evidence that would break the case. The three men in the Skoda had probably been Pratley, Wallace and Royce. That meant Royce was present at Payne's murder and might possibly have been one of the people who had held him down.

'Anything on the CCTV footage of the Skoda?' he asked O'Neill.

'We have it arriving and leaving, but I don't think we're going to be able to identify the driver. The plates are a dead end. Whoever was driving knew his business.'

'And the gun?'

Browne shook his head. 'Another dead end.'

'The person, or persons, who had climbed into the slurry

tank to hold Payne down must have been covered in pig shit,' Wilson said. 'How had they managed to clean themselves?'

Graham bowed his head. 'We're grasping at straws, Boss. It was too long ago to go around the car valeting companies and ask whether they'd had a Skoda in whose interior was covered in pig shit. The murderers could have used plastic jumpsuits and dumped them later.'

Wilson looked up at the board. He was having an episode of déjà vu. Pratley and Wallace looked like they were going to get away with murder. But he was damned if they were.

CHAPTER SEVENTY-SIX

Jennings watched Pratley the same way a biologist watches the antics of an insect. He could smell the fear and panic emanating from him. Fear in one's associates is dangerous. They had gone from safety to deadly peril since Royce's murder. The decision to take him out was going to prove disastrous for somebody and it wasn't going to be him. Pratley and Wallace were going to take the fall. But were they going to talk? Wallace knew nothing, but Pratley was a different kettle of fish altogether. It was a chance he couldn't take. But that wasn't the impression he wanted to transfer to Pratley.

'I've made arrangements,' Pratley said. 'As soon as they get close, I'm out of here. I've got a false passport and the money is already in Hong Kong.'

Jennings didn't tell him that Wilson was so close that Pratley should be feeling his breath on his neck. 'The last thing you must do is panic. The coroner has issued an open verdict. There's no evidence.'

'Royce had direct evidence on the Payne murder. I offered him money, but it wasn't about cash for him. He was on a crusade and he was going to turn us in come hell or high water.'

'But Royce is dead.'

Pratley let out a deep breath. 'Maybe you're right. Perhaps we can sit this one out.'

No, we can't, Jennings thought. There was far too much money involved. 'We must remain calm. It's possible that nothing will come of the investigation. Wilson reports to me so I'll let you know if you're in danger. Then you can run.'

'Thank you, Roy, I knew I could depend on you.'

It was like soothing a child, something Jennings had never done. 'In the meantime, our friend Best is expecting a large shipment from Holland next week and he would be very annoyed if anything should interfere with it.'

'I'll make sure it arrives safely.'

Jennings put on his most reassuring smile. 'Leave Wilson to me.'

Pratley started towards the door.

'Don't worry, George, I'll be in touch,' Jennings said. He watched Pratley leave. He was a dead man walking but he would just be a dead man if Best got wind that he was about to run. The updates from Davis on the Payne and Royce murders were encouraging. Wilson's team had made virtually no progress on the Royce murder and any evidence there had been in the Payne murder would have disappeared years ago. Why then did he feel so apprehensive? There was something he was overlooking. But what was it?

CHAPTER SEVENTY-SEVEN

Wilson was sitting on his couch looking across the river. The cold snap had returned but this time the snow hadn't stuck. The investigations were stalled and the only choice he had was to plod on. Reid was working late again, trying to catch up after California. He thought about their last day in Santa Monica, sitting in a restaurant facing the Pacific with the sun beating down while they tucked into a meal of fish and salad. Maybe it is time to leave the cold and wet island where he'd been born. The intercom sounded. If it was Jock McDevitt, he was going to be shown the door. He wasn't up for the journalist's probing this evening. He lifted the phone reluctantly.

'Are you fit for having a short word with me?'

'Not tonight, Jack.'

'We need to talk, Ian. Is Stephanie in?'

'No.'

'Then buzz me up.'

Wilson was bothered by the idea that Reid's absence was important. He left the door open and went into the kitchen. 'Can I get you a drink?' he said when he heard the door close.

'Not right now.' Duane walked into the living room.

'What's so important?'

'Maybe you should have a drink.'

'I don't like the sound of that.'

'Remember I told you we had intelligence on a meeting in the south of France concerning a hit on a police officer in Belfast.'

'I remember.'

'The contract has been made. The hit man is one of our usual suspects and he generally fulfils his contracts.'

'And this involves me how?'

'The information we're getting on the target has firmed up. It looks like it's you. What are you working on at the moment?'

'A murder case that might involve corruption in the Drugs Squad.'

'The guy who took out the contract is member of a Dublin drugs gang. That must be the connection.'

Wilson could think of another possibility, but he didn't care to mention it. He knew someone who lived in the south of France and who had a very good reason for wanting him dead. The murder of Jackie Carlisle would cause a major scandal closer to home. 'You passed along the intelligence?'

'What do you think?'

'Where do we go from here?'

'You watch your back and you keep your weapon handy.'

'For God's sake, Jack, this isn't the Wild West.'

'We've had fourteen murders in the south related to a gang war over drugs. They've turned Dublin into a war zone and they're not worried about collateral casualties. The money to be made from drugs is staggering. As far as they're concerned, if you're meddling in their business, you're a legitimate target.'

'I think I'm ready for that drink. What about you?'

'Jameson. Are we friends?'

'Always, Jack.'

Wilson poured two glasses of whiskey and went to the

picture window. 'How will it happen?' He handed Duane his drink.

'They'll try to get close.'

'Timing?'

'The meeting was yesterday. I don't think there was a time on it. You must be seriously pissing someone off.'

The door opened and Reid tossed her bag on a chair before taking off her coat. 'Hello, guys, it's a bitch out there.' She walked into the living room rubbing her hands together and saw the serious expression on both their faces. 'Okay, whose dog died?'

Wilson walked forward and kissed her. 'Jack, just dropped in to say hello.'

'I am not the little woman,' Reid said. 'And I never will be the little woman. What the hell has the two of you looking like a bomb just hit?'

Wilson and Duane looked at each other. 'She's one tough lady,' Duane said. 'I think you should tell her.'

'Jack has intelligence that there's a contract hit out on a PSNI detective,' Wilson said. 'He has no evidence who, but he's afraid it might be me. I've told him it's rubbish.'

Reid went to the bar and poured herself a drink. 'That settles it. I'm taking the job in Los Angeles, and you are not getting yourself killed for nothing. Maybe you should have left the Payne thing alone.' She came close to him. 'We're getting out of here tomorrow. I'll cancel the rental on the house in Venice Beach.'

'No we're not. We don't run.' He looked at Duane for support. 'We take it as it comes.'

Reid looked at Duane. 'What do you say, Jack?'

'It's one of those occasions when I have to agree with Ian.'

'There's a smell of testosterone in the air,' Reid said. 'And an excess of that hormone is not associated with good decision making.' She looked at Wilson. 'I don't want you to die.' Her eyes were glassy.

'It's not going to happen,' Wilson said. 'Jack has passed the intelligence to HQ and they'll act on it. There's no proof that it's me.'

'Tell me who else causes as much trouble?' she said.

Duane finished his drink. 'I have to go, but I'll stay in touch.'

Wilson walked him to the door. 'Thanks for the heads-up.'

'Stay safe, Ian, and remember to keep your weapon handy.'

Wilson closed the door and turned back to Reid. She was wiping tears from her eyes.

CHAPTER SEVENTY-EIGHT

Jackson and Leslie were sitting in a black SUV on the Shankill Road, fifty yards from the front door of the Mountainview Tavern. They were dressed in all-black gear and had balaclavas on their heads ready to be pulled down over their faces. Jackson had been following Davidson all day. It appeared that the detective was taking his retirement to heart and had embarked on a daylong pub-crawl. Since it was now late at night and Davidson was getting unsteady on is pins, Jackson had assumed that the Mountainview was the last stop. He'd called Leslie and asked him to join a little operation with him.

'You're sure the chief has approved this?' Leslie said.

'I wouldn't be here if he hadn't.' Jackson had learned in the army that sometimes you had to take the initiative when the officers dithered.

'So, run it past me again.'

'We lift Davidson, bring him to this abandoned house that I know, find out what he's been up to and what Wilson knows, and then we're out of there.'

Leslie stared at his superior. Something didn't feel right.

His first inclination on receiving Jackson's phone call was to call Rodgers for verification. He was beginning to regret not following his intuition. Although it was cold, Jackson was sweating and his eyes were wild. Leslie wondered whether he was on something. Was it too late to pull out now? 'I'll nip out and get us a couple of teas.'

'No, he could leave any minute. We have to be ready to roll.' Jackson had debated whether it was wise to use Leslie but lifting Davidson was a two-man job. Sometimes beggars can't be choosers. There was no way he was going to let a fucking has-been like Davidson put him in jail.

DAVIDSON HAD SPENT the day following Wilson's instructions, which involved him spending hours in various hostelries exchanging stories with old ex-coppers. He'd learned that Pratley was, by and large, deemed to be a worthless scumbag who had arrived at the rank of DCI by licking the arse of every superior he served under. None of the old timers had known Wallace, but it was their considered opinion that if he was close to Pratley, he must be as big an arsehole. While acquiring this information, Davidson had been required to drink an inordinate amount of beer. So much so that he had to cancel a date with Irene. There was no way he wanted her to see him in the state his investigation had left him in. It was after ten o'clock when he finally concluded his last 'interview'. After a day of reminiscing with multiple retirees, he was thinking how incredibly lucky he was to have tumbled into Irene Carlisle's arms. Not for him the worries of whether to put the heating on or eat something more nourishing than beans on toast. He was still bathing in the glow of his golden future when he left the Mountainview. He had chosen that pub because it was the closest to his residence, a two-bed terraced house in Ainsworth Drive, which he rented from a mate for the princely sum of one hundred and fifty pounds per month. He bundled himself up against the cold as soon as he closed the pub door behind him. He'd been a fool to cancel the date with Irene. He could do with her warm body curled round him.

Davidson's little house was across the street and he stepped gingerly into the road, aware that his senses weren't exactly on high alert. He reached the other side of the Shankill safely. The street ahead of him was dark and empty. He was halfway home when he heard a screech of brakes and turned to see a black SUV pulling up beside him. He blinked his eyes as he saw a figure dressed in black from head to foot jump out of the body of the car and hit him on the head before pulling him into the vehicle. Davidson's survival instincts didn't exactly spring into action and he was inside the SUV before he tried to push the black-clad figure off him. He received a second blow to the head for his trouble and the lights went out.

When he came to an hour or so later, Davidson had the mother of all headaches. He tried to move his hands, but they were secured with several turns of grey plastic adhesive tape to the arms of the chair in which he sat. The room was pitch black and he blinked his eyes in order to get better focus. He smelled vomit and he could taste bile in his mouth. He assumed he was the originator of the smell. His senses were still addled, but he knew that he was in considerable danger. He hadn't been a random pick-up on the street. The chickens associated with the Carlisle investigation were coming home to roost. He fought to clear his head, but his eyes kept closing and he found himself falling into short disturbed sleeps. Finally, he woke and started to recognise some of his surroundings. Directly ahead of him was a window that had been blocked up with concrete slabs. The chair he was sitting on was the only piece of furniture in the room. The floor was bare boards and the door to the room hung awkwardly off one of its hinges. The old floral wallpaper was peeling off the walls. His lips were dry and he felt his hair matted at the place where his assailant had hit him. He winced as his stomach cramped and he expelled a stream of vomit across the room directly in front of him. The last pieces fell on his chest. He'd never felt so tired in all his life, but he tried to keep his eyes open. There was no sign of the black-clad man who had bundled him into the back of the SUV. There had to be a driver because the man had jumped out as soon as the car stopped. That meant there were at least two of them. He couldn't keep his eyes open any longer.

The next time he woke, Davidson found two men dressed in black with balaclavas over their faces standing in front of him. His chair had been turned round one hundred and eighty degrees and he was now facing a wall instead of the blocked-up window. The smell of vomit was overpowering.

'You're a dirty bugger, Davidson,' Jackson said. 'You've made a right mess of this place. I suppose we should be grateful that you haven't shat yourself, yet.'

Davidson lifted his head as far as it would go. He was figuring the heights and weights of the two men for future reference. That was if there was going to be a future. He tried a smile. The man who spoke probably wasn't a native of Belfast, there was an English overlay on his accent.

'You've been playing in the wrong backyard. Get that fucking smile off your face.' Jackson punched him hard in the side of the head.

Davidson's head rocked and a pain shot through his body.

'Does your boss know what you've been up to?'

Davidson spat out a tooth and some blood. 'Fuck off.'

Leslie was moving round the room. Beating up a fellow officer wasn't on, but he wasn't about to get into an argument with Jackson. The man had a reputation and he looked like he was on the point of losing control.

Jackson punched Davidson hard in the ribs. Leslie thought he could hear a crack.

'Does your boss know what you've been up to?' Jackson said.

Davidson was wracked with pain. He'd never been known for taking a punch well, but he was damned if he was going to answer the question. They didn't know whether he was acting alone or under Wilson's orders. Maybe it was time to give them a lie. Then again, if he did that, there was very little chance he was getting out of this room alive. His head came up just in time for Jackson's next punch to land on the left side of his cheek. He shot back in the chair. The bugger really could hit. He was beginning to feel dizzy.

Leslie moved from the back of the room and pulled Jackson's arm. 'What the hell is going on here? I didn't sign up for this.'

'This,' Jackson pointed at Davidson, 'is what we do. You'd better get used to it.' He lifted Davidson's head. Why wouldn't the bastard answer the question? Davidson's eyes seemed to be disappearing up into his head. Jackson leaned in close to his ear. 'Does your boss know what you've been up to? Answer me and all this stops.'

Davidson was thinking of his wonderful future with Irene, but it was looking fuzzy like a mirage fading into the distance. Life isn't fair. Just when everything was going so well. He started feeling a searing new pain in his left arm. It was followed by a tightness in his chest and he was having difficulty breathing. Oh God no, he thought, I'm having a heart attack.

Davidson's head rolled and Jackson pulled back his first preparing to launch another punch.

Leslie grabbed his hand and pointed at Davidson. 'There's something wrong. Look at him! I think he's having a heart attack.'

'Saves us the problem,' Jackson said. 'Let him die.'

'No,' Leslie started pulling off the tape that bound Davidson's arms to the chair. He tried to pull Davidson to his feet, but they both tumbled to the floor.

'Leave the bastard,' Jackson shouted and launched a kick at Davidson's head that caught him a glancing blow on the temple.

Leslie pulled a gun from his jacket. 'I will fucking shoot you if you move even one inch. There's no way that the chief sanctioned this. You came here this evening intent on killing this man. It's not going to happen, I'm not going to be a part of that.'

'You fucking wimp, I should have chosen someone with a pair of balls. You have no idea who or what you're screwing with.' Jackson thought about rushing him, but the gap between them was too great. Even an amateur would get off a shot, and that might be enough. He stared into Leslie's eyes. He'd faced men with guns before and he reckoned the little bastard would fire.

Davidson was lying on the floor, wheezing. The room was getting dim. He could hear the men arguing, but he had no idea what they were saying.

Leslie kept his gun trained on Jackson while he removed his mobile phone from his pocket. He dialled 999 and asked for an ambulance at the address of the abandoned house. 'I think you should leave,' he said when he'd finished.

Jackson moved to the door. 'You have no idea what you've done. You're finished in Special Branch.'

'Get out. Neither of us should be here when the ambulance arrives.'

Jackson went through the door and Leslie returned the gun to his pocket. Maybe this was the end of his career in Special Branch. If it were, there would be repercussions.

Davidson's eyes had disappeared into his head and his breathing was barely discernible. Suddenly he stopped breathing. Leslie felt for a pulse in his neck and there was nothing. He quickly located Davidson's clavicle and moved two fingers up. He started to pump rhythmically, one hundred and twenty compressions per minute. 'Come on,' he shouted as he pumped. He was young and strong and he kept up the rhythm until Davidson gave a short breath. Leslie felt for the pulse in his neck and it was there. He could hear the siren of an approaching ambulance. It was time to split. 'Sorry pal, but you're on your own now,' he said as he stood up.

CHAPTER SEVENTY-NINE

Wilson glanced at the clock as the noise of the telephone at his bedside woke him. It was three o'clock in the morning, a bad time to get a phone call.

'Sorry for the call, sir, it's Sergeant Burns at the station.'

'Go ahead, sergeant.'

'It's DC Davidson, sir, he's in the Royal. The officers who attended say that he was pretty badly beaten and he appears to have suffered a heart attack.'

'Will he be okay?'

'I don't know, sir. The first responders said he was in a bad way.'

'Thanks for calling.'

'No problem, sir.'

Wilson swung out of bed, closely followed by Reid. 'It's Peter,' Wilson said. 'He's been badly beaten and suffered a heart attack. He's at the Royal.' He started putting his clothes on. 'It's all my fault.'

'I'll call on the way.' Reid was dressing quickly.

Reid got on the phone as soon as they were in the car. 'He's in surgery, which is already good news. It means that they've been through triage and they know what they have to do for him. The surgeon is one of the best heart men in the business.'

Wilson was driving like a maniac through the empty streets. She put her hand on his arm. 'There's no point in hurrying, he'll be in surgery for some hours yet.'

'I should have known better,' Wilson said, taking his foot a little off the accelerator. 'I knew it was dangerous, but I had no idea that it would end like this.'

'It's not the end. He's in good hands. And this isn't the time to start beating yourself up.'

When they arrived at the Royal, Wilson took Reid's parking space and followed her directly to the surgical ward. It paid to have a senior consultant as a partner. 'Sit here,' Reid instructed him. 'There's nothing you can do. I'll find out how he is.'

Wilson sat in the waiting area. If anything happened to Davidson, somebody was going to pay the price. What the hell was happening to the world? Davidson had just a few months to go before retirement and something like this happens. It had to be related to the Carlisle investigation. He'd known that they were rattling a cage containing dangerous animals. So had Davidson, and he'd been scared.

Reid returned and sat beside him. 'They're still in surgery and will be for the next few hours. Peter is pretty banged up. He had a compound fracture of the cheek, a couple of black eyes and some cracked ribs. It looks like someone was working him over when he had the heart attack. The surgeon is a top angioplasty man, they're putting in a couple of stents so that shouldn't be a problem. But it pretty much depends on what they find when they're inside. It appears that the ambulance got there in the nick of time.'

'Where the hell was he?'

'In an abandoned house beside the Peace Wall.'

'What was he doing there?'

'There are ligature marks on his wrists. It looks like he was tied up while he was beaten.'

'Fucking cowards.'

'We need to go home and get some sleep. As soon as he's out of surgery, they're taking him to the recovery room and then ICU. You won't be able to see him until tomorrow evening at the earliest.'

'I'm staying here.'

'I completely understand, but it's not the right move. You need to be rested for tomorrow.' She put her arm round him. He was like a big hurt teddy bear. 'Peter's in good hands.'

'I'm going to get whoever did this.'

CHAPTER EIGHTY

'What a cluster fuck.' Black Bob Rodgers had been roused from his bed just after one thirty by a babbling Leslie. It took a stiff brandy to get the full story out of the young man. 'Why the hell didn't you check with me?'

'He told me you were onside.'

'Well I bloody well wasn't.' Jackson had lost it big time. 'How was Davidson when you left?'

'He was alive but only just. If the first responders were any good, they'll have managed to get him to hospital.'

Rodgers wanted to check, but he knew the Royal probably wouldn't give him the information without knowing who he was, and that piece of information was off the table. He wouldn't like to be Jackson when Wilson found out, and Wilson was certainly going to find out. In the meantime, he had to find Jackson. Otherwise the whole Carlisle thing was going to unravel and that couldn't be allowed to happen. 'Where was Jackson when you last saw him?'

'Heading out the front door.' Leslie held out his glass for a refill. 'I skipped out the back and climbed over a few gardens before heading over here.'

He had to find Jackson before Wilson did. Otherwise they

were all screwed. Rodgers was feeling his age. He'd been involved in a lot of bad shit during his time in Special Branch, but the Carlisle affair could put him away. He didn't want to spend the cold night hunting Jackson. What he wanted to do was crawl back into a warm bed and cuddle up to his wife. 'Wait here until I get dressed.'

JACKSON HAD SLIPPED into a house two doors down from the one he had used for Davidson's interrogation. He crouched in the front room and watched the ambulance arrive closely followed by a police car. He waited fifteen minutes before leaving his hiding place. He moved out onto the street, approached the police car and took out his warrant card. 'What's happening? I heard the traffic on the radio.'

'Some poor bastard has been beaten senseless and managed to have a heart attack,' one of the officers said.

'Poor devil, is he going to make it?'

'Touch and go apparently.'

Just then paramedics hurriedly wheeled a stretcher out of the house and loaded it into an ambulance.

Jackson caught one of them on the arm and showed his warrant card. 'How is he?'

'I hope that there's a good surgeon on call,' the paramedic said and rushed away.

Jackson made his way back to the SUV and drove to his home in Mount Coole Park. He quickly filled a bag, picked up his passport and money and left immediately. Maybe he should have listened to Rodgers. But maybe he was going to jail anyway, so no real harm had been done. After all, he had just been following orders. And the people who had given him those orders had much more to lose than him. One thing was for sure, it was time to get out of Belfast, even if it was only until the heat went out of the situation.

. . .

RODGERS AND LESLIE arrived in Mount Coole Park a half an hour after Jackson had left. They used a pick to open the door and confirmed that Jackson wasn't there. Rodgers examined the house and concluded that Jackson had scarpered. There was evidence of a hasty exit. Where had he gone? It could be anywhere. He was a highly trained operative. He thought about putting an alert out for his car and then changed his mind. Jackson was in the wind. Wilson would have a hell of a job finding him, but that wouldn't stop him looking into Carlisle's death.

CHAPTER EIGHTY-ONE

It was seven o'clock when Wilson climbed out of bed. Reid was already up and he could hear her talking on the phone in the living room. He'd had great difficulty getting back to sleep and had fallen into a disturbed slumber at around five o'clock. He kept seeing a battered Davidson lying on a floor alone.

Reid was still on the phone when he entered the living room. She put her finger to her lips to shush him. 'Thanks, Jeffrey, go home and get some sleep.'

'How is he?'

'Out of recovery and settled in ICU. He's still not out of the woods and he was extremely lucky. His heart stopped during the operation, but they got him back again.'

'Thanks be to God. But the prognosis is good?'

'The prognosis is that he's in bad shape and the next twenty-four hours will be critical.'

'When can I see him?'

'He should be awake later this evening.'

'We need to know what happened before we can start looking for the people who did this.'

'You need to allow your emotions to calm down. Have a shower and I'll prepare breakfast.'

'How is he, Boss?' the duty sergeant asked when Wilson entered the station. 'The boys want to know.'

'He's on the flat of his back in ICU for the moment. The operation was a success, but he's still considered critical. I'll let you know more when I know.' He went to the squad room and had just taken his seat when Davis called.

'How is he?' Davis asked.

Wilson repeated the message he'd given the duty sergeant.

'I'll circulate an email and inform HQ. You and I need to discuss this.'

'Later.'

There was silence on the other end. 'Okay, later.'

Graham stood at the door. 'What's going on, Boss? It looks like Peter was targeted.'

'That's the way it looks. If it goes well today, we should be able to have a few words with him this evening. Maybe he'll be able to give us an idea of why.'

'I'll give Irene Carlisle a ring, she'll be worried sick.'

'What's Irene Carlisle got to do with it?'

'Peter has been having a thing with her for the past few months. He's been trying to tell you, but every time he's on the point of informing you something else comes up.'

'He's working on an investigation into her husband's death.'

'He knew their relationship was problematic, but I suppose he feels it's his last chance.'

Under the present circumstances, it was hard for Wilson to be angry with Davidson. He'd been the one to place a man about to retire in danger of his life. He hadn't believed it would go this far, but there was always the chance. He would bet a month's pay that Jackson was mixed up somewhere in the assault. He was the kind of bastard who would beat up a man twenty years his senior. 'Okay, give Mrs Carlisle the news.'

Browne and O'Neill were standing at the door.

'He's in ICU,' Wilson said. 'If it goes well today, he'll be awake by this evening. It's a crap break, but we have to keep going on both the Payne and Royce cases.'

'Do you think it has something to do with Payne and Royce?' Browne asked.

'I doubt it. I think it probably has to do with Peter investigating Jackie Carlisle's death.' He stood up from his desk. 'Rory, you mind the shop. There's somewhere I have to be.'

Tennent Street to Castlereagh is normally a twenty-minute drive. Wilson knocked five minutes off that despite the heavy morning traffic. He showed his warrant card at the entrance to Special Branch HQ and marched straight to Chief Superintendent Rodgers' office.

'You can't go in, he's in conference.' The secretary in the outer office stood and tried to bar Wilson.

He moved her away firmly but gently and entered the office. There was a young man sitting facing Rodgers. Wilson tapped him on the shoulder. 'Get out.'

Leslie looked at Rodgers, who nodded. He stood and left the room.

Wilson stood facing the desk. 'There's a piece of your handiwork lying in ICU this morning. And it's your bad luck that he happens to be one of my men.'

'I've seen the email from CS Davis. I hope everything goes well for him.'

'Where's Jackson?'

'I am your superior officer and you do not barge in here and speak to me like I'm something you found on the bottom of your shoe.'

'You forget that I've dealt with Jackson before. I know his type and I know what he was up to. He doesn't have the brains to act alone and that means that your dirty hands are in the business somewhere. Now, where is he?'

Rodgers sat back in his seat and stared at Wilson. 'I understand that you're upset. I've had men in the hospital, and I've given more than one oration at Roselawn Cemetery. Sergeant Jackson had nothing to do with what happened to your friend, and until you have proof to the contrary I would ask you to desist with the unfounded allegations.'

Wilson put his two hands on the desk and leaned forward until he was looking directly into Rodgers' face. 'Oh he had something to do with it all right. He had everything to do with it. If you don't hand him over today, I'll pull him out of here tomorrow by his rotten neck. You won't be able to hide him away indefinitely.'

Rodgers stood. 'We're done here. I'm making allowances for your fragile emotional state otherwise I would be bringing a charge. In any case, I'll be taking it up with CS Davis and I don't expect to see you barging into my office again.'

There was a sound at the door and Wilson turned to see the young man who had earlier left the office accompanied by two uniformed officers. 'I'll be back.' Wilson turned and pushed his way through the three men.

Rodgers indicated that the two uniformed officers could leave.

'I take it that was Ian Wilson,' Leslie said when the door was closed.

Rodgers nodded and retook his seat. 'I don't like having that bastard on my tail. Any word on Jackson?'

Leslie shook his head.

'Keep the enquiry low key but find out where the fucker is,' Rodgers said. 'When you find him don't tell anyone else, just me.' I want to kill him myself, he thought.

WILSON WAS on his way back to the station when his mobile rang.

'Remember that conversation we were going to have?' Davis said. 'Well we're going to have it as soon as you get back to the station.'

'Rodgers called?'

'He certainly did.'

'We don't need the conversation. I already know the content.'

'You're denying me the pleasure of rebuking you?'

'Isn't that what you're doing now?'

'No, this isn't even close. You are not to piss off your superior officers, do you get that?'

'I get it.'

'Then I won't expect any more calls from irate chief superintendents?'

There was silence on Wilson's side.

'This call doesn't end until I get some reassurance,' Davis said.

'No more calls.' Wilson was driving so he couldn't cross his legs.

CHAPTER EIGHTY-TWO

'How close is Wilson?' Davie Best was enjoying a full Irish breakfast in a room at the Merchant Hotel.

It sickened Jennings that he was at the beck and call of the biggest criminal in Belfast. He watched Best shovelling a piece of poached egg and bacon into his mouth. The man was a neanderthal, but all he had to do was make a phone call and Jennings was obliged to come running. 'He managed to get an open verdict on Payne from the coroner. That opens another front. Pratley swears that they didn't leave any evidence at the farm.'

'And you believe him?' Best dabbed with a perfectly white napkin at a piece of egg yolk on his chin.

Jennings thought for a moment. 'I have no reason to disbelieve him. It's been four years. Even if the place was covered with forensic evidence at the time it would have disappeared by now.'

'So, we're safe?' Best forked some bacon into his mouth and chewed noisily.

'Safety is an illusion.'

'We're not here for philosophical discussions. Are we safe?'

'It depends.'

'On what?'

'On whether Royce really had evidence and whether it still exists. Pratley scoured the shithole he was staying in and found nothing. Wilson and Graham found nothing. Maybe Royce was bluffing.'

'And if he wasn't?'

'Then we're not safe.'

Best pushed his breakfast plate away. 'How can we make ourselves safe?'

'Wallace knows nothing. All our dealings are with Pratley.'

'So, Pratley is the key.'

'No, waiting to see if Royce was lying is the key.'

'Waiting won't make us safe. Can we find the evidence?'

'I don't think so. Wilson is stumped and by extension so are we.'

'I want Pratley somewhere I can put my hands on him. It's time he took a holiday until the situation is clarified.' He looked at Hills. 'Pick him up and stow him somewhere safe, a cottage at the coast. Make sure he has some company.'

'You need him to assure your shipment,' Jennings said.

Best smiled. 'I brought the date forward. It arrived yesterday. Our arrangements are too lucrative to be disrupted by Pratley's current problems. Eddie will arrange a nice holiday for him. There'll be minimum disruption. What we're trying to avoid is total disturbance.'

Jennings would have to reassess Best. He stood up. 'I need to get to the office. Please don't call me to come here again.'

'I'll try,' Best said. 'But no promises.'

CHAPTER EIGHTY-THREE

Wilson was back in his office when Reid called. 'It's looking good. I just talked to the matron in ICU and he's responding well.'

Wilson let out a sigh, 'That's good.'

'He'll probably be awake sometime this evening, you can plan a visit. I'll keep you informed. Everything is going to be all right.'

'Thanks. I love you.' He put down the phone. She was wrong. Everything wasn't going to be all right. Wilson had the file on the Royce murder open in front of him and he was going through the pages when he came upon his report of the interview with Sharon Parnell, the ex-Mrs Royce. There was something in the exchange between them that bothered him. Then he saw it. He picked up his phone and called her. 'It's Detective Superintendent Wilson, Mrs Parnell, I'd like to talk with you again if that's convenient.'

'I thought that you might.'

Fifteen minutes later, Wilson was standing at the door of the Parnell residence on Shore Road.

'Come in.' Sharon Parnell opened the door and stood aside.

Wilson went directly into the living room. 'Why were you expecting me to return?'

'You're not the type who gives up easily.'

'You told me that you hadn't seen your husband since you divorced him,' Wilson said.

'Yes.'

'That was true, but you've been in contact with him.'

'A few times over the years.'

'And more recently.'

'Yes.' She sat down.

'You knew that he'd been on Rathlin?'

'That Pearson character is a conman. Hugh was completely taken in by him.'

'What did Hugh tell you the last time you spoke?'

'That he'd found God, and God had told him that he had to put things right. He swallowed the Pearson crap hook, line and sinker.'

'When you split, did he give you something for safe keeping?'

She sighed. 'You know, don't you?'

Wilson didn't know, but he wasn't going to say that. He nodded.

'He called the day he died,' she said. 'He wanted the book and the mobile phone he'd left with me. It was his evidence against Pratley, Wallace and himself. He was ready to go to jail for what he'd done, the stupid fool.'

'What did you tell him?'

'I told him that I needed money, but he said he didn't have any. I told him he couldn't have the book and phone unless I got paid.'

'How did he react to that?'

'Not well, he needed to purge himself of his crimes. He said he would try to get some money and asked how much I needed. I told him five hundred pounds would be enough.'

Wilson looked at her. If she'd have gone to the right place

she could probably have had a hundred times that. 'Then he got himself killed. He must have been stupid enough to reach out to Pratley.'

She bent her head. 'I suppose.'

'Why didn't you go to Pratley?'

'He would have killed me, just like he must have killed Hugh.'

'Why didn't you give me the book and phone when I was here earlier?'

'When Hugh was killed, he was out of the picture. I still needed the money and I kept it as my ace in the hole.'

'Go and get them for me.'

She stood up and left the room. He could hear her footsteps climbing the stairs. He'd wasted a lot of precious time because he hadn't realised the only safe place had been the Parnell house.

She returned and handed him a woollen pouch. He opened it and took out Royce's notebook and phone. She had retaken her seat. 'I'm sorry.'

Wilson knew that being angry wouldn't solve anything. 'Thank you for your cooperation,' he said. At the door to the living room he turned. 'I've been to Rathlin and I've met Pearson. It's not all crap. I think he genuinely helps people.'

CHAPTER EIGHTY-FOUR

Pratley was in his office when he received the call from Best. He was needed for an urgent conference on next week's shipment. He put on his cashmere coat and made his way to the car park. Sometimes Best could be a real pain in the arse. Donaghadee was eighteen miles away on the Ards Peninsula. Surely there was someplace closer to Belfast for a confab. It took him half an hour before he arrived in the car park of the Grace Neills pub. He climbed out of his car and was about to enter the pub when Eddie Hills appeared at his side.

'Change of plan,' Hills said and held out his hand. 'Car keys.'

'What the fuck,' Pratley said. 'I'm here to meet Davie.'

'Davie's waiting down the coast,' Hills said. 'You're coming with me. Car keys.'

Pratley put his keys into Hills' hand. Hills passed them directly to one of the two men standing behind him and ushered Pratley towards a black BMW.

Pratley had to fight to stop his bowels from evacuating. 'I need to speak to Davie,' he babbled.

'All in good time.' Hills had to force Pratley into the car. A second man sat in the rear.

They left the car park and travelled along the coast until they turned into a road leading to a deserted caravan park. Hills pulled up at a caravan. 'Home sweet home,' he said as he exited the car. Pratley's car pulled up beside the BMW. Hills nodded at the two men who took Pratley out of the car and went with him into the caravan. Pratley had to be half-led half-carried. Hills took out his phone and dialled. 'Honey, we're home.'

CHAPTER EIGHTY-FIVE

B ack at the station, Wilson called Browne into his office. 'We have what we need for the Payne murder.' He showed him Royce's notebook and phone. 'The phone is dead. Get Siobhan to charge it and find out what's on it. Give Harry the notebook and have him go through it. I need you to organise a couple of uniforms. As soon as we've got the evidence, we're going to Musgrave Street to pick up Pratley and Wallace for questioning. Get Lucy too, I want her with us. Tell Harry and Siobhan that time is of the essence.'

Browne left the office with the notebook and phone in hand.

Wilson watched Browne issuing orders to Graham and O'Neill. He was growing into the job. Davidson would not be returning to active service, which meant that there was going to be a vacancy sooner than expected. He wondered how Browne would cope with a returning Moira McElvaney. He tried to keep himself busy while waiting anxiously for Graham and O'Neill to finish.

Graham came to the door. 'We've got them, Boss. Royce's written up how every bust went down. I've only had a chance to look at the first few pages, but there's already enough to pick up Pratley and Wallace.' He put some photocopied pages in front of Wilson. 'I'll go through the rest and photocopy the juicy parts.'

Wilson picked up the pages. 'Good man, Harry, keep at it.' He started reading. It was apparent that Pratley had been in league with the Rice and McGreary gangs from the beginning.

He was still examining the pages when O'Neill came to the door. 'The phone contains video footage from the Bagnell farm the day Payne was murdered. It's pretty graphic. I'll print off some stills.'

'Well done, let me have them as soon as they're ready, the more graphic the better. I need clear shots of everyone involved.'

Wilson went upstairs and entered Davis's office. 'I have enough to bring in Pratley and Wallace for the Payne murder. We have Royce's notebook and even more importantly a video of Payne's murder at the Bagnell farm. I'm heading over to Musgrave Street now to pick the bastards up.'

'No, you are not,' Davis said. 'Before you arrest serving police officers on their own turf, there are steps to be taken.'

'I'm not arresting them. I'm asking them to come to the station to help us with our enquiries into two murders. Being PSNI officers doesn't give them a free pass.'

'Same difference, their boss will go ballistic just as I would if someone came for you. Is Kane and PS in the loop?'

'Yes,' Wilson lied. 'Ma'am, these guys have been on the take for years. They must have amassed a significant amount of money. It's possible that their chief superintendent is involved. If we warn them, they'll run.' If he were them, he would.

'I'll have to discuss this with HQ.'

'That's the last thing you should do.'

Her eyes widened. 'Then who the hell can I call?'

'Baird is in the loop.'

'You're joking,' she scoffed and then looked hard at Wilson. No, you're obviously not. Since when?'

'Not long.'

'You are some boyo. You sit there while I make the call.'

Wilson listened as she spoke to Baird. She explained the developments in the Payne case and what Wilson wanted to do.

'Yes, sir,' she said eventually. 'Your staff will make the arrangements.'

'Baird doesn't want you arresting Pratley and Wallace at Musgrave Street. He's arranging for uniforms to bring them here within the hour.'

'I can live with that.'

'Yes, you can. You are trouble on the hoof, Ian.'

'I know, ma'am.'

Wilson was standing in the corridor outside the interview rooms and wasn't overly surprised when only Wallace was marched in by a brace of uniforms. Wilson, Browne and Kane moved to an observation room and watched on CCTV as Wallace, his face as white as a ghost, was led into an interview room and installed at the table. Wilson left and accosted the uniforms as they exited. 'Where's Pratley?'

'Not at the station, sir,' one of the uniforms said. 'He left some time ago. The chief super is trying to raise him on his mobile. But no luck so far.'

Wilson returned to the observation room. 'Pratley's done a bunk. But we'll get him.' He was about to start the interview when O'Neill entered the room and laid a file in front of him. He opened it and looked at a series of pictures from the Bagnell farm. They would make a hell of an impression on a jury, if the case ever got that far. He passed the file to Browne who examined the photos. Wilson didn't take the file back when it was offered. 'I think that you're owed this one. Take DS Kane with you.'

Browne and Kane entered the interview room and sat across from Wallace, who at this stage was sweating profusely.

'Your boss has skipped,' Browne said. 'He walked out of

Musgrave Street a couple of hours ago and I don't think he plans to come back. The reason I'm telling you this is that you are in a unique position. Whoever speaks to us first will get the best treatment. DS Kane perhaps you could do the honours.'

Kane turned on the video equipment. 'John Wallace, you are now under arrest on suspicion of the murder of Colin Payne. You do not have to say anything, but it may harm your defence if you do not mention when questioned something which you later rely on in court. Anything you do say may be given in evidence.'

'Do you want to tell us about the murder of Colin Payne?' Browne asked.

'Solicitor,' Wallace replied.

Browne opened the file and withdrew a photo, which he put on the table. 'I am showing DS Wallace a photo of him in a plastic jumpsuit covered in pig slurry standing over a prone body in a slurry tank. The photo appears to have been taken at the Bagnell farm in Ballyward. The prone figure has not yet been identified but is believed to be DC Colin Payne. Do you recognise yourself in this photo?'

Wallace sat back in the chair. 'Solicitor.'

'Do you have any idea what the cons do to jailed police officers?' Browne said.

'Solicitor.'

'Okay, let's get DS Wallace a solicitor. In the meantime, we'll print out a few of the more graphic images. The jury will be very interested in seeing them.' Browne stood up and started for the door.

'Hold on,' Wallace said.

Browne turned.

'Can we make a deal?' Wallace asked.

'We don't do deals with scum,' Browne said. 'That's one for the DPP.' He returned to the table and sat down. 'Now that we know you were at the farm and involved in Payne's murder, it's only a matter of time until we corroborate the evidence from the video we have of the murder. We're going to dig into every facet of your life, and we're going to turn up evidence of corruption and murder. Talk to us now and maybe it'll influence the DPP to go easy on you.'

Wallace's head fell. 'Okay, what do you want to know?'

'Everything,' Browne said. 'Let's start with Payne's murder.' He nodded at Kane to turn on the equipment.

'The three of us were there,' Wallace said. 'Pratley, Royce and me. Royce was on the junk at the time and he was fuck all use. We tossed Payne into the slurry tank and stood on his back until he drowned.'

'How did you know that Payne was the whistle-blower?' Kane asked.

'Pratley was the centre of the whole operation,' Wallace said. 'I have no idea where he got the information on Payne, but he has lots of contacts. Royce and I did the heavy lifting. Pratley was the pivot, he took the money from the dealers and divided it up. Some went down to us and some went up to more important people.'

'So there is someone above Pratley?' Kane said.

'I don't know, but Pratley was pretty confident we wouldn't be caught.'

'What did the dealers pay for?' Browne asked.

'We let the big shipments through and every now and then they let us hit a small shipment, maybe one out of ten. Sometimes we didn't hand up whatever we seized and sold them back their own junk.'

'Who did Pratley work with?'

'Rice and McGreary and later Best.

'What about Royce?' Browne asked.

'Royce was a fuck-up. He had some sort of mental problem and Pratley slipped him some heroin. He took to it like mother's milk. When PS started looking into us, Royce agreed to take the blame as long as Pratley continued to supply him with money and junk. He was kept on the payroll until he disappeared.'

'And what happened when he reappeared?' Browne asked.

'Yeah, he'd kicked the junk and he was full of remorse for what he'd done. He said he was going to confess and that we'd have to pay for our misdeeds.'

'And that didn't suit Pratley?' Browne said.

'Not really, Royce was okay while he was a junkie but not when he was clean.'

'So, Pratley decided he had to die.'

'Something like that. Pratley asked Royce to meet at the pub. You know the rest.'

'You had no part in the Royce murder?'

'No.'

'That'll do for the present,' Browne said.

Kane turned off the machine.

'We'll get you a solicitor for the next session.' Browne collected up the pictures from the file. 'In the meantime just sit there and think of all the jolly nights you're going to spend with the boys inside.'

Browne and Kane left the room.

'That was dynamite,' Kane said.

Wilson turned to Browne. 'We need to find Pratley. Wallace was only a soldier.' He switched on his mobile and it immediately indicated the arrival of a message. He clicked on it and smiled when he read the message. 'Peter is out of danger. He's stable and will be transferred to an ordinary ward tomorrow.'

'That's fantastic,' Browne said. He noticed Wilson wipe a tear from his eye.

CHAPTER EIGHTY-SIX

Jennings held his head in his hands. It was Armageddon. Jackson on the run and God knows where, Pratley under guard by Eddie Hills, and Wallace being interviewed by Wilson in Tennent Street. It had all the portents of the end of his world. Had he had left himself too exposed? He was in so deep that he was now responding to events instead of shaping them. Wallace was a very small cog in a very big machine and he was sure that Pratley had kept him ignorant of the bigger picture. One couldn't say the same about Pratley himself. If Wilson got his hands on him, the whole house of cards could come tumbling down. And that would be the end of Jennings and his dream of becoming chief constable. Pratley had to go, it was a no-brainer. He had passed the word to Best about Wallace being lifted, and that had signed Pratley's death warrant, as he had known it would. He felt no remorse. This situation meant what the French call *sauve qui peut*, each man has to do what is necessary to save himself. Best would take care of Pratley, but Jackson was still out there somewhere. And while he lived, the danger persisted. They were beginning to eat their own children. He wondered when it would be his turn.

. . .

PRATLEY LOOKED out the window of the caravan at the slate-grey waters of the Irish Sea. It was a bright winter's day and he fancied he could see the lighthouse on the Mull of Galloway. But that might just have been wishful thinking. The last time he'd been in Donaghadee had been with his parents almost thirty years previously. He wondered what they would make of him if they saw him now. They had been so proud when he had passed out of Police College. He'd certainly let them down. The two men guarding him were sitting at the table in the main room playing interminable games of cards. He had been in the bedroom praying that, somehow, he would escape from this predicament., but being a realist he knew he was about to pay the price for his misdeeds. He thought about the house he had bought in Koh Samui and the money he had stashed in Hong Kong. He would give it all up to walk out of this caravan alive. But that wasn't going to happen. He knew it in his bones and he saw it in the eyes of his captors. He fantasised about overpowering his captors and managing to get away. But this was not a James Bond film where death is avoided by some last-minute intervention. As he stared out the window, a car pulled up and he saw Hills exiting. The Grim Reaper arriving to claim his next client. His stomach churned. He hadn't flinched when it came to killing Payne and Royce and now the boot was on the other foot. He thought about offering his money for leniency, but he knew the runes had been cast.

Hills didn't say anything when he entered the caravan. His men scooped up the cards without finishing the game or speaking. They moved to the rear of the caravan and stood in the doorway of the bedroom. Hills removed a gun from his pocket and wiped it carefully with a rag.

Pratley watched in fascination. He was going to die.

'You have to do it yourself,' Hills said. 'We don't want to

have to force you but will if necessary.' He held out the gun towards Pratley. 'There's one bullet in the chamber. In the mouth pointing upwards and it'll be over in a second. Please don't try anything stupid.'

Pratley held out his hand and took the gun. He looked at it. It was his own Browning. They had been to his house and found the gun he had shot Royce with. That would close a loop. He respected their attention to detail. He looked into Hills eyes and confirmed there would be no last-minute reprieve. It was over. Slowly he put the gun in his mouth, pulled the trigger and blew the top of his head off.

Hills looked at the scene in front of him and nodded. It looked right. There was no need to feel for a pulse in Pratley's neck, there would be none, he turned to the other men. 'Make sure there's no sign of us having been here.'

CHAPTER EIGHTY-SEVEN

Wilson had gathered the team at the whiteboard. 'Harry, pick up a couple of uniforms and go to Pratley's house. He may be there, but I think not. Check the garage for a Skoda. If it's not there, find out if he has a lock-up somewhere. We need to find that car.'

'On it, Boss,' Graham went to his desk and got on the phone.

'Rory, get over to Musgrave Street and get Pratley's and Wallace's computers. Lucy will go with you, I'm sure she's interested to see what's on them. And clean out both of their desks.'

'What are we going to do, Boss?' O'Neill said.

'Siobhan and I are going to the Royal to see how Peter's getting on. I'm sure he'd be happier to see a pretty face as well as my old scowl.'

Reid met them at the hospital entrance and led them to the waiting room for ICU. There was a middle-aged woman sitting there when Wilson and O'Neill entered.

'Detective Superintendent Wilson,' Irene Carlisle stood.

'Please sit, Mrs Carlisle. I hope you haven't been here all day.'

'Since DC Graham called me.'

Wilson turned to O'Neill. 'Siobhan, would you fetch Mrs Carlisle a cup of tea and a biscuit.'

'You're very kind,' Irene said. 'I haven't eaten since breakfast.'

'He's going to be all right.'

'I know, they told me. But I want to see him for myself.'

'You realise it's going to be a shock.' Wilson hadn't recognised his own father when he had seen him in the morgue, so extensive where his injuries. 'He's going to look a lot worse than he actually is. It's important that you don't show too much emotion.'

'Don't worry, I'm aware.'

'Has he been keeping you up to date on the investigation into your husband's death?'

'No, he only told me that he'd proved it was murder.'

'Aye, he did, and he almost died because of it.'

O'Neill returned with a cup of tea and a chocolate bar.

'Thanks, dear.' Irene took them and sat down.

Reid came into the room. 'One of you can go inside for a few minutes only. He's still very poorly, but every day is going to be better.'

Wilson introduced the two women.

'I'm not going home until I see him,' Irene said.

'I'm sorry,' Wilson said. 'But I have to see him urgently.'

Reid handed him a surgical mask and led him to the door of the ICU.

Wilson walked along the beds until he saw someone who looked like Peter Davidson. He was badly beaten about the face and only bore a pale resemblance to the man who had been in Wilson's office the previous day. His body appeared to have shrunk and the dapper Davidson was a dishevelled old man. Davidson's eyes opened when Wilson stood beside him.

'Boss.' Davidson's voice was weak.

'It's going to be okay, Peter. We're going to get the bastard who did this to you. Do you have any idea who it was?'

'Two, they wore balaclavas, big guy slapped me about, could have been Jackson. They wanted to know what you knew about Carlisle.' He was straining to speak. 'When you find them, I'd like to book a few minutes with them. And I want to be holding a baseball bat.'

My sentiments exactly, Wilson thought. He put a hand on Davidson's arm. 'I'll be back tomorrow and we'll talk some more. Irene Carlisle is outside, apparently she's been here all day.'

'Tell her I love her.' His eyes closed.

He went back to the waiting room where the three women were in conversation. He hunkered down in front of Irene. 'He's very weak now, but he's going to get better. You won't be able to see him today, so maybe you should go home and rest. He'll be in a ward tomorrow and you'll be able to sit with him a while. He told me to tell you that he loves you.'

Irene stood up and began to cry.

Wilson hugged her. 'I can get a police car to take you home.'

Irene stood up straight. 'No thank you, I'll take a taxi and I'll be back first thing in the morning.'

Reid removed a card from her pocket. 'If you have any problems, give me a call.'

Irene put the card in her handbag and left.

'What did he say?' O'Neill asked.

'There were two of them wearing balaclavas. I have a pretty good idea who one of them was.'

CHAPTER EIGHTY-EIGHT

Harry Graham walked around Pratley's house. There was no sign of the owner, but the breakfast dishes were unwashed in the sink. It didn't look like Pratley had departed in haste. Graham explored the rooms, opening drawers and cupboards. Everything appeared intact. If Pratley has run, he is travelling light. Upstairs in the bedroom, he found two passports on the dressing table, one was Pratley's British passport, the second was issued by the Irish Republic for a George McGrath whose photo bore an uncanny resemblance to Pratley. He took an evidence bag from his pocket and dropped both passports into it. He went downstairs and locked the front door. Forensics would give the place a complete examination. There was a garage to the side of the house. He used a lock pick to open the door. Inside was a 2004 Skoda Octavia and nailed to the wall were a series of licence plates. Graham took out his mobile phone and took a photo of the interior. He texted Wilson the news and included the photo. At last they had found the Skoda.

THE MOOD in the Drugs Squad's room at Musgrave Street was

sullen when Browne and Kane entered. Rumours had been flying after the uniforms had taken Wallace away. Then the word came through that he had been arrested and was being questioned at Tennent Street. The rank and file of the squad were confused as to why their leaders had been lifted. Browne ignored the muttering of the detectives and produced his warrant card. 'DS Browne and this is DS Kane from Professional Services. Please pick up your items of clothing only and leave the office. The squad room will be sealed and you will be informed by the chief constable as to when you can return.' He looked straight at two of the men who had been at the table in the cafeteria on his last visit. 'You may spend the next few hours drinking tea in the cafeteria and thinking about what you have to say when DS Kane interviews you. Now please leave.' He got busy wrapping the computers in plastic sheeting. Then he and Kane carried the computers to the door and handed them to uniformed officers from Tennent Street. They returned to Pratley's office and began filling cardboard boxes with the contents of the office.

CHAPTER EIGHTY-NINE

PC Francis Cole drove into the caravan park just outside the village of Millisle. He'd been at the station in Donaghadee when he received a report that a gunshot had been heard in the vicinity of the park. It was probably a car backfiring, but it was a slow day and the drive along the coast broke the monotony. He was surprised to find a car parked close to one of the caravans. Nobody in his right mind would be caravanning here in the middle of winter. He parked beside the car and knocked on the caravan door. When he didn't receive a response, he tried the handle but the door was locked. He walked around the outside of the caravan until he came to the large window at the rear. It looked like someone had thrown a can of tomato juice against the window. He peered inside and immediately recoiled. He pressed the button on his radio and made a frantic call to the station.

WHEN WILSON ARRIVED at the scene, the uniform from Donaghadee had been augmented by two squad cars from Bangor and crime scene tape had already cut off the entrance to the park. As soon as he had heard the news from

Donaghadee, he'd called Graham and told him to meet him at the caravan park. He'd then called Forensics and asked for a team, and Reid.

Wilson slipped on his plastic overshoes and his latex gloves before approaching the caravan. He noted the churned-up ground beneath his feet. Forensics would not be at all pleased.

He tried the door of the caravan before taking a lock pick from his pocket and opening the door. Inside, he walked down the van to the bedroom at the end. George Pratley was splayed out on the double bed. Pieces of his brain were spread over the rear window of the caravan. Wilson looked at the gun in Pratley's hand, a Browning Hi-Power that he was sure would turn out to be the weapon that had killed Royce. He would wait for the forensic report and Reid's opinion, but he had a feeling that he was looking at a genuine suicide. He was immediately drawn back to the sight of his father sitting in his chair in the potting shed of their house in Lisburn with his brain splattered on the wall behind him. There was a similar bloody mess in the back room of the caravan. There was going to be a hell of a clean-up job here. He wondered who had cleaned the shed in Lisburn and realised that his mother had probably spared him the full horror of his father's suicide. When Pratley had disappeared, Wilson had three scenarios in mind, he'd run, he'd killed himself or he'd been murdered. He'd was willing to accept either suicide or murder. He walked back down the van and stepped gingerly onto the ground. He didn't want to compromise the scene any more than had already been done.

'Who is it, Boss?' Graham said as he joined Wilson.

'Pratley, blew the top of his head off.'

Graham held up the evidence bag containing the passports. 'Looks like he planned to run.'

'Then he was overtaken by events and took the easy way out.'

'I wouldn't call that the easy way out.'

'He was done once we had Wallace inside. He would have

gone down for Payne and we would eventually have got him for Royce. Especially after we tied the Skoda to him. He shot himself with a Browning Hi-Power and I'd bet a month's pay it's the gun that killed Royce. Maybe the thought of a lifetime in prison was too much for him.'

They walked to the entrance of the park. 'Who found him?' Wilson asked.

'I did.' Cole came forward from a group of uniforms. 'PC Francis Cole.'

'Harry, please take a statement from PC Cole and don't forget the name of the person who made the call.'

Wilson sat into his car to await the arrival of the forensic team and Reid. It was always the same. You plod away for ages trying to put the evidence together and developing prime suspects, then all of a sudden the pace of the investigation goes into overdrive. Wallace would go down for his part in Payne's murder and the other two participants were now dead. Case solved. Pratley was the middleman in the corruption within the Drugs Squad, but he was lying with his brains blown out and his hand still round the gun that killed Royce. Second case solved. The forensic van arrived and pulled up at the entrance to the caravan park. It was the same team that had been at O'Reilly's pub. Wilson watched them suit up. Finlay briefed his team and then joined Wilson.

'Is it a suicide?' Finlay asked.

'Apparently.'

'Not sure?'

'I'm pretty certain. I'd like to know whether he was alone when he died.'

Finlay looked over at the caravan. 'That might be difficult. My guess is that there are dozens of latents in that caravan. Either that or it was thoroughly cleaned after the last renting season, and I have yet to meet a caravan owner who does that.'

'Get his car towed in, I want it checked out and printed.'

'We'll do our best. Any sign of the pathologist?'

'She'll be here any minute.'

'We'll take the photos but leave the body where it is.' Finlay marched off in the direction of the caravan.

It was all neat and clean. Wilson knew that he should be happy, but he wasn't. An ambulance arrived at the entrance but neither attendant exited. He went back to the car and found Graham sitting in the passenger seat.

'Anonymous caller,' Graham said as Wilson slid into his seat. 'Reported a shot fired in the vicinity of the caravan park.' Graham turned to face Wilson. 'I don't like that look on your face, Boss. We've got a result on both killings.'

'Cases closed, Wallace goes down for Payne's murder, the corruption case on the Drugs Squad will be investigated by Professional Services. I don't think we're the only ones who got a result.'

'There's someone else?'

'I think there may be lots of someone elses. Pratley was a cog in a machine. Wallace says he was the middleman collecting the money from the drug peddlers and passing it upstairs. I'd like to know who was upstairs. Also, I think that Lucy is aware that not all her colleagues are as squeaky clean as she is.'

There was a rap on the driver's side window and Wilson looked out to see a smiling Reid looking in at him. He lowered the window.

'We've got to stop meeting like this,' Reid said.

'He's in the caravan,' Wilson said. 'Don't bother about time of death, we had an anonymous call about a shot fired. Cause of death was a bullet in the brain.'

'Looks like I'm superfluous. Are you coming along, or is it too cold for you?'

Wilson raised the window and opened the door.

'Peter is doing well,' Reid said as they walked towards the caravan.

Wilson was giving himself his umpteenth metaphorical kick in the arse. 'Shit. I'd forgotten about Peter.'

'You are tired.' She let her free hand touch his.

'This has been a tough one. Pratley, Royce and Wallace were all dirty coppers. How many more of them are out there?' He thought about Jennings suborning perjury from Whiticker.

'Cleaning up the PSNI isn't your job.'

He opened the caravan door and they both climbed in. Two CSIs were working the interior. One was taking photographs and the other was collecting fingerprints.

Reid moved to the bedroom and examined the corpse. She took the dead man's temperature and examined the wound in his head before standing up. 'The gun was in his mouth and I think you'll find that it's a clear case of suicide.' She packed up her case. 'He can be taken away as soon as you're finished inside.'

They left the caravan. 'Maybe you'll start sleeping at night now,' Reid said as they walked towards their cars.

Wilson gave her a comforting smile. He felt a complete cheat. His phone rang and he took the call. 'I'll be there as soon as I can?'

'Jennings?' Reid asked.

'Baird.'

CHAPTER NINETY

'I'm resigning.' Rodgers was sitting in Jennings' office facing the DCC. 'The fuckers can learn to watch their own backs and do their own dirty work.'

'Don't be an idiot. You wouldn't last a wet week. You know too much. That knowledge helped you climb the ladder, but now it's become your death warrant. As long as you're useful, you'll be alive. So I don't think it's a good plan to talk about retiring.'

Rodgers slumped in his chair. Jennings was right. The little bastard was always right. It wasn't only the IRA that had the motto, 'once in never out'.

'No sign of Jackson then?' Jennings asked.

Rodgers shook his head. 'We put an APB out on the van, but so far nothing has turned up.'

'We need to find him. Wilson knows about his role in Carlisle's death. I hope to God that's all he knows.'

'Jackson won't talk, if that's what's worrying you.'

'That's exactly what's worrying me. You and I both know that Wilson will never let the Carlisle affair go. He has evidence that Jackson is involved and he'll worry that until he finds out why Carlisle had to die and who has the power to use Special Branch to get the job done. So go and find Jackson.'

Rodgers pushed himself out of the chair. 'I'll see what can be done.'

'And no more talk of resigning, you're much too important to a lot of people.' Jennings watched Rodgers as he left the office, his shoulders were rounded and he looked ten years older than he had the previous week. He would have to keep an eye on him. There was still the possibility that everything might eventually go pear-shaped. It all depended on what Wilson knew. Jackson's ill-advised action had thrown the spotlight on him and Davidson. Word from the hospital was that Davidson would survive, but he would never return to active duty. He would do whatever was necessary to ensure that outcome. It all hinged on Wilson. If only he could be removed from the equation.

CHAPTER NINETY-ONE

The object of Jennings' musing was sitting in the chief constable's office not fifty metres away.

'Thank God Davidson is going to be all right,' Baird said. 'That's a relief. I'll drop by and see him later this evening. I suppose a return to active duty is out of the question considering that he'll be retiring in a few months.'

'I'll be sad to lose him,' Wilson said. 'He's done a very good job.'

'And you're sure he was beaten up by a Special Branch colleague?'

'Not sure, but there's a strong probability.'

'Find him and drag him in. We can't have PSNI officers beating each other up.'

Or murdering each other, Wilson thought.

'Are you ready to tell me the background to this whole incident?'

'Not until I speak to Jackson.'

'Then pull him in and ask him the questions.'

'I would, if I could find him.'

Baird picked up the phone on his desk. 'I'll call Rodgers and get him to present Jackson to you.'

'Don't waste your breath. Rodgers doesn't know where he is either.'

'Are you telling me that a PSNI officer has gone missing?'

'That's correct.'

'That's it. Tell me exactly what's going on.'

'Davidson has uncovered evidence that Jackie Carlisle was murdered.'

'Good God, man, do you realise what you're saying. That was an open-and-shut verdict of suicide.'

'And it appears that Jackson may have been involved.'

'Involved how?'

'He was at the scene dressed as a hospice nurse. I think he gave Carlisle the hot shot.'

'You have more evidence?'

Wilson didn't reply immediately. 'Nothing substantial.'

Baird ran his fingers through his hair. 'Does CS Davis know about this investigation?'

'No, it was off the books.'

'Then let's keep it that way. Does this tie in to Pratley?'

'I don't think so. Pratley was the middleman for a corrupt link between the PSNI Drugs Squad and big dealers in the city. He, Wallace and Royce murdered Payne because he blew the whistle on them. Someone in Professional Services leaked Payne's name to Pratley. Royce was about to reveal all until Pratley murdered him and now Pratley has killed himself.'

'This is going to cost me my job.'

Spoken like a true politician, Wilson thought. If Baird were removed, Jennings would be the obvious replacement. That wasn't a scenario he could countenance. 'It all depends how you spin it.'

'I'm listening.'

'You're a new broom intent on cleaning up the PSNI. Professional Services uncovered corruption in the Drugs Squad. The DCI in charge of that squad took his own life when he realised he was about to be exposed. Another officer is in custody and will be charged accordingly. Wallace will plead so there will be no show trial.'

'That might fly.'

'There are two dead men, both killed by serving PSNI officers. That might be a little more difficult to gloss over. Also, Pratley was the middleman between someone more senior and the dealers. Wallace has no idea who controlled Pratley and I doubt if we'll ever know. And someone compromised Professional Services by giving Pratley the whistle-blower.'

'So, it's not over.'

'It is for me. I have the murderers of the two men. I've secure the football, but now I'm passing it on to you.'

'Who can I trust?'

'That's your problem.' Wilson rose. 'I promised Peter that I'd pass by the hospital on my way home.'

Baird extended his hand and Wilson took it. 'I had lunch with CS Davis last week. She wondered whether you were worth the trouble you cause, but on balance she thought you were. I agree with her. If there's something rotten in this organisation, I'm going to do my best to root it out.'

Good luck, Wilson thought but didn't say. 'I do have a small request.'

'Go ahead, you earned it.'

'We're agreed that Peter Davidson will not be returning to duty.'

Baird nodded.

'My old sergeant, Moira McElvaney, has returned from a sabbatical and is currently working in Vice. I'd like to have her back in my squad.'

Baird wrote a note. 'You have it. And keep me informed on the Carlisle non-investigation. You've done a hell of a job. I'm glad you're working for me.'

CHAPTER NINETY-TWO

Reid was waiting for him at the entrance to the Royal and she led him to one of the private rooms on the second floor. Davidson was awake and propped up on pillows. His eyes were black and puffy and his cheeks were badly bruised. He looked like he had gone a couple of rounds with Mike Tyson but had lived to tell the tale. Irene Carlisle was fussing over him like a mother hen. Reid drifted away to have a word with Davidson's doctor and Irene installed herself in the chair beside his bed.

'I hear that you're out of the woods,' Wilson said, sitting on the edge of the bed.

'So they tell me,' Davidson slurred. The swelling around his jaws made his speech sound like Daffy Duck.

'We're looking for Jackson, but he's missing. You think it was him that worked you over?'

Davidson nodded. 'Walked like he had a stick up his arse.' He laughed and then stopped abruptly because of the pain.

'Sounds like him.'

'The other guy with him hung back. I don't think he'd signed on for the beating. I have a recollection of someone giving me CPR before the ambulance arrived.'

Wilson made a mental note to check with the first responders. 'You'll soon be back on the job.'

'He certainly will not,' Irene said. 'As soon as he's out of this bed, I'm taking him to Spain to recuperate. He'll be retiring as soon as he's better.'

Reid had re-entered the room and was standing beside Wilson. She punched him in the arm. 'Stop teasing.' She turned to Irene. 'Don't worry, Peter won't be going back to work.'

Davidson tried a smile, but it hurt. 'Sorry, Boss, looks like I'm through.'

Wilson grasped his shoulder. 'I'm sorry, Peter, I should never have put you in danger. All this is my fault.'

Davidson put his hand out to Irene who held it. 'It was worth it, Boss.'

Reid tugged at Wilson's arm. 'Let's leave these two love birds alone.'

'I'll be back tomorrow.' Wilson allowed Reid to pull him away.

'Peter was lucky,' Reid said as they walked towards the lift. 'The heart attack was coming. One of his arteries was totally closed and another was ninety per cent closed. It was going to happen and it could have been fatal.'

'He said that someone gave him CPR at the scene.'

'Probably a first responder. Is it important?'

'I'd like to find out.'

'There'll be a log.'

'I'll have a look tomorrow.' Wilson's phone rang. It was Graham. He listened and then hung up. 'It looks like our presence is required.'

THE MURDER SQUAD had taken over one corner of the Crown. Davis was in the middle of the group, which included Browne, O'Neill, Kane, Graham and McElvaney.

Graham came forward to greet Wilson and Reid. 'How's Peter doing?'

'Great,' Wilson said. 'Irene will have him away to Spain as soon as he's out of hospital. I think he may have landed on his feet there.'

'It's about bloody time. I took the initiative of inviting Lucy and Moira,' Graham said. 'It was a hell of a result, Boss.'

'You did right, Harry, it was a hell of a result.' But not only for us, Wilson thought. 'Lucy was part of the team and Moira is replacing Peter as soon as the paperwork is through.'

'What are you having, Boss?' Graham said. 'The CS has put two hundred quid behind the bar and the wife has given me a pass for the evening. I might have to take a sick day tomorrow.'

'Need to know, Harry. Get me a pint like a good man and a gin and tonic for my lady friend.'

'On it, Boss.'

Wilson wondered how long Graham had been celebrating. Davis came over and joined him and Reid. 'I hear Peter is making good progress,' she said.

'Aye, he is,' Wilson said. 'But he won't be back.'

'I had a call from Baird. You shook him up a bit.'

'Apparently it's what I do.' He reached past her and passed a gin and tonic to Reid before accepting a pint of Guinness.

'The apple cart is well and truly upturned,' Davis said. 'But on the other hand, two murders have been cleared up and a cabal of corrupt police officers exposed. I think the chief constable will be able to sell it as a major result.'

Reid had drifted over to the group at the bar. Wilson toasted her with his drink. 'All in a day's work, ma'am. But I think we might have had a little help along the way.'

Davis sighed. 'I don't think I want to know what you mean by that.'

'Pratley didn't strike me as the suicidal type.' Wilson had already checked with Finlay and there was no indication of others present in the caravan. Nevertheless, Wilson suspected that Pratley had been induced to kill himself to protect his masters.

'Here we go again. Can't you just accept that we've had a damn good result.'

Wilson looked over at Reid and saw that she was motioning for him to join the party. 'I'm being instructed to forget about work and join the celebrations. How are things going with Jack?'

'Mind your own business. I have to leave now as I have another appointment, but I hope you all enjoy the rest of the evening.'

Wilson walked over to stand beside Reid. Graham threw his arms round his boss. 'Here he is, the best fucking detective in Northern Ireland.'

'Only Northern Ireland?' Reid said.

JACKSON LEFT the A8 and headed in the direction of the Baie des Anges at Cap d'Antibes in the south of France. He had put the address of the villa he was seeking into the Satnav. It led him directly to a set of nine-feet-high iron gates. He stepped out of the car and pressed the intercom set into the wall.

'*Oui*,' the voice came over the intercom.

'I'm here to see Mrs McCann,' Jackson said.

'Madame is not receiving today.'

'Please tell her that Simon Jackson from Belfast is here.'

'And what is the purpose of your visit, Mr Jackson.'

'Tell her I'm looking for a job.'

Author's note

I hope you enjoyed this book. As an independent author, I very much rely on readers' feedback. I know it's a hassle, but I would be very grateful if you would take the time to pen a short review on Amazon. This will not only help me but will also indicate to others your feelings, positive or negative, on the work. Writing is a lonely profession, and this is especially true for indie authors who don't have the back-up of traditional publishers.

Please check out my other books on Amazon, and if you have time visit my web site (derekfee.com) and sign up to receive additional materials, competitions for signed books and announcements of new book launches.

DEREK FEE IS a former oil company executive and EU Ambassador. He is the author of seven non-fiction books. *Dead Rat* is the ninth book in the Wilson series, there are two novels featuring Moira McElvaney as the main character and two standalone books. Derek can be contacted at http://derekfee.com.

NOTE: This is a work of fiction. Names, characters, places and incidents are a product of the author's imagination. Locales and public names are sometimes used for atmospheric purposes. Any resemblance to actual people, living or dead, or to businesses, companies, events, institutions or locales is completely coincidental.

AUTHOR'S PLEA

I hope that you enjoyed this book. As an indie author, I very much depend on your feedback to see where my writing is going. I would be very grateful if you would take the time to pen a short review. This will not only help me but will also indicate to others your feelings, positive or negative, on the work. Writing is a lonely profession, and this is especially true for indie authors who don't have the backup of traditional publishers.

Please check out my other books , and if you have time visit my web site (derekfee.com) and sign up to receive additional materials, competitions for signed books and announcements of new book launches.

You can contact me at derekfee.com.

ABOUT THE AUTHOR

Derek Fee is a former oil company executive and EU Ambassador. He is the author of seven non-fiction books and sixteen novels. Derek can be contacted at http://derekfee.com.

SAMPLE MY NEXT BOOK

COLD IN THE SOUL

DEREK FEE

PROLOGUE

He whistled as he dug. He had selected an area where the ground was loose and the digging was easy. Progress had been better than he'd expected. A hole three feet deep should do the job. Six feet long by two feet wide by three feet deep was the ideal in his experience. No inquisitive dog would ever stumble on a grave he had dug. He stopped digging and leaned on his shovel. The whistling had been unconscious. He recognised the tune as 'You are my sunshine'. Where the hell had that come from? Was he ever anyone's sunshine? Did he ever make anyone happy? He wasn't about 'happy'; he was about hate and about pain. He thought people should be able to see the hate in his face, but they didn't seem to and that was to his advantage. He laughed at the body in the wheelbarrow. I'm certainly not going to make you happy. Or perhaps I did for a while. But it was always going to end like this. He wiped the sweat from his brow with the back of his hand and then returned to digging, changing the whistling to humming and singing a few words in between. The hole was taking shape. The evening was still bright and the air was still heavy after a day of blazing sunshine.

He had contemplated using a chainsaw to cut the bodies

up and had even purchased a plastic jacket and trouser combination for the task. Then a police officer on a reality television show had said that murderers who use a chainsaw are stupid. Sawing the body simply spreads blood spatter all over the place and leaves lots of forensic evidence. He had reluctantly reconsidered his plans, realising it was better to be safe than sorry. His safety was always the primary consideration.

Ten minutes later he stuck the shovel into the loose earth he had piled up beside the hole and went over to the body. A pair of startled eyes stared back at him. The eyes could see and the brain could register, but the drug had paralysed the body. He saw a tiny movement and wondered what was happening behind those staring eyes. There was certainly fear, but there would also be horror at the prospect of being interred while still alive. He felt exultation. It was the feeling he lived for. No stimulant he had taken had ever come anywhere close to the feeling he got from taking a life.

Eager to finish, he began to dig with more gusto and a louder hum. It reminded him of the way black members of the chain gangs in the films sang to establish the rhythm of their work. Small droplets of sweat fell from his face into the hole. Another couple of inches and it would be perfect. He looked again at Browne's body. Bye bye, Rory, he whispered and blew a kiss.

UNTITLED

Two weeks earlier

93

CHAPTER 1

Detective Superintendent Ian Wilson's eyelids fluttered and he forced himself to concentrate on what was happening around him. He was sitting in Chief Superintendent Yvonne Davis's office and enduring the weekly senior officers' meeting. It was an event he normally avoided like the plague, but he had run through his full list of excuses and was, therefore, obliged to spend a precious two hours of his life listening to the drivel spewed out by his colleagues. His own contribution had been the minimum acceptable. He had two active cases: the search for Sammy Rice, the former Shankill gang lord, and the ongoing investigation into the body found in a burned-out car in Helen's Bay. There was a third investigation, but that wasn't to be discussed, even with the senior officers. One of his detectives had proved that former political bigwig Jackie Carlisle had not died by suicide but had been sent to his maker with a hot shot administered by a Special Branch officer who was now missing. Davis and he had not informed HQ of the progress of that investigation. In the meantime, the colleague who established that murder had been committed, Peter Davidson, had retired and was sunning himself on a beach in Spain. Wilson glanced at his watch, hoping the officer speaking would take the hint. Davis looked as bored as him, but he supposed that she was responding to some edict from HQ saying she should meet with her senior staff once per week to prove that she had her finger on the pulse of her station. He pitied her.

Wilson came out of his reverie when he realised that everyone around the table except him was standing up. He thanked God under his breath and stood. He picked up one of the pads that had been left in front of every participant and slipped it into his jacket pocket. It was virginal and he didn't want to advertise the fact by leaving it behind him. He was a member of the management team as Davis called it, and members of the management team took notes.

'Ian, would you mind staying behind for a few minutes,' Davis said as she moved towards her desk.

The rest of the management team filed out and closed the door behind them. They cast envious glances at him before they left. He supposed he was developing a reputation as the chief super's pet.

'Have you seen Jack?' Davis sat behind her desk.

Wilson didn't have to ask which Jack she was referring to. DCI Jack Duane of the Garda Special Branch appeared to spend as much time in Belfast as he did in Dublin, particularly since he and Davis had become an item. Wilson sat in a visitor's chair. 'I haven't seen him in a week or so. Why do you ask?'

'He's been around for the past few days.'

Wilson had been surprised when Duane and Davis got together. Jack was a bit of a rough diamond, whereas she was a cool intellectual. Whatever the chemistry was between them, it was certainly working on Davis. When she had taken over as chief superintendent from Wilson's old mentor Donald Spence, she often dithered, but lately she exuded confidence. She had also adopted a decidedly more female look in her fashion choices. 'Is he here socially or on business?'

'Both.'

'And you're telling me because … ?'

'There was a briefing at HQ yesterday from DCC Jennings. He slipped in a piece of intelligence from Dublin that a police officer's life is in danger. He made little of it by saying that the life of every police officer in the province is in danger. Then he cited the trouble in Derry. There was a smile on his face that I didn't like. Jack's sure it's you who is in danger. Do you keep your weapon handy?'

He opened his jacket to show there was no gun.

'That's downright stupid. Jack says the hitman is well-known to the Garda Síochána and he's the kind that over-weapons.'

'And that's why Jack's in town?'

'I think it's part of it. He likes you and I don't think he wants to see you dead; neither do I.'

She looked genuinely worried. 'Okay, if it makes you happy, I'll carry my gun.'

Her face creased in a smile. 'Good man, with a bit of luck you won't need it. I suppose the threat is linked to the Carlisle investigation. Davidson was getting too close to the real culprit and that's why he was assaulted.'

If she only knew who the real culprit was, maybe she wouldn't sleep so well at night, thought Wilson. 'I think you're right. He did a hell of a job. We wouldn't be where we are on the investigation if it wasn't for him. Thank God he didn't pay the ultimate price for his good work.'

'Any news from him?'

'Just a postcard, one of those where you send a photo to some digital company and they make up an individual card. It's a picture of him and Irene Carlisle sitting by a pool in Spain toasting us with cocktails. He looks pretty well recovered.' Wilson was glad Davidson was happy.

'It's an ill wind that blows nobody any good.'

'The pity is that Simon Jackson's in the wind. I'd like to give that bastard a taste of what he gave Peter.'

'No sign of him?'

'Disappeared off the face of the earth.'

'How are things downstairs? Is Moira McElvaney fitting in okay?'

'I don't think that DS Browne is happy with the new situation.'

'That I can imagine. How about the others?'

'Harry worked with her before, so there's no problem there. But Siobhan doesn't appear to be onside just yet.'

She glanced at the papers in her tray. 'Keep in touch, and the next time I see you I want to see a bulge in that jacket.'

He stood up. 'Your concern is both touching and appreciated.'

'You're too much, Ian. Get back to work.'

94

CHAPTER 2

He heard the argument before he opened the door to the squad room. Detective Sergeants Moira McElvaney and Rory Browne were standing in front of a whiteboard shouting at each other. The other members of the squad, Detective Constables Harry Graham and Siobhan O'Neill, were spectating. It was not the best example of team spirit he'd ever seen. He knew that reintegrating Moira into the team that already had a sergeant might prove problematic, but to say that she and Browne hadn't exactly hit it off would be an understatement.

He marched up to the arguing couple. 'Enough! I could hear you two down the hall. We have a rule in this squad: arguing is okay but shouting isn't.'

'Sorry, boss,' Moira said. 'You asked me to take a look at the murder book on the body found in the boot at Helen's Bay. I was just pointing out some holes in the investigation and Rory took it as a personal slight.'

'She seems to believe that she can make much more progress than me,' Browne said. 'Maybe I should just quit and leave everything to her.'

Wilson had huge respect for Moira's ability as a detective

and was sure that she might well have done better than Browne, but he wasn't about to say that. 'We're a team, and if we perform well individually that means the team performs well collectively. So when we review our performance, it's with a view to doing better next time. We don't take offence. We move on.' If the argument had happened on the rugby field, the referee would have asked the participants to shake hands. However, Wilson wasn't ready to play referee in an argument between his sergeants. 'What's your point, Moira?'

'There was a giant conflagration on the edge of the sea and yet nobody at the café down the road saw anything. I don't buy it. Whoever set the fire must have left in that direction. I think we should interview the café staff again. There were also two patrons and we should check in with them again as well. Maybe they have remembered something in the meantime.'

'That's the argument?' Wilson said. 'If you have the time, it might not be a bad idea to have another word with them. If I were to hazard a guess as to who we're talking about, I'd say Eddie Hills. Moira hasn't met Eddie yet, so she's a fresh pair of eyes. Go talk to the people at the café and the patrons. It's worth a try. Rory, let's go to my office.'

Wilson motioned to Browne to close the door behind him. 'Take a seat. Look, I get it that Moira has ruffled your feathers a little, but we can't go on like this.' He saw Moira pick up her jacket and head for the door. She glanced into his office as she passed.

'She can be so bloody superior, boss. She thinks she knows everything.'

'That's not the picture I have of her. She's a first-class detective who gets results. And up to now, she's been a good colleague. She's not taking your job. She's taking Peter David-son's place and we're lucky to have her. You two will have to get along sooner or later and I'd prefer if it was sooner.'

'Yes, boss.'

'Don't think of her as a threat, think of her as an opportunity. You're a smart guy and part of being smart is learning from others.' Browne was sitting with his head bent. 'And stop looking like an errant schoolboy. I want Moira to cast an eye over both the Sammy Rice murder and disappearance and the body in the burned-out BMW. You never know, fresh eyes might give us a lead.'

'I am sorry, boss.'

'There are two of you in it. I'll have a word with her as well when she gets back.'

Browne stood and left the office.

Wilson swivelled in his chair and took a small key from his pocket. He opened a locked steel box attached to the wall behind him, removed his PSNI issue Glock 17, two magazines and a shoulder holster, and laid them on the desk in front of him. He didn't like guns. Maybe it was because his father had put one into his mouth and blown the top of his head off. He moved the slide on the top of the pistol and verified that there was nothing in the chamber. He handled the gun and found that it still fitted his hand like a glove. As a trained athlete, he had excellent hand–eye coordination, and he was one of the best shots on the range. He removed a box of 9 mm shells and loaded each of the magazines with a full load, seventeen. Then he slapped a magazine into the gun and put it into the shoulder holster. It was a hell of a bind having to carry a gun on his person, but he had made a promise. He put the holster on and settled the gun underneath his left armpit. A fully loaded Glock 17 weighs about two pounds, so when people tell you you won't notice it when it's under your armpit, they're not exactly telling the truth. He knew he would get used to it; however, as far as he was concerned, it was an interim measure until they discovered that the whole hitman/assassination thing was a figment of someone's imagination. At that point, the Glock would be back in the box and could stay there as far as he was concerned. He slipped on his jacket and looked across at the glass door where Graham was looking in. He motioned for him to enter.

'What's up, boss?' Graham asked. 'I saw you tooling up. There must be something serious on the cards.'

'Nothing. It's just been a while since I wore the damn thing and I have to go to the range next week. I thought I'd get used to the feel.'

'That's why you loaded a full magazine?'

'Look, Harry, it doesn't concern you and it's on a need-to-know basis.'

'Peter reckoned he could remain safe and it almost cost him his life. What's going on, boss, maybe I can help?'

'It's probably nothing, but there's a threat against a PSNI officer and the chief super thinks it may be me. It's all a load of crap.'

'You got to be kidding me, boss. The people who put Jackie Carlisle in the ground know you're after them. They murdered one of the biggest politicians in the province, and you're not afraid of them? Those people would off you in a heartbeat. What if the chief super's right?'

'And what if she's wrong? All this is for nothing.'

'Holy shit, I thought after Peter that things couldn't get worse, but as long as you investigate Carlisle's death they will. Give it up, boss. Whoever killed him has the power and is not afraid to use it.'

'Don't involve yourself in this, Harry. You've got the kids to think about.' He stood up. 'I feel like Wyatt Earp walking around with this thing under my arm. Concentrate on giving the kids their tea and help them with their homework and stay lucky.'

ALSO BY DEREK FEE

The Wilson Series

Nothing But Memories

Shadow Sins

Death To Pay

Deadly Circles

Box Full of Darkness

Yield Up the Dead

Death on the Line

A Licence to Murder

Dead Rat

Cold in the Soul

Border Badlands

Moira McElvaney Books

The Marlboro Man

A Convenient Death

* Crispy Calamari
Japanese Spring Roll
. Angel Wings Rolls
Seafood Tempura Ap't
House Fried Rice
Hibachi Shrimp + Scallop
    Combo

Seafood Tempura Boat

Steak + Shrimp Hibachi;

Made in the USA
Monee, IL
11 May 2022

96239470R00215